Grace Livingston Hill

MIRANDA

BARBOUR BOOKS
Westwood, New Jersey

CHAPTER 1

MIRANDA GRISCOM opened the long wooden shutters of the Spafford parlor and threw them back with a triumphant clang, announcing the opening of a new day. She arranged the slat shades at just the right angle, gave a comprehensive glance at the immaculate room, and whisked out on the front stoop with her broom.

Not a cobweb reared in the night remained for any early morning visitor to view with condemning eye, no, not if he arrived before breakfast, for Miranda always descended upon the unsightly gossamer and swept it out of existence the very first thing in the morning.

The steps were swept clean, also the seats on either side of the stoop, even the ceiling and rails, then she descended to the brick pavement and plied her broom like a whirlwind till every fallen leaf and stray bit of dust hurried away before her onslaught. With an air of duty for the moment done, Miranda returned to the stoop, and leaning on her broom gazed diagonally across the street to the great house set back a little from the road, and surrounded by a row of stately stiff gray poplars.

Just so she had stood and gazed every morning, briefly, for the past five years; ever since the owner of that stately mansion had offered her his heart and hand, and the opportunity to bring up his family of seven.

It had been a dark rainy night in the middle of November, that time he first came to see her. All day long it had drizzled, and by evening settled into a steady dismal pour. Miranda had been upstairs, when he knocked, hovering over the baby Rose, tucking the soft blankets with tender brooding hand, stooping low over the cradle to catch the soft music of her rose-leaf breath; and David Spafford had gone to the door to let his neighbor in.

Nathan Whitney, tall, gaunt, gray and embarrassed, stood under his streaming umbrella on the front stoop with a background of rain, and gravely asked if he might see Miss Griscom.

David, surprised but courteous, asked him in, took his dripping umbrella and overcoat from him, and escorted him into the parlor; but his face was a study of mingled emotions when he came softly into the library and shut the door before he told his young wife Marcia that Nathan Whitney was in the parlor and wanted to see Miranda.

Marcia's speaking face went through all the swift changes of surprise and wonder, but without a word save a moment's questioning with her eyes, she went to call Miranda.

"Goodness me!" said that dazed individual, shading the candle from her eyes and looking at her mistress—and friend—with eyes that were almost frightened. "Goodness me! Mrs. Marcia, you don't mean to tell me that Nathan Whitney wants to see *me?*"

"He asked for you, Miranda."

"Why Mrs. Marcia, you must be mistooken. What would he want of me? He must uv ast fer Mr. David."

"No, Mr. David went to the door," said Marcia smiling,"and he distinctly asked for Miss Griscom."

"Griscom! Did he say that name? Didn't he say Mirandy? Then that settles it. It's sompin' 'bout that rascally father uv mine. I've ben expectin' it all along since I was old 'nough to think. But why didn't he go to Grandma? I couldn't do nothin'. Ur—D'you 'spose, Mrs. Marcia, it could be he's a lawin' fer Grandma, tryin' to fix it so's I hev to go back to her? He's a lawyer y'know. But Grandma wouldn't go to do a thing like that 'thout sayin' a thing to Mr. David, would she?"

Miranda's eyes were dilated, and her breath came fast. It seemed strange to Marcia to see the invincible Miranda upset this way.

"Why of course not, Miranda," she said soothingly. "It's likely nothing much. Maybe he's just come to ask you to look after his baby or something. He's seen how well you cared for Rose, and his baby isn't well. I heard today that his sister has to go home next week. Her daughter is going away to teach school this fall."

"Well, I ain't a reg'lar servant, I'll tell him that," said Miranda with a toss of her head, "an' ef I was, I wouldn't work fer him. He's got a pack of the meanest young ones ever walked this earth. They ought to be spanked, every one o' them. I'll just go down an' let him know he's wasting his time comin' after me. Say, Mrs. Marcia, you don't *want* me to go, do you? You ain' *tired* of me, be you? 'Cause I kin go away, back to Gran'ma's ef you be, but I won't be shunted off onto Nathan Whitney."

Marcia assured her that it was the one dread of her life that Miranda would leave her; and comforted, the girl descended to the parlor.

Nathan Whitney, tall, pale, thin, blue-eyed, scant-straw-colored of hair and eyebrow, angular of lip and cheek bone, unemotional of manner, came to his point at once in a tone so cold that it seemed to be a part of the November night sighing round the house.

Miranda, her freckled face gone white with excitement, her piquant, tip-tilted nose alert, her blue eyes under their red lashes keen as steel blades, and even her red hair waving back rampantly, sat and listened with growing animosity. She was like an angry lioness guarding her young, expecting momentarily to be torn away, yet intending to rend the hunter before he could accomplish his intention. Her love in this case was the little sleeping Rose upstairs in the cradle. Miranda did not tell him so, but she hated him for even suggesting anything that would separate her from that beloved baby. That this attempt came in the form of an offer of marriage did not blind her eyes to the real facts in the case. Therefore she listened coldly, drawing herself up with a new dignity as the brief and chilly declaration drew to its close, and her eyes flashed sparks at the calmly confident suitor.

Suddenly, before her gaze, had come the vision of his second wife not dead a year, brown eyes with golden glints and twinkles in them, but filled with sadness as if the life in them were slowly being crushed out; thin cheeks with a dash of crimson in their whiteness that looked as if at one time they might have dimpled in charming curves, lips all drooping that had yet a hint of cupid's bow in their bending. Her oldest boy with all his mischief looked like her, only he was bold and wicked in place of her sadness and submission. Miranda bursting with romance herself, had always felt for the ghost of young Mrs. Whitney's beauty, and wondered how such a girl came to be tied as second wife to a dried-up creature like Nathan Whitney. Therefore, Miranda held him with her eye until his well-prepared speech was done. Then she asked dryly:

"Mr. Whitney, did Mis' Whitney know you wuz cal'clatin' to git married right away agin fer a third time?"

A flush slowly rose from Nathan Whitney's stubbly upper lip and mounted to his high bare forehead, where it mingled into his scant straw-colored locks. His hands, which were thin and bony and showed the big veins like cords to tie the bones together, worked nervously on his knees.

"Just why should you ask that, Miss Griscom?" he demanded, his cold voice a trifle shaken.

"Wal, I thought 't might be," said Miranda nonchalantly, "I couldn't see no other reason why you should come fer me, ner why you should come so soon. 'Tain't skurcely decent, 'nless she 'ranged matters, 'n made you promus. I've heard o' wives doin' thet frum jealousy, bein' so fond o' their lovin' husband thet they couldn't bear to hev him selec' 'nuther. I thought she might a-picked me out ez bein' the onlikeliest she knowed to be fell in love with. Folks don't gen'lly pick out red hair an' freckles when they want to fall in love. I never knowed your fust wife but you showed sech good taste pickin' out the second, Mr. Whitney, I couldn't ever think you didn't know I was homebley, n'less your eyesight's begun failin'."

Nathan Whitney had flushed and paled angrily during this speech, but maintained his cold self-control.

"Miss Griscom, we will not discuss my wife. She was as she was, and she is now departed. Time goes slowly with the bereaved heart, and I have been driven to look around for a mother to my children. If it seems sudden to you, remember that I have a family to consider and must put my own feelings aside. Suffice it to say that I have been looking about for some time and I have noticed your devotion to the child in your care in this household. I felt you would be thoroughly trustworthy to put in charge of my motherless children, and have therefore come to put the matter before you."

"Wal, you kin gather it right up agin and take it home with you," said Miranda with a toss. "I wasn't thinkin' of takin' no famblies to raise. I'm a free an' independent young woman who can earn her own livin', an' when I want to take a fambly to raise I'll go to the poor farm an' selec' one fer myself. At present I'm perfickly confort'ble a livin' with people 'at wants me fer *myself*. I don't hev to git married to some one thet would allus be thinkin' uv my red hair an' freckles, and my father that ran away—"

"Miss Griscom," said Nathan Whitney severely, "I thoroughly respect you, else I should not have made you the offer of my hand in marriage. You are certainly not responsible for the sins your father has committed, and as for your personal appearance, a meek and quiet spirit is often a better adorning—"

But Miranda's spirit could bear no more.

"Well, I guess you needn't go on any farther, Mr. Whitney. I ain't considerin' any sech offers at present, so I guess that ends it. Do you want I should git your ombrell? It's a rainy evenin', ain't it? That your coat? Want I should hep you on with it? Good even'n', Mr. Whitney. Mind thet bottom step, it gits slipp'ry now an' agin."

Miranda closed and bolted the front door hard, and stood with her back leaning against it in a relaxation of relief. Then suddenly she broke into clear merry laughter, and laughed so hard that Marcia came to the library door to see what was the matter.

"Golly! Mrs. Marcia, wha' d'ye think? I got a per*po*sal. Me, with my red hair'n all, I got a perposal! I never 'spected it in the world, but I got it. Golly, ain't it funny?"

"Miranda!" said Marcia coming out into the hall and standing in dismayed amazement to watch her serving maid. "Miranda, what in the world do you mean?"

"Jest what I say," said Miranda. "He wanted to marry me so's I could look after his childern," and she bent double in another convulsion of laughter.

"He wanted you to marry him? And what did you tell him?" asked Marcia, scarcely knowing what to think as she eyed the strange girl in her mirth.

"I told him I had a job I liked better, 'r words to that effect," said Miranda suddenly sobering and wiping her eyes with her white apron. "Mrs. Marcia, you don't think I'd marry that slab-sided tombstone of a man ennyhow he'd fix it, do you? An' you ain't a-supposin' I'd leave you to tend that blessed baby upstairs all alone. Not while I got my senses, Mrs. Marcia. You jest go back in there to your readin' with Mr. David, an' I'll go set the buckwheats fer breakfast. But, Golly! Ain't it funny? Nathan Whitney perposin' to *me!* I'll be *swithered!*" and she vanished into the kitchen laughing.

It was the next morning, when she opened the shutters to the new fresh day with its bright cold air and business-like attitude of having begun the winter, that Miranda began those brief matinal surveys of the house across the way, taking it all in, from the gable ends with their little oriole windows, to the dreary flags that paved the way to the steps with the lofty pillared porch suggestive of aristocracy. It was an immense satisfaction to Miranda's red-haired, freckled-faced soul, to reflect that she might have been mistress of that mansion. It was not like thinking all her life that nobody wanted her, nobody would have her, and she could never be married because she would never be asked. She *had* been asked. She had had her chance and refused, and her bosom swelled with pride. She was here because she wanted to be here on this side of the street, but she might have been there in that other house if she had chosen. She might have been stepmother to that little horde of scared straw-colored girls, and naughty handsome boys who scuttled out of the gate now and then with fearful backward glances toward the house as if they were afraid of their lives, and never by any chance meant to do what they ought to if they could help it. The girls all looked like their drab-and-straw-colored father, but the boys were handsome little fellows with eyes like their mother and a hunted look about their faces. Miranda in her reflections always called them brats!

"The idea uv him thinkin' I'd swap my little Rose fer his spunky little brats!" That was always her ejaculation before she went in and shut the door.

Five separate times during the five years that had intervened, had Nathan Whitney taken his precise way across the street and preferred his request. In varied forms, and with ever increasing fervor he had pressed his suit, until Miranda had come to believe in his sincere desire for her as a housekeeper, if not as a companion, and she held her head higher with pride, as the proposals increased and the years passed by. Day after day she swept the front stoop, and day after day looked over toward the big house across the way with the question to her soul, "You might uv. Ain't you sorry you didn't?" And always her soul responded, "No, I ain't!"

The last time he came Miranda had her final triumph, for he professed that he had conceived a sort of affection for her, in spite of her red hair and questionable parentage, and the girl had sense enough to see that the highest this man had to give he had laid at her feet. She was gracious, in her quaint way, but she sent him on his way with so decided a refusal that no man in his senses would ever attempt to ask her to marry him again; and after the deed had been done she surveyed her wholesome features in the mirror with entire satisfaction. Not a heartstring of her well packed outfit had been stirred during the five years' courting, only her pride had been rippled pleasantly. But now she knew that it was over; no more could she look at the neglected home across the way and feel that any day she might step in and take possession. She had cut the cold man to his heart, what little chilly heart he had, and he would look her way no more, for she had dared to humble him to confessing affection, and then refused him after all. He would keep his well-trained affections in their place hereafter; and would look about in genuine earnest now to get a housekeeper and a mother for his wild flock which had been making rapid strides on the downward course while he was meandering through the toilsome ways of courtship.

Nathan Whitney looked about to such purpose that he was soon able to have his banns published in the church, and everybody at once began to say how altogether suitable and proper it was for Nathan Whitney to take another wife after all these five long years of waiting and mourning his sweet Eliza; and who in all that country round so fit as Maria Bent to deal with the seven wild unruly Whitneys, young and old. Had she not been mistress of the district school for well nigh twelve years gone, and had she not dealt with the Whitneys time and time again to her own glory and the undoing of their best-laid schemes? Maria Bent was just the one, and Nathan Whitney had been a fool not to ask her before. Maybe she might have saved the oldest boy Allan from disgrace.

Strange to say, as soon as Miranda felt herself safe from becoming related to them, her heart softened toward the little Whitneys. Day after day as she swept the front stoop, after the banns had been published, and looked toward the great house which might have been hers, but by her own act had been put out of her life forever, she sighed and thought of the little Whitneys, and questioned her soul: "Could I? Ought I to uv?" but always her soul responded loyally, "No, you couldn't uv. No, you oughtn't uv. Think o' him! You never could uv stood him. Bah!"

And now on this morning of Maria Bent's wedding day Miranda came down with a whisk and a jerk, and flung the blinds open triumphantly. The deed was almost done, the time was nearly over. In a few more hours Maria Bent would walk that flagging up to the grand pillared porch and enter that mansion across the way to become its mistress; and she, Miranda Griscom, would be Miranda Griscom still, plain, red-haired, freckled—and unmarried. No one would ever know, except her dear Mrs. Marcia and her adored Mr. David, that she had "hed the chancet an' never tuk it." Yet, Miranda, on her rival's wedding day, looked across at the great house, and sang, *sang* her joy of freedom.

"I might uv endured them brats, poor little hanted lookin' creatoors, but I never could a-stood that slab-sided, washed-out, fish-eyed man around, nohow you fixed it. My goody! Think o' them all 'long side o' my little Rose!"

And Miranda went into the house, slamming the door joyfully and singing. David upstairs shaving remarked to Marcia:

"Well, Miranda doesn't seem to regret her single blessedness as yet, dear."

Marcia, trying a bright ribbon on little Rose's curls, answered happily:

"And it's a good thing for us she doesn't. I wonder if she'll go to the wedding."

Miranda, later, after the breakfast was cleared away, announced her intention.

"Yes, I'm goin' jest to show I ain't got no feelin's about it. 'Course she don't know. I don't s'pose he'd ever tell her, 'tain't like him. He's one o' them close, sly men thet think it's cost him something ef he tells a woman ennythin', but I'm goin' jest fer my own satisfaction. Then 'course I'll own I'd kinder like to watch her an' think thet might o' ben me ef I ben willin' to leave little Rose, an' you an'—well, ef I'd a ben *will*in'—which I never was. Yes, course I'm goin'."

CHAPTER 2

THE ceremony was held in the schoolhouse in the afternoon. Maria Bent lived with her old mother in two small rooms back of the post-office, not a suitable place for the wedding of Nathan Whitney's bride; so Maria, by reason of her years of service as teacher, was granted permission to use the school-house.

The joyful scholars, radiant at the thought of a new teacher,—any teacher so it be not Maria Bent,—and excited beyond measure over a holiday and a festivity all their own, joyously trimmed the schoolhouse with roses, hollyhocks and long trailing vines from the woods, and for once the smoky walls and much hacked desks blossomed as the rose smothered in the wealth of nature.

The only children who did not participate in the noisy decorations were the young Whitneys. Like scared yellow leaves in a hurricane they scurried away from the path of the storm and hid from the scene of action, peering with jealous eyes and swelling hearts from safe coverts at the enemy who was scouring the woods and gardens in behalf of her who was about to invade the sacredness of their homes. Not that they had hitherto cared much about that home; but it was all they had and the world looked blank and unlivable to them now with the terror of their school days installed for incessant duty.

The little girls with down-drooped yellow lashes, and peaked, sallow faces strangely like their father's, hurried home to hide away their treasures in secret places in the attic, known only to themselves, and to whisper awesomely about how it would be when "she" came.

"She smiled at me in school yesterday," whispered Helena, the sharp fourteen year old. "It was like a gnarled spot on a sour apple that falls before it's ripe."

"Oh, be careful," hushed Prudence, lifting her thin little hands in dismay. "What if Aunt Jane should hear you and tell her. You know she's going to be our mother, and she can do what she likes then."

"Mother nothing!" flouted Helena grandly, "she'll not mother me, I can tell you that. If she lets me alone I'll stay, but if she tries to boss me I'll run away."

Nevertheless Helena took the precaution to tiptoe lightly to the head of the stairs, to be sure the attic door was closed so that no one could hear her.

"Helena!" gasped Prudence, beginning to cry softly. "You wouldn't dare! You wouldn't leave me alone?"

"Well, no," said Helena relenting. "I'd take you with me p'raps; only you'd be so particular we'd get caught like the time I stole the pie and had it all fixed so Aunt Jane would think the cat got it, and you had to explain because you thought the cat might get whipped!"

"Well, you know Aunt Jane hates the cat, and she'd have whipped her worse'n she did us. Besides—"

"Aw, well you needn't cry. We've got enough to do now to keep quiet, and keep out of the way. Where's Nate?"

"I saw him going down toward the saw mill after school—"

"Nate won't stay here long," stated Helena sagely. "He just despises Maria Bent."

"Where would he go?" said Prudence, drying her tears as her little world broke up bit by bit. "Helena Whitney, he's only ten years old!"

"He's a man!" snapped Helena. "Men are diffrunt. Come on, let's go hide in the bushes and see what they get. The idea of Julia Fargo and Harriet Wells making all that fuss getting flowers for her wedding when they've talked about her so; and only last week she took that lovely book away from Harriet Wells just because she took it out in geography class and began to read."

Hand in hand, with swelling throats and smarting eyes filled with tears they would not shed, the motherless children hurried away to the woods to watch in bitterness of spirit the preparations for the wedding, which was almost like watching the building of their own funeral pyres.

Nevertheless the time of hiding could not be for always and the little brood of Whitneys were still under stern discipline. Aunt Jane held them with no easy hand. Promptly at half-past two they issued forth from the big white house clothed in wedding garments, their respective heads neatly dressed in plait or net or glossy ringlet, or firmly plastered down. Young Nathan's rebellious brown curls were smooth as satin the water from their late anointing trickling down his clammy back as with dogged tread and downcast, insurgent look he marched beside his frightened, meek little sisters to the ceremony which was to them all like a death knell.

The familiar old red school-house appeared in the distance down the familiar old street, yet the choking sensation in their throats, and the strange beating and blurring of their eyes gave it an odd appearance of disaster. That surely could not be the old hickory tree that Nate had climbed so often and hidden behind its ample friendly trunk to watch

Maria Bent as she came forth from the school-house door in search of him. How often had he encircled its shielding trunk to keep out of sight when he saw her looking for him! Now, alas, there would be no sheltering hickory for sanctuary from her strong hand, for Maria Bent would be no longer the school marm merely; she would be at close range in their only home; she would be mother! The name had suddenly taken on a gruesome sound, for they had been told that morning by Aunt Jane as she combed and scrubbed and arrayed them, that such address would be required of them henceforth. Call Maria Bent mother! Never!

Nate as he trudged, thought over all the long list of disrespectful appellations that it had been their custom among themselves to call their teacher, beginning with "Bent Maria" and ending with "M'wry-faced-straighten-er-out"; and inwardly resolved to call her nothing at all, or anything he pleased, all the time knowing that he would never dare.

Miranda, on the other side of the street, watched the disconsolate little procession, with their Aunt Jane bringing up the rear, and thanked her stars that she was not going forth to bind herself to their upbringing.

She had purposely lingered behind the Spaffords as they started to the wedding, saying she would follow with little Rose; and she came out of the front door and locked it carefully, just as the Whitneys issued forth from Aunt Jane's grooming. Rose jumped daintily down the steps, one at a time, watching the toes of her little new pink slippers, and tilting the ruffed pink silk parasol her father had brought her from New York. She looked like a sweet pink human rose, and the little prim Whitneys, sleek and scared though they were, turned envious eyes to watch her, almost forgetting for the moment the lump in their throats and the hot, angry feeling in their hearts, while they took in the beauty of the parasol, the grace of the small light feet, and the bobbing floss of golden curls as Rose skipped along by Miranda's side.

Miranda herself was wearing a new green and brown plaid silk, the pride and glory of her heart, bought with her own money and selected by her beloved Mrs. Marcia on her last trip to New York. Her bonnet was green shirred silk with a tiny green feather, and her red hair looked like burnished copper glinting out beneath. Miranda did not know it, never would, but she was growing to be a most attractive woman, and the twinkle of mischief in her eyes made one always look a second time at her cheerful freckled face.

Proudly she looked down at the dainty Rose, and compared her with the unhappy Whitneys doing the funeral march to their father's wedding. Not for any money would she be today in Maria Bent's place, but she walked the prouder and the more contented that she had had the chance.

There was a pleasant bustle about the school-house door when they all arrived. But the little Whitneys, their feuds laid aside at this time of their common sorrow, huddled together just inside the door of the school room, as far from the scene of action as possible, with dropped eyes and furtive sidewise glances, never daring even to whisper.

There were wreaths of flowers on each desk, zinneas, peonies, asters, roses, pansies, larkspurs and columbine; some of the smaller flowers were wreathed around a plateau of velvety moss on which in white pebbles and with varying designs the letters M.B. and N.W. were tastefully entwined. Each scholar had taken pride in getting up an original design for his or her own desk, and the result was unique and startling.

"How touching of them to want to please teacher!" exclaimed Ann Bloodgood, who lived in the next township and therefore did not know the current feeling.

But, however touching, the decorations only served to remind the three older Whitneys of their own mother's funeral. Nate hung his head and frowned hard behind the goldenrod-embowered stove, trying not to see or think of that other day five years ago when odors of flowers filled the air and he had had that same lump in his throat and gasp in his chest. That had been bad enough, but this day was worse. He had half a mind even now to bolt through that school-house door and never come back. But when he looked out to calculate how likely he was to get off without being seen, his father came walking up the school-house path. Maria Bent was hanging on his arm, in bright blue silk with a white lace bonnet, white kid gloves and a lace parasol. She was smirking and smiling to this side and that, and bestowing unwontedly loving greetings on the festive row of school girls lined up on either side of the path, stiff and straight all in their best dresses. "Walking pride," Miranda called it, and secretly exulted that she might have been there if she would; yet did not regret her choice.

Miranda had taken up her position where she could stand Rose on a desk to get a good view of the ceremony, and from her point of vantage she also got a vision of handsome little Nathan Whitney, his well-brushed Sunday suit squeezed between the stove and the wall, his soapy curls rumpled by the goldenrod, his stiff collar holding up a very trembling chin surmounted by hard little lips and an angry frown. It was plain that young Nathan was by no means happy at his father's wedding. Something in the whole slouch of his sturdy little figure touched Miranda and she watched him with a hitherto unsuspected sympathy. It was not to be expected of course that a bad boy like Nate Whitney would like to have a stern schoolteacher for his new mother. A gleam of something like pity shone in her eyes as she reflected how often Maria Bent would probably get her "comeuppance" for marrying Nathan Whitney; and how often little Nate Whitney would probably get his "comeuppance" for his pranks. Of the two Miranda was just the least bit inclined to side with the boy for the sake of his half-brother Allan with whom she had gone to school.

Miranda looked up to find him again after the prayer was over, but though her eyes searched quite carefully behind the stove, and under the bowers of goldenrod, he was gone. High in the branches of the friendly hickory, his Sunday clothes bearing a jagged tear in the seat of the trousers, his collar awry, and the shine of his Sunday shoes hopelessly marred and scratched, Nathan Whitney the second surveyed the scene. The prayer had been long enough for him to reach his old shelter in safety, and only the Whitney twins, Julia and Julius, and the five-year-old brother Samuel had seen his escape; and they were too frightened to tell. Miranda's searching gaze finally caught the uplifted look of the twins and Sammy, and following it presently saw the tremble of old hickory. She quickly lowered her eyes, knowing instinctively what had happened, but before she lowered them she caught the gleam of a pair of sorrowful brown eyes so like another pair of brown eyes she knew, looking between the leaves, and they haunted her all through the day.

The ceremony was long over and all the guests had gone home to discuss at length how "he looked," and how "she looked," and the prospect of happiness for the two who had been united in marriage.

Miranda had changed her green and brown plaid silk for a brown calico and a white apron, and was stirring up muffins for tea when she thought she saw a stealthy little figure stealing through the yard close by the hedge, but the early dusk was coming down and it was quite easy to fancy it had been only the shadows on the grass. Miranda was just about to light a candle and begin to set the table, but it was early yet for Mr. David would be late coming home from the office today on account of the time he had taken off for the wedding; and instead she took a bowl and went out to see if she could find some late yellow raspberries on the vines, though she knew quite well there were not likely to be any.

Humming a lively little tune she approached the berry vines, her sharp eyes studying the while the great leaves of pieplant growing next the hedge. They were moving now, stirring gently, almost imperceptibly, one minute, the next bobbing vigorously back and forth as if they had suddenly become animate. Miranda watched them stealthily, the while walking deliberately past them and humming her tune. The leaves became absolutely still as she passed them, though she did not turn her eyes down to them noticeably, but went on a little further and knelt down by the berry bushes voicing her tune in words now:

> "Thur wuz a man in our town,
>   An' he wuz wondrus wise,
> He jumped into a bramble bush
>   An' scratched out both his ey-i-es;
> An' when he saw his eyes were out
>   'ith all his might an' main,
> He jumped into another bush
>   An' scratched 'em in again."

"Land sakes!" she ejaculated suddenly. "Wisht I hed a boy t'hep hunt berries. Guess I'm gettin' nearsighted in the dark. Here's three whole ras'berries right clost together an' I come real nigh missin' 'em."

She cast an eye toward the pieplant leaves, but they remained motionless. Perhaps she had made a mistake after all. Perhaps there had been no dark little figure stealing along by the hedge. Perhaps her imagination had played her false.

She kept on feeling after berries that were not there, and finally after having secured not more than a handful, she crept softly back by the pieplant bed, for she thought she had heard a soft gasp like the catching of breath, and something stirred within her. She must find out what was moving the leaves.

Suddenly she set her bowl down on the grass and made a soft dive with her hands, lifting up two or three broad leaves and peering under.

It was almost dark now and the forlorn little figure close under the hedge could scarcely be seen, but Miranda's eyes were keen and kind, and she made out the outline of Nate Whitney's curly head, so sleek in the morning, now tousled and rough. He shrank back with his face in the grass, as she lifted the leaves, hoping to escape her notice, but she reached out her two strong hands and drew him forth resisting furiously.

"Lemme alone. I ain't doin' you any harm!" he declared sulkily as she drew his head and shoulders out from the entangling stalks.

There was light enough in the garden to see his face, tear-stained and smeared with mud streaks. His collar was crushed and twisted awry, and his jacket had a great jagged tear in one elbow.

"You poor little motherless sinner!" ejaculated Miranda in a tone she had never used in her life before except for little Rose.

Suddenly she sat down plump on the garden walk and took the forlorn little fellow into her arms, at least as much as she could get hold of, for he was still wriggling and twisting away from her strong hand with all his discomfited young might.

She stooped over his dirty fierce young face and laid her lips on his forehead.

"You poor little soul, I know how you feel and I don't blame you one mite," she whispered, her strong young arms enwrapping him gently.

Then quite suddenly the struggling ceased, the fierce wiry body relaxed, the dirty face and curly head buried themselves quite childishly in her arms, the boy sobbed as if his heart would break, and clung to her as if his life depended on it.

Something wonderfully sweet and new sprang up in Miranda's breast, motherhood stirring in her soul. The clinging hands, the warm wet face, the pitiful sight of this sorrowful child in place of the saucy, impudent, self-possessed boy who dared any mischief that his bright restless mind suggested, touched her heart in a new way. A fierce desire seized her to protect and love him, this boy who needed someone sorely, and for the first time a regret stole into her heart that she was not his new mother. What a thing it would be to have those clinging arms belong to her! Then a wicked exultant thrill passed through her. She had not "walked pride" with Nathan Whitney, but his son had turned to her for comfort, and she loved the boy for it with all her heart. Maria Bent might hold her head high and reign severely in his home, but *she*, Miranda Griscom, would love the little son and help him out of his scrapes from this time forth.

"There, there," she soothed, passing her rough, work-worn hand over the tumbled curls and exulting in their tendency to wrap about her fingers. How soft they were, like a baby's, and yet they belonged to that hard, bad, little boy she had always called a "brat!"

"There, there! Just cry it out," she murmured. "I know. I jest guess I know all how you feel. You needn't to mind me. I've been fixed myself, so I didn't like things pretty much, an' I kin see you ain't overly pleased at the change over to your house. You jest cry good an' hard oncet, an' it'll make you feel better. Ef you can't do it hard 'nough by yerself I'll hep you—" and Miranda laid her freckled face on the little muddy cheek of the boy and let her tears mingle with his.

Perhaps it was those hot tears falling on his face, tears that were not his own, that called him back to his boy senses and brought to an end the first crying spell he remembered since he was six years old when Aunt Jane sneered at him and called him a cry-baby, that time he had cut his foot on a scythe. He had been a self-contained, hard, bad, little man ever since till now, when all the foundations of his being seemed shaken with this unexpected sympathy from one whom he had hitherto ranked among his enemies.

His sobs stopped as suddenly as they had begun and for some time he lay still in her arms, his head pressed against her shoulder where she had drawn it, his breath coming hot and quick against her face.

"Can't you tell me what's the matter? Is't anythin' special?" asked the girl gently. One would scarcely have known Miranda's voice. All the hardness and sharpness and mirth were gone. There was only gentleness and tenderness, and a deep understanding. "Course I know 'tain't altogether pleasant hevin' a stranger—especially ef she's one you've known afore an' ain't fond of—"

"I *hate* her!" came with sudden fierce vehemence from the lips of the boy. There was a catch in his throat, but his lips were set and no more tears were allowed to come.

"Well, 'course that ain't the way you're expected t' feel, but I onderstand, and I guess they wouldn't enny of 'em do much better in your place. I never did admire her much myself, so I ken see how you look at it."

"I hate her!" reiterated the boy again, but this time not so fiercely. "I hate her and I won't let her be my mother, ever! Say, why didn't *you* be it?"

The question was balm and pride to the heart of Miranda. She put her arms the closer around the lonely boy and rocked him gently back and forth, and then smoothed his hair back from his hot dirty forehead. The marvel was he let her do it and did not squirm away.

"Why didn't I? Bless him! Well, I didn't think I'd like it enny better'n you do her. B'sides, ef I had, you'd a hated *me* then."

The boy looked at her steadily through the twilight as though he were turning it over in his mind and then suddenly broke into a shy smile.

"Mebbe I would," he said with honest eyes searching her face, and then half shamefaced, he added shyly: "But anyhow I like you now."

A wild sweet rush of emotion flooded Miranda's soul. Not since she left her unloved, unloving grandmother Heath who lived next door, and came to live with David and Marcia Spafford receiving wages, doing honest work in return, and finding a real home, had such sweet surprise and joy come to her. Sweeter even than the little cherished Rose's kisses was this shy, veiled admiration of the man-child whose lonely life she seemed somehow strangely to understand. All at once she seemed to know how and why he had got the name of being a bad boy, and her heart went out to him as to a kindred spirit. She had seen the soul of him looking out of his beautiful brown eyes in the dusk at her, and she knew he was not all bad, and that it had mostly been the fault of other people when he had really done wrong.

Miranda's arms in their warm pressure answered the boy's words, and she stooped again and laid her lips on his forehead lingeringly, albeit as shyly as a boy might have done it. Miranda was not one to show deep emotion and she was more stirred than ever before.

"Well, I guess we sort o' b'long to each other somehow. Ennyhow we'll be friends. Say, didn't you tear your cloes when you went up that hick'ry?"

The child in her arms suddenly straightened up and became the boy with mischief in his eyes and a knowing tilt to his handsome head.

"Say, did you see me go up that tree?"

"No, but I saw you gone; and I saw Sammy's eyes lookin' up, an' I saw the hick'ry movin' some, so I calc'lated you was up there, all right."

"An' you won"t tell?" doubtfully.

"Course I won't tell. It's none o' my business, an' b'sides I could see you wasn't enjoyin' yerse'f to the weddin'. What's more, I'll mend them cloes. There ain't no reason fer M'ria Bent as was, to come inspectin' you yet a whiles. You kin shin up the kitchen roof, can't yeh, to my winder, an' you take off them rips an' tears an' hop into my bed? I'll come up an' mend yeh so's she won't know. Then you ken shin up a tree to yer own winder t' hum an' go to bed, an' like's not she'll never notice them cloes till yer Aunt Jane's gone, an' she'll think they been tore an' mended sometime back, an' she ain't got no call to throw 'em up to yeh. Hed yer supper?"

"Naw. Don't want any."

"That's all right. I'll bring you up some caraway cookies. You like 'em don't yeh? Er hev yeh et too much weddin' cake?"

"Didn't touch their old wedding cake," said the boy sulkily.

"Boy, didn't you go home 'tall since you was in the hick'ry? Wall, I swan! To think you'd miss the reception with all them good things to eat! You must a felt pretty bad. Never mind you, honey. You do's I tell yeh. Just shin right up that roof. Here, eat them raspberries first, they ain't many but they'll stay yeh. I got some fried chicken left over. Don't you worry. Now, let's see you get up there."

Miranda helped Nate from the back kitchen window to mount to the roof and saw him climb lightly and gleefully in at her window, then she bustled in to put supper on the table. Mr. David was not home yet when everything was ready, so with a glass of milk, a plate of bread, jelly, and chicken, and another of cookies she slipped up the back stairs to her small boy, and found him quite contentedly awaiting her coming, his eyes shining a welcome to her through the gathering darkness of the room, as he might have done to any pal in a youthful conspiracy.

"I've got a boarder," she explained grimly a few minutes afterward to the astonished Mrs. Marcia, coming downstairs with her lighted candle, a small pair of trousers and a jacket over her arm.

"A boarder!" Mrs. Marcia had learned to expect the unusual from Miranda, but this was out of the ordinary even for Miranda, at least without permission.

"Yes, you ken take it off my wages. I don't guess he'll remain more'n an hour or so, leastways I'll try to get him off soon fer his own sake. It's that poor little peaked Nate Whitney, Mrs. Marcia. He's all broke up over hevin' that broomstick of a M'ria Bent fer his mother, an' seein' as I sorta shirked the job myself I thought 'twas only decent I should chirk him up a bit. He was out behind the pieplant cryin' like his heart would break, an' he ast me, why didn't *I* be his mother 'at he *hated* her, an' he was all tore up with climbin' trees to get out of sight, so I laid out to mend him up a little 'fore he goes home. I know M'ria Bent. I went to school to her one year 'fore I quit, an' she's a tartar! It ain't reasonable fer him to start in with her the first day all tore up. She'd get him at a disadvantage. Ain't you got a patch would do to put under this tear, Mrs. Marcia? I took him up some supper. I knowed you wouldn't care, an' I want you should take it off my wages. Yes, that's right. I'll feel better about it ef you do, then I could do it agin ef the notion should take me. I owe a little sumpin' to that boy fer my present state of freedom an' independence, an' I kinda take a likin' to him when he's cryin' you know. After all, I do' no's'e was ever so awful bad."

Mrs. Marcia laid a tender understanding touch on her handmaiden's arm, and with a smile in the dimple by the off-corner of her mouth, and a tear in the eye that Miranda could not see, went to get the patch.

Young Nathan inside of two hours departed by the way of the roof, washed and combed, mended and pressed, as well as Aunt Jane could have done it; but with more than he had had for years, a heart that was almost comforted. He felt that now he had at least one friend in the world who understood him, and meditated as he slid down the kitchen-shed roof, whether it might not be practicable for him to grow up fast and marry Miranda so no one else would carry her off. By the time he had scaled his own kitchen roof and cautiously removed his clothing, hung it up and crept to his own little bed, he had, it is true, quite forgotten this vague idea; but the comfort in his heart remained, and made it possible for him to waken cheerfully the next morning to his new world without that sinking feeling that had been in his heart and stomach ever since he knew that Maria Bent was to be his father's wife.

So that was how it all came about that Miranda Griscom became mother-confessor and chief-comforter to Nathan Whitney's second son, and Nathan became the slave and adorer of little Rose Schuyler Spafford when she was five-years-old-going-on-to-six; and it all began in the year 1838.

CHAPTER 3

THERE was a chapter in Miranda's life that she had never told to a living soul, and which only on rare occasions did she herself take out of her heart and look over. It was only when the wellsprings of her very being were deeply touched in some way as in the quiet and dark of her starlit window; or when she was on her knees at her queer devotions, that she let her mind dwell upon it.

Miranda was twenty-two years old, and entirely heart whole, yet there had been and still was a romance in her life as sweet and precious as any that more favored girls had experienced. That it had been sad and brief, and the hope of its ever coming to anything had long since departed from her heart, made it no less precious to her. It was on account of her strength and sweetness of character, her bubbling good nature and interest in others, and her keen sense of humor that her experience had not hardened or sharpened her one mite. She was one of those strong souls who through not having has learned to forget self, and be content in the joy of others. There was not a fibre of selfishness in the whole of her quaint, intense, delightful make-up. She lived her somewhat lonely life and picked up what crumbs of pleasure she could find; fought her merry, sometimes questionable, warfare for those she loved; served them worshipfully; would give her life for theirs any day; yet kept in her heart one strong secret shrine for the love of her young heart furnished royally with all the hopes and yearnings that any girl knows.

Years ago, it seemed centuries now, before David had brought his girl bride to the old house next door to Grandmother Heath's, where Miranda had been a schoolgirl, eleven—twelve—thirteen years old, there had been a hero in her life. No one had known it, not even the hero. But no knight of old ever was beloved or watched or exalted by fair lady more than was Allan Whitney, half brother of young Nathan—for Maria Bent was of course old Nathan Whitney's third wife.

Allan Whitney was tall and strong, with straight dark hair that fell over his forehead till he had continually to toss it back; a mouth that drooped pathetically above a strong purposeful chin; eyes that held depths of fierceness and sadness that only a passionate temperament knows how to combine; and a reputation altogether worse than any boy that had ever been brought up in the town.

Allan had been kind to his stepmother when his father was cold and hard, and had in some way cheered her last days; but she never had time or fortitude to do much in the way of bringing him up. In fact he never was brought up, unless he did it himself. If one might judge by his strong will, if it was his inheritance from his own mother, she alone might have been able to do something toward moulding him. Certainly his father never held the slightest influence with the boy. Nathan Whitney could make money and keep it, but he could not make boys into good men.

Allan Whitney had been quick and bright, but he would not study at school, and he would not go to work. He had been very much in his time as young Nathan was not, only more so, Miranda thought as she placed the facts honestly before her in the starlight, while she watched to see if there would be a light in the boy's window across the way.

Allan had been in continual rebellion against the universe. In school he was whipped whenever the teacher felt out of sorts with anybody, and he took it with the careless jocular air of one who knows he could "lick the teacher into the middle of next week" if he undertook the job. As it was he generally allowed the chastisement for the sake of the relief from monotony for the rest of the scholars. He would wink slyly at Miranda who sat down in a front seat demurely studying her spelling, as he lounged forward and held out his hand. By a sort of freemasonry he knew her to be of the same temper as himself, and that she both understood and sympathized with him. Five desks back Rowena Higginson was in tears on account of his sufferings, and gentle Annetta Bloodgood turned pale with the sound of each blow from the ferrule, half shuddering in time to the chastisement; but Allan Whitney hugely enjoyed their sentimental sufferings. He knew that every boy in the room admired him for the way he took his whippings, and sought provocations for like martyrdom, that they might emulate his easy air of indifference. When his punishment was over Allan would seek his seat, lazily, a happy grimace on his face, another wink for Miranda, with sometimes a lollipop or some barley sugar laid surreptitiously on her desk as he passed by, and a knowing tweak of her red pigtails, which endearments were waited for on her part with a trembling eagerness that he never suspected. She was only a smart child who knew almost as much as a boy about a boy's code of life, and took his good-natured tormentings as well as a boy could have done; therefore he enjoyed tormenting her.

Nevertheless, though Miranda witnessed his punishments with outward serenity and gloried in his indifference to them, her young soul was filled with bitterness against the teachers for their treatment of her hero, and many a hard knock of discipline did she lay up in store for those same teachers in the future if ever it came her way to give it; and she generally managed sometime, somehow to give it.

"Miss Menchant, is this your hankercher?" she asked sweetly one day after Allan had retired indifferently from a whipping which Miranda knew must have hurt, given merely because Miss Menchant found a large drawing of herself in lifelike lines on the blackboard near Allan's desk, and couldn't locate the artist.

Miss Menchant said severely that it was—as if Miranda were in some way to blame for it's having been on the floor—as indeed she was, having filched it from her teacher's pocket in the coat-room and brought it into the schoolroom ready bated for her prey.

A moment later Miss Menchant picked up the handkerchief from where Miranda had laid it on the desk at her hand, and wiped her face, immediately thereafter dropping it in haste with aloud exclamations and putting her hand with pain to her nose, while a fine large honeybee flew away through the open door of the schoolhouse.

"Miranda!" called the suffering teacher. "Miranda Griscom!" But Miranda, like a good child, had taken her dinner pail and gone home. Her bright brown eye might have been seen taking observations through a knothole at the end of the schoolhouse, but Miss Menchant didn't happen to be looking that way, and when the next morning the teacher asked the little girl if she noticed anything on the handkerchief when she picked it up, Miranda's eyes were sweetly unconscious of the large red knob on the teacher's nose as she answered serenely:

"I didn't take notice to nothin'."

The next time that Allan Whitney was called up for discipline the ruler which usually played a prominent part in the affair was strangely missing, and might have been found in Miranda Griscom's desk if anyone had known where to look for it. It met a watery grave that night in the old mill stream down behind the mill wheel, in company with several of its successors of later years.

Time cures all things, and they usually had women teachers in that school. Allan presently grew so large that few women teachers could whip him and it then became a vital question, when engaging a new teacher, as to whether or not she would be able to "lick" Allan Whitney. One winter they tried a man, a little, knotty shrimp of a man he was, with a high reputation as to intellect, but no more appreciation of a boy than if he had been a boiled owl. Those were days that delighted the souls of the scholars of that school, for it was soon noised abroad that every day was a delight because every day a new drama of contest was flung on the stage for their delectation.

Now, there was behind the platform, where the teacher's desk and chair were placed, a long dark room where coats and dinner pails were kept. It had a single small, narrow window at one end, and the other end came up to a partition which cut off the teacher's private closet from it. This was the girls' cloak room, and was a part of the improvements made on the old red school-house about the time that Miranda began to go to school. The boys had a small closet at the back of the room, so they never went to this, but as the school grew crowded this cloakroom was well filled, especially in winter when everybody had plenty of wraps. To make more light, there had been made an opening from it into the schoolroom, window-like, with a wide shelf or ledge behind the teacher's desk. This was frequently adorned with a row of dinner pails. A door to the right of the platform opened into the teacher's closet, and was usually kept closed, while that to the left opened into the girls' cloak room and was usually standing open. Miranda's desk was directly in front of this door, the teacher having found it handy to have Miranda where he could keep a weather eye out for plots under a serene and innocent exterior.

When the man teacher, Mr. Applethorn by name, had been in the school about three weeks and had tried every conceivable plan for the conquering of Allan Whitney save the time-worn one of "licking" him, it became apparent that the issue was to be brought to a climax. Miranda had heard low words from Allan to his friend Bud Hendrake concerning what he meant to do if "old Appleseed tried it," and while the little girl had great faith in Allan's strength of body and quickness of mind over against the little flabby body and quickly aroused temper of the teacher, she nevertheless reflected that behind him were all the selectmen, and authority was always at war with poor Allan. It would go hard with him this time, she knew, if the matter were put in the hands of the selectmen. She had heard Grandfather Heath talking about it. "One more outrage and we're done with him." That sentence sent terror to the heart of Miranda, for the long stretches of school days unenlivened by the careless smile and merry sayings of Allan Whitney were to her unbearable to think about. Something must be done to save Allan, and she must do it, for there was no one else to care. So Miranda had lain awake for a long time trying to devise a plan by which the injustice done by the teacher to Allan could not only be avenged, but the immediate danger of a fight between Allan and the teacher averted, at least for a time. If Allan fought with the teacher and "licked" him everybody would be sorry for the teacher, for nobody liked Allan; that is, nobody that had any authority. There it was, always authority against Allan! Poor little Miranda tossed on her small bed and thought, and finally fell asleep with her problem unsolved; but she started for school the next morning with firmly set lips and a determined frown. She would do something, see if she wouldn't!

And then Grandmother Heath called her back to carry a pail of sour cream to Granny MacVane's on her way to school.

Now ordinarily Miranda would not have welcomed the errand away around by Granny MacVane's *before school*—and grandmother was very particular that she should go before school—she liked to get to school early and play hide and seek in the yard, and Grandmother Heath knew it and disapproved. School was not established for amusement, but for education, she frequently remarked when remonstrating with Miranda for starting so early; but this particular morning the girl's face brightened and she took the shining tin pail with alacrity and demurely responded, "Yes ma'am," when her grandmother repeated the command to be sure and go *before* school. She was so nice and obedient about it that the old lady looked after her suspiciously, having learned that the ways of Miranda were devious, and when her exterior was calm, then was the time to be on the alert.

For Miranda had suddenly seen light in the darkness with the advent on the scene of this pail of sour cream. Sour cream would keep. That is it would only grow sourer, which was desirable in a thing like sour cream. There was no reason in the world why that cream had to go to Granny MacVane's before school, especially when it might come in handy for something else besides making gingerbread for Granny MacVane. Besides, Granny MacVane lived beyond the school-house and Grandmother Heath would never know whether she went before or after. Sour cream was a delicacy frequently sent to old Mrs. MacVane, and if she brought the message, "Granny says she's much obliged Gran'ma," there would be no question, and likely nothing further ever thought about it.

Besides, Miranda was willing to take a chance if the stakes were high enough, so she hurried happily off to school with her head held high and the sour cream pail clattering against her dinner pail with reckless hilarity; while Miranda laid her neat little plans.

Arrived at the school-house, she deposited the pail of sour cream together with its mate the dinner pail inconspicuously on the inner ledge of the window over the teacher's desk-chair. The ledge was wide and the pails almost out of sight from the schoolroom. At noon, however, Miranda, after eating her lunch, replaced her empty dinner pail and made a careful rearrangement of all the pails on the ledge, her own and others, so that they were grouped quite innocently nearer to the front edge. Miranda herself was early seated at her desk studying demurely when the others came in.

The very atmosphere that afternoon seemed electric. Even the very little scholars seemed to understand that something was going to happen before school "let out," and when just as the master was about to send the school out for afternoon recess he paused and announced solemnly, "Allan Whitney, you may remain in your seat!" they knew it was almost at hand.

CHAPTER 4

MIRANDA had played her cards well. She sat studiously in her seat until everybody was out of the schoolroom but Mr. Applethorn, Allan and herself, and then she raised her hand demurely for permission to speak:

"Teacher, please may I go's soon 'z I finish my 'gzamples? Grandma wants me to go to Granny MacVane's on a errand, an' she don't want me to stay out after dark."

The teacher gave a curt permission. He had no time just then to fathom Miranda Griscom's deeps, and had always felt that she belonged to the enemy. She was as well out of the room when he gave Allan Whitney his dues.

Miranda worked away vigorously. The examples were already finished, but she had no mind to leave until the right moment. Such studious ways in Miranda were astonishing, and if Mr. Applethorn had not been otherwise occupied he would certainly have suspected something, seeing Miranda, the usually alert one, bending over her slate, a stubby pencil in her hand, her brows wrinkled hard over a supposedly perplexing question, her two red plaits sticking out at each side, and no eyes nor ears for what was going on in the playground.

Allan Whitney sat serenely whittling a small stick into a very tiny sword, and half whistling under his breath until the master, in a voice that was meant to be stentorian, uttered a solemn: "Silence, sir! I say, *Silence!*"

Allan looked up pleasantly.

"All right sir, just as you say sir."

The master was growing angry. Miranda saw it out of the tail of her eye. He glowered at the boy a minute.

"I said *silence,*" he roared. "You've no need to answer further. Just keep silence!"

"Very well, sir, I heard you sir, and I said all right sir, just as you say sir," answered Allan sunnily again, with the most aggravating smile on his face, but not a shade of impudence in his voice. Allan knew how to be impudent in a perfectly respectful way.

"Hold your tongue, sir!" fairly howled the master.

"Oh, thank you, I will sir," said Allan, but it was the teacher who, red and angry, found he had to hold his, while Allan had the last word, for just then the boy who had been appointed to ring the bell for recess to be over, appeared in the doorway and gave it three taps, and the eager scholars who had been hovering in excited groups hurried back to their seats wondering what was about to happen.

They settled into quiet sooner than usual and sat in breathless attention, their eyes apparently riveted on their books, awaiting the call to the last class of the afternoon, but in reality watching alternately the angry visage of the teacher, and the calm pale one of Allan Whitney who now drew himself to his full height and sat with folded arms.

The master reached into his desk, drew forth the ferrule, and threw it with skilful twirl straight into the face of the boy. Then Allan, accepting the challenge, arose and came forward to the platform, but he did not stoop to pick up the ruler and bring it with him according to custom. Instead he came as a man might have come who had just been insulted, his head held high, his eyes glowing darkly in his white set face, for the ruler had struck him across the mouth, and its sting had sunk into his soul. In that blow seemed concentrated all the injustices of all the years when he had been misjudged by his teachers and fellow-townsmen. Not but that he had not been a mischievous, bad boy often and often, but not always; and he resented the fact that when he did try to do right nobody would give him credit for it.

It was just at this crucial moment that Miranda arose with her completed arithmetic paper and fluttered conspicuously up to the desk.

"May I go now, teacher?" she asked sweetly, "I've got 'em all done, every one."

The master waved her away without ceremony. She was to him like a gadfly annoying when he needed all his senses to master the trouble in hand.

Miranda slipped joyously into the cloak room apparently as unconscious of Allan Whitney standing close beside her, as if he had been miles away; and a moment thereafter those who sat in the extreme back of the room might have seen the dim flutter of a brown calico sunbonnet landing on top of the dinner pails just over the master's head, if they had not been too occupied with the changing visage of the master, and the quiet form of Allan standing in defiant attitude before him. Mr. Applethorn was a great believer in deliberation, and was never afraid of a pause. He thought it impressive. At this moment, while he gathered all his courage for the encounter that he knew was before him, he paused and expected to quell Allan Whitney by the glance of his two angry eyes.

The schoolmaster was still seated, though drawn up to his full height with folded arms, looking dignified as he knew how to look, and far more impressive than if he had been standing in front of his tall pupil. Suddenly, before a word had been spoken, and very quietly for a thing of metal, the tin pail on the ledge over his chair began to move forward, as if pushed by a phalanx of its fellows from behind. It came to the edge,—it toppled,— and a broad avalanche of thick white substance gushed forth, preceded by a giddy tin cover, which reeled and pirouetted for a moment on the master's astonished head, took a step down his nose, and waltzed off to the platform and under the stove. This was followed by a concluding white deluge as the pail descended and settled down over the noble brows of Mr. Applethorn, who arose in haste and horror, dripping sour cream, spluttering and snorting like a porpoise, amid a howling, screaming, shouting mob of irreverent scholars who were laughing until the tears streamed down their cheeks.

Miranda, appearing penitently at the door of the cloak room, her brown sunbonnet in her hand, ready tears prepared to be shed if need be, at the loss of her precious sour cream,—accidentally knocked over when she went to get her sunbonnet which some malicious girl must have put up high out of her reach,—found no need for any further efforts on her part. Obviously the fight was over. The schoolmaster was in no condition to administer either justice or injustice to anybody.

Allan Whitney at this crisis arose magnificently to the occasion. With admirable solicitude he relieved the schoolmaster of his unwelcome helmet, and with his own soiled and crumpled handkerchief wiped the lumps of sour cream from his erstwhile adversary's features.

For one blessed hilarious moment the schoolmaster had stood helpless and enraged, blinded and speechless, choking and gasping and dripping sour cream from every point of his hair, nose, collar, chin, and the tips of his very fingers; and the wild mob of hysterical pupils stood on the desks and viewed him, bending double with their mirth, or jumping up and down in their ecstasy. The next moment Allan Whitney had taken command, and with one raised hand had silenced the hilarity, with a second motion had cleared the room, and a low word to one of his devoted slaves brought a pail of water to his side. Then in the seclusion of the empty schoolroom he applied himself to the rescue of Mr. Applethorn.

Miranda, in the shelter of the cloak room door, secure for the moment from the cream-filled eyes of the teacher, watched her hero in awe as he mopped away at his enemy, as tenderly and kindly as if he had been a little child in trouble. She was too filled with mixed emotions to care to play the guileless, saucy part she had prepared for herself in this comedy. She was filled with dread lest after all Allan did not approve of what she had done, and did not like it. That he would be in the least deceived by her sunbonnet trick she never for a moment expected. That he would be angry because she had stopped the fight had not crossed her mind before. Now she stood in an agony of fear, forgetting the comical sight of the schoolmaster done in sour cream, and trembled lest she had hopelessly offended her hero. Perhaps after all it wasn't fair to interfere with the game. Perhaps she had transgressed the rules of the code and lost her high place in his estimation. If she had, no punishment would be too great, no penance suffice to cover her transgression. The sun would be blotted out of her little world, and her heart broken forever.

At that instant of dejection Allan turned from wiping out the victim's left eye and gave the cringing Miranda a large, kind, appreciative wink. Suddenly her sun rose high once more, and her heart sprang lightly up again. She responded with her tongue in her cheek, and a knowing grimace, departing, warmed and satisfied, taking the precaution to make her exit through the window of the cloak room. Down behind the alders by the creek, however, her natural man asserted itself, and she sat down to laugh till she cried over the spectacle of her teacher in a tin pail enveloped in sour cream. Next morning she found a large piece of spruce gum in her desk with a bit of paper wrapped around it on which was written in Allan's familiar scrawl:

"You are a little brick."

The strange thing about it all was that Allan and Mr. Applethorn became excellent friends after that; but the selectmen, though they offered every inducement in their power, could not prevail upon the teacher to remain longer than the end of the month. Poor little Mr. Applethorn could not get over his humiliation before his scholars, and he never quite understood how that sour cream got located over his head, though Allan gave a very plausible explanation and kept him in some mysterious way from making too close an investigation.

After that Allan Whitney always had a glance and a wink, and on rare occasions, a smile, for Miranda, but the boy did not come back to school again after Mr. Applethorn left, and the little girl seldom saw him except on the street. However, her worship of him relaxed no whit and her young heart resented the things that were said about him. Always she was on the watch to do him a good turn, but not for a long time did it come and then it came with a vengeance, a short, sharp trial of her loyalty.

CHAPTER 5

IT was a bitter cold night in November and Miranda had crept up close to the fireplace with her spelling book—not that she cared in the least for her spelling lesson, though there was to be a spelling-down contest the next day in school, but her spelling book was always a good excuse to Grandma Heath for not knitting or spinning of an evening.

Grandpa Heath came in presently, stamping away the snow, and shutting the outside door noisily. One could see he was excited. He strode across the room and hung up the big key that locked the old smokehouse door. Mr. Heath was constable and the old smokehouse was being used for a lockup. It was plain that something had happened.

Miranda looked up alertly, but cast down her eyes at once to her book and was apparently a diligent scholar, even conning her words half aloud. She knew by experience that if she appeared to be listening, all the news would be saved till she was sent off to bed, and then she would have to lie on the floor in the cold with her ear to the pipe hole that was supposed to warm her room in order to get necessary information. If she kept still and was absorbed in her work the chances were her grandfather would forget she was there.

He hung up his coat, muffler and cap, and sat down heavily in his chair across the table from his wife, who was diligently knitting a long gray stocking. The light of the one candle that was frugally burning high on the shelf over the fireplace, flickered fitfully over the whole room and made the old man's face look ashen gray with shadows as he began to talk, nervously fingering his scraggly gray beard:

"Well, I guess we've had a murder!" he spoke shakily, as if he could not himself quite comprehend the fact he was imparting.

"You *guess!*" said his wife sharply, "Don't you *know?* There ain't any halfway about a murder usually."

"Well, he ain't dead yet, but there ain't much chance fer his life. I guess he'll pass away 'fore the mornin'."

"Who? Why don't you ever tell the whole story?" snapped Grandmother Heath excitedly.

"Why, it's old Enoch Taylor. Didn't I say in the first place?"

"No, you didn't. Who done it?"

"Allan Whitney,—leastways he was comin' away with a gun when we found him, an' we've got him arrested. He's down in the smokehouse now."

"H'm!" commented his wife. "Just what I expected he'd come to. Well, the town'll be well rid of him. Ain't he kinda young though to be hung?"

"Well, I guess he's about seventeen, but he's large fer his age. I don't know whether they ken hang him er not. He ain't ben tried yet of course, but it'll go against him, no question o' that. He's ben a pest to the neighborhood fer a long, time—"

At this point Miranda's spelling book fell clattering to the hearth, where it knocked off the cover from the bowl of yeast set to rise by the warmth, but when her startled grandparents turned to look at her she was apparently sound asleep, sitting on her little cushion on the hearth with her head against the fire jamb.

Her grandmother arose and gave her a vigorous shaking.

"M'randy, git right up off'n that hearth and go to bed. It beats all how a great girl like you can't keep awake to get her lessons. You might a fell in the fire. Wake up, I tell you, an' go to bed this minute!"

Miranda awoke with studied leisure, yawning and dazed, and admirably unconscious of her surroundings. Slowly she picked up her book, rubbing her drowsy eyes, lighted her candle and dragged herself yawning up the stairs to her room, but when she arrived there she did not prepare for bed. Instead she wrapped herself in a quilt and lay down with her ear to the stovepipe hole, her whole body tense and quivering with agony.

The old couple waited until the stair door was latched and the girl's footsteps unmistakably toward the top of the stair, then the Grandmother spoke:

"I'm real glad he's got caught now 'fore he growed up any bigger. I always was afraid M'randy'd take a notion to him an' run off like her mother did. He's good lookin',—the kind like her father was, and such things run in the blood. She was real fond of him a couple of years back— used to fly up like a scratch cat every time any body mentioned his cuttin's up, but she ain't mentioned him lately."

"Aw—you didn't need to worry 'bout that I guess," said her husband meditatively, "he wouldn't ever have took to her. Red hair and a little turned up nose like hers don't go down with these young fellers. Besides, she ain't nothin' but a child, an' he's most a grown man."

"She ain't so bad looking," bristled her grandmother with asperity, and it is a pity that poor, plain Miranda, who fancied herself a blot on the face of the earth for homeliness, could not have overheard her, for it would have softened her heart toward her hard, unloving grandmother to an astonishing degree. Miranda knew that she was a trial to her relatives, and never fancied that they cared for her in the least.

But though Miranda lay on the floor until her grandparents came upstairs for the night, she heard no more about the murder or Allan. Wrapped in her quilt she crept to the window and looked out through the snowy night. There was no wind, and the snow came down like fine powder, small and still, but invincible and steady. Out through the white veil she could dimly see the dark walls of the old smokehouse, white-capped and still.

Out there in the cold and dark and snow was Allan,—her fine, strong, merry Allan! It seemed incredible! He was there charged with murder! and awaiting the morrow! As had happened before, she, Miranda, was the only one in the whole wide world who seemed to have a mind to save him.

When she had first heard her grandfather's words downstairs her heart had almost frozen within her, and for once her natural cunning had almost deserted her. When her book fell it was with difficulty that she kept herself from crying out; but she had sense enough left to put her head against the fireplace and pretend to be asleep. As she closed her eyes the vision of the great black key hanging on the wall beside the clock seemed burned into her brain. It was the symbol of Allan's imprisonment, and it seemed to mock her from its nail, and challenge her to save her hero now if she could.

She had known from the first instant that she would save him, or at least that she would do all in her power to do so. The key had flung her the challenge, and her plan had been forming even as she listened to the story. Now she went over it carefully in every detail.

Out there in the smokehouse Allan was stiff and cold. She knew the smooth, chilly floor of hard clay, the rough, unfriendly feel of the brick walls with the mortar hanging in great blotches over their surface. On the dim raftered ceiling still hung a ham or two, because it was nearer to the house than the new smokehouse, where most of the winter stores were kept—for the lockup was seldom used, in fact had only been called into requisition twice in the three years that Mr. Heath had been constable— and it was handy to run to the old smokehouse door when they needed a slice of ham. Ah, that was an idea. Allan would need food. He could take one of those hams. Her busy brain thought it all out as an older girl might have done, and as soon as she heard the distant rumble of her grandfather's comfortable snore, she crept softly about her preparations. It was too early to make any very decided moves, for her grandmother, though quite deaf, was not always a ready sleeper, and had a way of "sensing" things that she could not hear. It would not be well to arouse grandmother's suspicions and spoil the whole scheme, so she moved cautiously.

Under the eaves, opening through her tiny closet, there stood a trunk containing some of the clothes that used to be her mother's, and she remembered that among them was an old overcoat of her father's. It was not fine nor handsome but it was warm; and from all she knew of Allan's habits he had probably worn no overcoat when he was out that afternoon, for it had not been so very cold then, and the snow had not begun to fall. He would be needing something warm this very minute. How her heart yearned to make him a good, hot cup of coffee and take it out to him, but she dared not attempt it. If her grandmother's ears were growing dim, at least her nostrils were not failing, and she would scent the smell of coffee in the middle of her night's sleep. There was no use at all in attempting that, even if it were safe for Allan to delay to drink it, which it was not. But the overcoat he could wear away and no one be any the wiser. Grandmother would not overhaul that trunk for any vagrant moths until next spring now, and what mattered it then what she thought about its absence? As like as not she would be glad to have it gone because it belonged to the hated man who had run away from their daughter, and left her and her little red-haired child to be a burden.

She hesitated about lighting a candle, finally deciding not to risk it, and crept softly into the eaves closet on her hands and knees in the dark, going by her sense of feeling straight to the little hair trunk, and finding the overcoat at the very bottom. She put the other things carefully away, and got back quietly to her room again with the coat, hugging it like a treasure. She laid her cheek for an instant against the worn collar and had a fleeting thrill of affection for the wanderer who had deserted his family, just because the coat was his and was helping her to help Allan.

People were "early to bed and early to rise" in those days. Mr. and Mrs. Heath had retired to their slumber at nine o'clock that night. It was ten before Miranda left her window to stir about the room. The old clock in the kitchen had struck eleven before she found the overcoat and had put everything back in the trunk.

She waited until she had counted out the slow strokes of twelve from the clock before she dared steal down-stairs and softly take the key from its nail by the clock. The cold iron of the key bit into her trembling fingers as if it had been alive, and she almost dropped it. She stood shaking with cold and fright, for it seemed as if every board in the floor that she stepped upon creaked. Once she fell over her grandmother's rocking chair and the rockers dug into her ankles as if they had a grudge against her. Her nerves were so keyed up that the hurt brought tears to her Spartan eyes, and she had to sit down for a minute to bear the pain.

She had carefully canvassed the idea of going out of the door downstairs and had given it up. There was too much risk. First the door opened noisily, and the bar that was put across it at night fitted tightly. It was liable to make a loud grating sound when it was moved. Also, the snow was deep enough that footprints by the door would be noticeable in the morning unless it snowed harder than it was doing now and the wind blew to cover them up. Besides, it would be terrible if any one should see her coming out the door and it should come to her Grandfather's ears that she had done this thing. He would never forgive her and she would have to run away. But worst of all, she dreaded being seen and stopped before she had accomplished her purpose, for the downstairs door was just under her grandmother's window. Therefore, the key secure, she slipped softly into the pantry, found half a loaf of bread, two turnovers and some cookies, and with her booty crept back upstairs again.

When she was at last safely back in her room she drew a long sigh of relief and sat down for a moment to listen and be sure that she had not disturbed the sleepers, then she tied the key on a strong string and hung it around her neck. Next, she wrapped the bread, turnovers and cookies in some clean pieces of white cloth that were given her for the quilt she was piecing, stuffed them carefully into the pockets of the old overcoat, and put on the coat.

It was entirely dark in her room, and she dared not light her candle lest some neighbor should see the light in the window and ask her grandmother next morning who was sick.

Cautiously, with one of her strange upliftings of soul that she called prayer, Miranda opened her window and crept out upon the sill. The roof below her was covered with snow, three or four inches deep, but the window and roof were at the back of the house and no one could see her from there. It was not going to be an easy job getting back with all that snow on the roof, but Miranda wasn't thinking about getting back.

Clinging close to the house she stepped slowly along the shed roof to the edge, trying not to disturb the snow any more than she could help. She had taken the precaution to slip on a pair of stockings over her shoes so that their dampness in the morning might not call forth any comments from her grandmother. At last she reached the cherry tree that grew close to the woodshed roof, and could take hold of its branches and swing herself into it. Then she breathed more freely. The rest was comparatively easy.

Carefully she balanced in the tree, making her way nimbly down, her strong young body swinging lithely from limb to limb unmindful of the snow, and dropped to the snowy ground beneath. She took a few cautious steps as far apart as she could spring, but once out from under the tree she saw that if it continued to snow thick and fast and fine as it was doing now there would be little danger that her footsteps would be discovered in the morning. However, she took the precaution to reach the smokehouse by a detour through the corn patch where tracks in the snow would not be so noticeable. Then, suddenly, she faced a new difficulty. The great old rusty padlock was reinforced by a heavy beam firmly fixed across the door, and it was all the girl could do, snow-covered as it was, to move it from the great iron clamp that held it in place. However, a big will and a loving heart can work miracles, and the great beam moved at last, with a creak that set Miranda's heart thumping wildly. But the still night was deadened with its blanket of snow, and the sound seemed shut in with her in a small area. She held her breath for a minute to listen, then thankfully fitted the key into the padlock, her trembling fingers stiff with cold and fright.

The lock was set high in the door and it was all the girl could do to reach it and turn the key, but at last the big door swung open, creaking noisily as it swung, and giving her another fright.

With her hand on her heart, and her eyes straining through the darkness, Miranda stepped inside, her pulses throbbing wildly now, and her breath coming short and quick. There was something awfully gruesome about this dark silent place; it was like a tomb.

CHAPTER 6

THERE was no sound nor movement inside, and at first the girl began to think her quest had been in vain; or perhaps the prisoner had already escaped. If there was a way of escape she made sure Allan would find it; but after a second her senses cleared and she heard soft breathing over in the corner. She crept toward it, and made out a dark form lying in the shadow. She knelt beside it, put her hand out and touched his hair, his heavy beautiful hair that she had admired so many times in school when his head was bent over his book and the light from the window showed purple shadows in its dark depths. It thrilled her now strangely with a sense of privilege and almost of awe to feel how soft it was. Then her hand touched the smoothness of his boy face, and she bent her head quite close, so that she felt his breath on her cheek.

"Allan!" she whispered, "Allan!"

But it was some minutes before she could get him awake with her quiet efforts, for she dared not make a noise, and he was dead with fatigue and anxiety, besides being almost numb with the cold. His head was pillowed on his arm and he had wrapped around him some old sacking that had been given him for his bed. Grandfather Heath as constable did not believe in making the way of the transgressor easy, and he had gone contented to his warm comfortable bed leaving only a few yards of old sacking and a hard clay floor for the supposed criminal to lie upon. This was not cruelty in Grandfather Heath. He called it Justice.

At last Miranda's whispered cries in his ear, and her gentle shakings aroused the boy to a sense of his surroundings. Her arms were about his neck, trying tenderly to bring him to a sitting posture, and her cheek was against his as though her soul could reach his attention by drawing nearer. Her little freckled saucy face, all grave and sorrowful now in the darkness, brought to him a conviction of sympathy he had not known in all his lonely boyhood days, and with his first waking sense the comfort of her presence touched him warmly. He held himself utterly quiet just to be sure that she was there touching him and it was not a dream, somebody caring and calling to him with almost a sob in her breath. For an instant a wild thought of his own mother whom he had never known came to him and

36

then almost immediately he knew that it was Miranda. All the hideous truth of his situation came back to him, as life tragedies will on sudden waking, yet the strong young arms, that with their efforts were warm, and the soft breath and exquisitely soft cheek were there.

"Yes," he said very softly but quite distinctly in her ear, not moving yet however, "I'm awake. What is it?"

"Oh, I'm so glad," she caught her breath with a sob, and instantly was her alert business-like self again, all sentiment laid aside.

"Get up quick and put on this overcoat," she whispered, beginning to unbutton it with hurried fingers. "There's some things to eat in the pockets. Hurry! You ain't got any time to waste. Grandma wakes up awful easy and she might find out I had my door buttoned and get Grandpa roused up. Or somebody might a heard the door creak. It made a turrible noise. Ain't you most froze? Your hands is like ice—" she touched them softly and then drew them both up to her face and blew on them to warm them with her breath. There's some old mittens of mine in the pocket here, they ain't your size, but mebbe you ken git into 'em, and anyhow they're better'n nothin'. Hurry, cause it would be all no use ef Grandpa woke up—"

Allan sprang up suddenly.

"Where is your grandfather?" he asked anxiously, "Does he know you're here?"

"He's abed and asleep this three hours," said the girl holding up the coat and catching one of his hands to put it in the sleeve. "I heard him tell about you bein' out here, and I jest kep' still and let 'em think I was asleep, so Grandma sent me up to bed and I waited till they went upstairs and got quiet, then I slipped down an' got the key and some vittles, and went back and clumb out my window to the cherry tree so's I wouldn't make a noise with the door. You better walk the rails of the fence till you get out the back pasture and up by the sugar maples. Then you could go through the woods and they couldn't track you even ef it did stop snowin' soon and leave any kind of tracks. But I don't guess it'll stop yet awhile. It's awful fine and still like it was goin' on to snow fer hours. Hev you got any money with you? I put three shillin's in the inside coat pocket. It was all I hed. I thought you might need it. Reach up and git that half a ham over your head. You'll need it. Is there anythin' else you want?"

While she talked she had hurried him into the coat, buttoning it around him as if he had been a child and she his mother; and the tall fellow stooped and let her fasten him in, tucking the collar around his neck.

He shook his head, and softly whispered a hoarse "No" to her question, but it caught in his throat with something like a sob. It was the memory of that sound that had sent the sobs of his young brother Nathan piercing to the soul of her, years later, down beside the pieplant bed.

"Don't you let 'em catch you, Allan," she said anxiously, her hand lingering on his arm, her eyes searching in the dark for his beloved face.

"No, I won't let 'em catch me," he murmured menacingly, "I'll get away all right, but Randa"—he had always called her Randa though no one else in the village ever called her that—"Randa, I want you to know I didn't do it. I didn't kill Enoch Taylor, indeed I didn't. I wasn't even there. I didn't have a thing to do with it."

"O' course you didn't!" said Miranda indignantly, her whole slender body stiffening in the dark. He could feel it as he reached out to put a hand on either of her shoulders.

"Did you 'spose I'd think you could? But ef you told 'em, couldn't you make 'em prove it? Ain't there any way? Do you hev to go away?" Her voice was wistful, pleading, and revealed her heart.

"Nobody would believe me, Randa. You know how folks are here about me."

"I know," she said sorrowfully, her voice trailing almost into tears. "And anyhow" he added, "I couldn't because—well Randa—*I know who did it* and I wouldn't tell!" His voice was deep and earnest. She understood. It was the rules of the game. He had known she would understand. "Oh!" she said in a breath of surrender. "Oh! of course you *couldn't tell!*" then suddenly rousing—"But you mustn't wait," she added anxiously, "somebody might come by, and you ain't got a minute to lose. You'll take care o' yourself, Allan, won't you?"

"Course," he answered almost roughly, "course, Randa. And say, Randa, you're just a great little woman to help me out this way. I don't know's I ought to let you. It'll mebbe get you into trouble."

"Don't you worry 'bout me," said Miranda. "They ain't going to know anything about me helpin' you, and ef they did they can't do nothin' to a girl. I'd just like to see 'em tryin' to take it out o' me. Ef they dare I'll tell 'em how everybody has treated you all these years. You ain't had it fair Allan. Now go quick—"

But the boy turned suddenly and took her in his arms, holding her close in his great rough overcoated clasp, and putting his face down to hers as they stood in the deepest shadow of the old smokehouse.

"There wasn't ever anybody but you understood, Randa," he whispered, "and I ain't going to forget what you've done this time—" The boy's lips searched for hers and met them in a shy embarrassed kiss that sought to pay homage of his soul to her. "Goodbye, Randa, I ain't going to forget, and mebbe—mebbe, some day I can come back and get you—that is ef you're still here waiting."

He kissed her again impetuously, and then as if half ashamed of what he had done he left her standing there in the darkness and slipped out through the blackness into the still, thick whiteness of the snow; stepped from the door to the rail fence as she had suggested and rapidly disappeared into the silence of the storm in the direction of the sugar maples.

Miranda stood still for several minutes unconscious of the cold, the night, and her loneliness; regardless of the fact that she had taken off a warm overcoat and was without any wrap over her flimsy little school dress. She was not cold now. A fine glow enveloped her in its beautiful arms. Her cheeks were warm with the touch of Allan's face, and her lips glowed with his parting kiss. But most of all his parting words had filled her with joy. He had kissed her and told her he would come back and get her some day if she were still there waiting. What wonder! What joy!

It was the memory of those words that hovered about her like some bright defending angel when Allan's father came six years later to ask her to marry him, and taught her that fine scorn of him. It was what had kept her in her place waiting all the years, and what had drawn her to the younger brother, who was like and yet so unlike Allan.

When Miranda realized where she was standing, and that she must finish her work and get back to her room before she was discovered, she raised both hands to her face and laid them gently on her lips, one over the other, crossed, as if she would touch and hold the sacred kiss that had lain there but the moment before. Then she lifted her face slightly and with her eyes open looking up at the dark rafters, and her fingers still laid lightly on her lips, she murmured solemnly:

"Thanks be!" Gravely she came forth to the business of the night. She reached and fastened the padlock, her warm fingers melting the snow that already again lay thick upon it, and made sure the key was safe about her neck and dropped inside her dress against her warm, palpitating breast to keep it from getting wet and telling tales. She struggled back the beam into place, forcing it into its fastening with all her fierce young might until it rested evenly against the door as before. With her hands and feet she smoothed and kicked the snow into levelness in front of the door. She mounted the fence rail for just an instant and glanced off toward the sugar maples, but there was no sign of a dark figure creeping in the blanketed air of the storm, no sound but the steady falling, falling, of the snow, grain by grain, the little, mighty snow! In a few minutes all possible marks of the escape would be utterly obliterated. With a sigh of relief Miranda stole quickly back to the cherry tree. She had intended to smooth her tracks in retreat one at a time so that the snow would have less to do, but it was not necessary except just about the door of the smoke-house. The snow was doing it all and well. Ten minutes would cover everything; half an hour would make it one white level plain.

The climbing of the cherry tree was a difficult task with chilled body and numb hands, but she accomplished it swiftly, and crept back over the roof and into her own window. Fortunately the snow was dry and brushed off easily. Her dress was not wet so there was no need to invent an excuse for that. With deep thanksgiving she dropped on her knees beside her bed and sobbed her weary heart out into her pillow. Miranda was not one who often cried. In a crisis she was all there and ready for action. She could bear hardships with a jolly twinkle and meet snubbing with a merry grimace, but that kiss had broken her down and she cried as she had never cried before in her life; and prayed her queer heartfelt prayers:

"Oh, God, I didn't never expect no such thing as his being good to me. It was turrible good of you to let him. An' I'm so glad he's safe. So glad! You won't let him get caught will you? He didn't do it you know—say, did you know that I wonder?—'thout his tellin' you? I 'spose you did but I like to think you would a' let me save him anyway, even ef he had. But he didn't do it. He *said* he didn't, and you know he *never* told what wasn't so—he never minded even when it made out against him. But who did do it? God—are you going to let Enoch Taylor die? Allan can't never come back ef you do, he said mebbe—but then I don't suppose there could ever be anythin' like that fer me. But please, I thank you fer makin' him so kind. I can't never remember anybody to huv kissed me before. Of course it was dark an' he couldn't see my red hair,—but then he knowed it was there—he couldn't forget a thing like that—an' it was most as if I was real folks like any other girl. An' please, you'll take good care of him, won't you? Not let him get lost er froze, er hungry, an' find him a nice place with a warm bed an' work to do so's he can earn money, 'cause it ain't in conscience people'll find out how folks felt about him here. He ain't bad, you know, and anyhow you made him, and you must 'uv had some intrust in him. I guess you like him pretty well, don't you, or you wouldn't uv let me get him away 'thout bein' found out. So please, I thank you, and ef you've got anythin' coming to me any time that's real good, jest give it to him instead. Amen."

The prayer ended, she crept into her head, her heart warm and happy, but though the hour was well on to morning she could not sleep, for continually she was going over the wonderful experience in the smokehouse. Allan's tired, regular breathing, the soft feel of his hair when she touched it, and his cheek against hers; his lips when they kissed her, and his whispered words. What it had meant to her to have him take her in his arms and thank her that way and be so kind and glad for what she had done, nobody but a lonely, loveless girl like herself could understand. Over and over her heart thrilled at the wonder of it all—that she had been permitted to save him. She felt as she thought it over that she would have been willing to lay down her life to save him.

That was twelve long years ago and not a word had been heard from Allan since, yet still Miranda on starlit nights looked out, remembered, and waited. Long ago she had given up all hope of his return. He was dead or he was married, or he had forgotten, she told herself in her practical daytime thoughts; yet when night came and the stars looked down upon her she thought of him, that perhaps he was somewhere looking at those same stars, and she prayed he might not be in want or trouble—so she waited. Somehow she found it hard to believe that Allan could easily die, he was so young and strong and vivid—so adequate to all situations. It was easy to find excuse for his not coming back. The world was large and far apart in those days of few railroads, expensive travel, and no telegraph. Even letters were expensive, and not unduly indulged in. There would still be danger for him in return, for old Enoch Taylor's sudden and tragic death, shot in the back near the edge of the town just at the time of early candlelight, was still remembered; and the shadow of young Allan's supposed crime and mysterious disappearance had fallen over his younger brother's reputation and made it what it was. Even his father spoke of him only to warn his younger sons now and then that they follow not in his footsteps. Only in Miranda's heart he really lived, and that was why his younger brother, slender and dark and in many ways much like him, had found a warm place in her heart and love, for he seemed somehow like Allan come back to her again.

Love wasn't in just getting it back again to yourself. It was great just to love; just to know that a beloved one existed.

Not that Miranda ever reasoned things out in so many words. She was keen and practical in daily life, but in her dreams strange fancies floated half formed amid her practicalities, and great truths loomed large upon her otherwise limited horizon. It was so she often caught the meaning of life where wiser souls have failed.

The world is not so large and disconnected after all. One evening just after Miranda had gone next door to live with David and Marcia she heard David reading the *New York Tribune* aloud to his wife while she sewed; little scraps of news and items of interest; what the politicians were doing, and how work was progressing on the canal locks.

"Listen to this," he said half amusedly:

"A boy has travelled through England, Ireland and Wales with only fifty-five dollars in his pocket when he started, and has returned safely. He says he is only five dollars in debt, and gives as his reason for going that he *wished to see the country!"*

Miranda did not understand at all the sympathetic glance of amusement that passed between husband and wife. Her attention had been caught by the facts. A boy! Travelled through all those countries! How very like Allan to do that, and to go on just a little money! It was like him, too, to want to go to see things. It was one of the things in him that had always made good practical people misunderstand him—that wanting to do things just because it was pleasant to do them, and not for any gain or necessity. Miranda smiled to herself as she set the heel of the stocking she was knitting; but she never saw how strange it was that she, the most practical of human beings, should heartily understand and sympathize with the boy who was an idealist. Perhaps she had the same thing in her own nature only she never knew it.

Nevertheless, it became a pleasant pastime for Miranda to look up at the stars at night and share with them her belief that it was Allan who had journeyed all that way, and her pleasure in feeling that he was back in his own land again, nearer to her. All these years she had dreamed out things he might have done, until as the years passed and he did not come, her dreaming became a thing almost without a foundation, a foolish amusement of which she was fond, but ashamed, and only to be indulged in when all the world was asleep and no one could possibly know.

It was so Miranda watched for the light in the gable window across the way, and when it did not come she knew Nathan had crept to his bed without a candle. She went by and by to her bed, and dreamed that Allan came and kissed her just as he had done so long ago when she was but a little girl.

CHAPTER 7

FOR the next few years after his father's marriage to Maria Bent young Nathan Whitney lived two distinct lives. One, in the village and the red. schoolhouse, where he was rated the very worst boy in the town, all the more despised and hunted by every one in authority because he was bright enough to be better; the other in the company of Miranda and little Rose, out in the woods and fields, down by the trout brook fishing, or roaming through the hills watching birds and creeping things; and sometimes sitting at the feet of little Mother Marcia as she told beautiful stories to Nate and Rose, while she held in her arms the sleeping baby brother of little Rose. Here he was a different being. Every hard handsome feature of his face softened into gentleness and set with purpose. All the stubbornness and native error melted away, and his great brown eyes seemed to be seeing things too high for an ordinary boy to comprehend. One could be sure he almost worshipped Mother Marcia, the girl-wife of David Spafford, and looked into her madonna face as she talked or sang softly to her baby, with a foreshadowing of the look that the man he was to be would have some day for the mother of his children.

As for little Rose she was his comrade and pet. With her, always accompanied by Miranda carrying a generous lunch basket, he roamed all the region round about on pleasant holidays. He taught her to fish in the brook, to jump and climb like any boy and to race over the hills with him. Miranda, well pleased, would stray behind and catch up with them now and then, or sit and wait till they chose to race back to her. Rose thought Nathan the strongest and the best boy in all the town, or the wide world for that matter. He was her devoted slave when she demanded flowers or a high branch of red leaves from the tall maple. It was for her sake he applied himself to his lessons as he had never done in his life before, because the first day of her advent in school he had found her with red eyes and nose weeping her heart out at the reprimand he had received for not knowing his spelling lesson. Spelling was his weakest point, but after that he scarcely ever missed a word. His school life became decidedly better so far as knowing his lessons was concerned; though his pranks still kept up. Rose, in truly feminine fashion, rather admired his pranks, and he knew it; though he had always tried to keep them under control since the day when the teacher started to whip him and Rose walked up the aisle with flashing eyes and cheeks like two flames, and said in a brave little voice:

"Teacher, Nate didn't throw that apple core at all. It was Wallie Eggleston. I saw him myself!" And then her lip trembled and she broke down in tears. Nate's face turned crimson and he hung his head, ashamed. It was true that he had not thrown the apple core, but he had done enough to deserve the whipping and he knew it. From that day he refrained from over-torment of the teacher and kept his daring feats for out of school. Also he taught Rose by that unspoken art of a boy, never to "tell on" another boy again.

Mother Marcia watched the intimacy of the little girl and big boy with favor. She felt it was good for Rose, and good for the boy also. Always Miranda or herself was at hand, and never had either of them had reason to doubt the wisdom of the comradeship that had grown between the two children.

But matters were not likely to continue long in this way without the interference of some one. Nathan Whitney got into too many scrapes and slid out of their consequences with a too exasperating skill to have many friends in town. His impudence was unrivalled and his daring was equalled only by his indifference to public opinion. Such a state of things naturally did not tend to make him liked or understood. No one but the three, Rose, her mother and Miranda, ever saw the gentle look of holy reverence on his handsome face, or heard the occasional brief utterances which showed his thoughts were tending toward higher ambitions and finer principles. No others saw the rare smile which glorified his face by a gleam of the real soul of the boy. In after years Marcia often recalled the beautiful youth seated on a low stool holding her baby boy carefully, his face filled with deep pleasure at the privilege, his whole spirit sitting in his eyes in wonder, awe and gentleness as he looked at the little living creature in his arms, or handled it shyly, with rarely tender touch, while Rose sat close beside him well content. At such times the boy seemed almost transfigured. Neither Marcia nor Miranda knew the Nathan who broke windows, threw stones, tied old Mr. Smiles' office door shut while he was dozing over his desk one afternoon; and who filed a bolt, letting out a young scapegrace from the village lockup and helping him to escape from justice and an unappreciative neighborhood into the wide world. They saw only the angelic side to Nathan, the side that nobody else in the wide world dreamed that he possessed.

Nathan spent little time in his home. Shelter during his sleeping hours, and food enough to keep him alive was all he required of it, and more and more the home and the presiding genius there learned to require less of him; knowing that she did not possess the power to make him do what she required. Nathan would not perform any duties about the house or yard unless some one stood over him and kept him at it. If his stepmother attempted to make him rake the leaves in the yard and took her eyes from him a minute he was gone, and would not return until sometime the next day. An appeal to his father brought little but a cold response. Nathan Whitney senior was not calculated by nature to deal with his alert temperamental son and he knew it. He informed his wife concisely that that was what he had married her for, or words to that effect, and she appealed no more. Gradually Nathan Whitney, Jr. had his way and was let alone, for what could she do? When she attempted to discipline him he was not there, neither would he return for hours, sometimes even days afterward, until she would become alarmed lest he had run away like his older brother and she might be blamed for it. She found that her husband was not as easily ruled as she had supposed, and that her famous discipline of schoolday times must be limited to the little girls and baby Samuel. Nathan seemed to know by instinct just when it was safe to return and drop into family life as if nothing had happened, and be let alone. One word or look and he was off again, staying in the woods for days, and knowing wild things, trees and brooks as some men know books. He could always earn a few pennies doing odd jobs for men in the village, for he was smart and handy, and with what he earned kept himself comfortably during his temporary absences from the family board. As for sleeping, he well knew and loved the luxury of a couch on the pine needles under the singing, sighing boughs, or tucked under the sheltering ledge of a rock on a stormy night. His brooding young soul watched storm and lightning with wide eyes that held strange fancies, and thought much about the world and its ways. Now and again the result of these thoughts would come out in a single wise sentence to Miranda or little Rose; rarely, but sometimes, to Mrs. Marcia, always with shyness and as if he had been surprised out of his natural reserve.

Nathan made no display of his intimacy at the Spaffords. When he went there it was usually just at dusk, unobtrusively slipping around to Miranda at the back door. When they went a-roaming on the hills, or fishing, he never started out with them. He always appeared in the woods just as they were beginning to think he had forgotten. He usually dropped off their path on the way home by going across lots before they reached the village, having a fine instinct that it might bring criticism upon them if they were seen with him. And thus, because of his carefulness, the beautiful friendship of Rose and the boy went on for some years and no one thought anything about it. Nathan never attempted to walk home from school with

Rose as other boys did with the girls they admired. Once or twice when an unexpected rain came on before school closed he slid out of his last class and whirled away through the rain to get her cloak and umbrella, returning just as school "let out," drenched and shamefaced; but he let the little girl think her father had brought them and asked him to give them to her.

One unlucky day, toward evening, Nathan slipped in at the side gate and brought a great bag of chestnuts for Rose, while Mr. David's two prim maiden aunts, Miss Amelia and Miss Hortense Spafford, were tying on their bonnets preparatory to going home after an afternoon call. When Nathan perceived the guests his face grew dark and he backed away toward the door, holding out the bag of nuts toward Rose, and murmuring that he must go at once. By some slip the bag fell between the two and the nuts rolled out in a brown rustling shower over the floor. The boy and girl stooped in quick unison to pick them up, their golden and brown curly heads striking together in a sounding crack, making both forget the presence of their elders and break forth into merry laughter, as they ruefully rubbed their heads and began to gather up the nuts. Nathan was his gentle best self for three or four whole minutes while he picked up nuts and made comical remarks in a low tone to Rose, unconscious of the grim visages of the two aunts in the background, who paused with horrified astonishment in their tying of bonnet strings, to observe the evident intimacy between their grandniece and a dreadful boy whom they recognized as that scapegrace son of Nathan Whitney's.

Marcia did not notice their expressions at first. She was standing close by with her eyes on the graceful girl and alert boy as they struggled playfully for the nuts; she liked to see the two together in the entire unconsciousness of youth playing like children.

But Nathan, sensitive almost to a fault, was quick to feel the antagonistic atmosphere, and suddenly looked up to meet those two keen old pairs of eyes focussed on him in disapproval. He colored all over his handsome face, then grew white and sullen as he rose suddenly to his feet and flashed his defiant habitual attitude, never before worn in the Spafford house.

Standing there for an instant, white with anger, his brows drawn low over his fine dark eyes, his chin raised slightly in defiance (or was it only haughtiness and pride?) his shoulders thrown back, his hands unconsciously clenched down at his sides, and looking straight back into those two pairs of condemning, disapproving eyes, he seemed the very embodiment of the modern poem Invictus, and if he had been a picture it should have borne the inscription, "Every man's hand is against me."

There was utter silence in the room, while four eyes condemned and two eyes defied—offending anew by their defiance. The atmosphere of the room seemed charged with lightning, and oppression sat sudden upon the hearts of the mother and daughter who stood by, oppression and growing indignation. What right had the aunts to look that way at Nathan in the house of his friends?

In vain did Rose summon a merry laugh, and Mrs. Marcia try to say something pleasant to Nathan about the nuts. It was as if they had not spoken. They were not even heard. The contest was between the aunts and the boy, and in the eyes of the two who watched the boy came off victor.

"What right have you to look at me like that? What right have you to condemn me unheard, and wish me off the face of the earth? What right have you to resent my friendship with your relatives?" That was what the boy's eyes said; and the two narrow-minded little old ladies, red with indignation, cold with pride and prejudice, declined to look honestly at the question, but let their eyes continue to condemn merely for the joy of having a chance to condemn him whom they had always condemned.

The boy's haughty undaunted look held them at bay for several seconds, before he turned coolly away and with a bow of real grace to Marcia and Rose he went out of the room and closed the door quietly behind him.

There was silence in the room. The tenseness in all faces remained until they heard him walk across the kitchen entry and close the outside door, heard his quick, clean step on the flagstones that led around the house; and then heard the side gate click. He was gone out of hearing and Rose drew a quick involuntary sigh. He was safe, and the storm had not broken in time for him to hear. But it broke now in low oncoming threats of look and tone. Rose was shriveled to misery by the contemptuous glances of her aunts, coming as they did in unison, and meaning but one thing, that she was to blamed in some way for this terrible disgrace to the family. Having disposed of Rose to their satisfaction they turned to her mother.

"Well, I must say I'm surprised, Marcia." It was Aunt Amelia as usual who opened up the first gun, "In fact, to be plain, I'm deeply shocked! Living as you have in this town for thirteen and a half years now—[Aunt Amelia always aimed to be exact]—you cannot fail to have known what a reputation that boy has. There is no worse in the county, I believe. And you, the mother of a sweet daughter just budding into womanhood [Rose was at that time nearly eleven], should be so unwise, nay even wicked and thoughtless, as to allow a person of the character of Nathan Whitney to enter your house intimately. I observed that he entered the back door unannounced—and to present your daughter with a gift! I am shocked beyond words to express—" and Aunt Amelia paused impressively and stood looking steadily at the indignant Marcia, shaking her head slightly as if the offense were too great to be quite comprehended in a breath.

Then Aunt Hortense took up the condemnation.

"Yes, Marcia, I am deeply grieved," she spoke weepily, "to think that our beloved nephew's wife, who has become one of our own family, should so forget herself and her position, and the rights of her family, as to allow that scoundrel to enter her doors, and to speak to her child. It is beyond belief! You cannot be ignorant of his character, my dear! You must know that all the outrages that have been committed in this town have been either perpetrated by him, or he has been their instigator, which in my mind is even worse, because it shows cowardice in not being willing to bear the penalty himself—"

At this point Rose, with flashing blue eyes and cheeks as red as the flowers she was named after, stepped indignantly forward.

"Aunt Amelia, Nathan *isn't* a coward! He isn't afraid of *any*thing in the whole world! He's brave and splendid!"

Miss Amelia turned shocked eyes upon her grandniece; and Miss Hortense, chin up, fairly snuffed the air:

"In my day little girls did not speak until they were spoken to, and never were allowed to put in when their elders were speaking!" "Yes, Marcia," put in Miss Hortense getting out her handkerchief and wiping her eyes offendedly, "you see what your headstrong ideas have brought upon you already. You cannot expect to have a well-behaved child if you allow her to associate with rough boys, and especially when you pick out the lowest in the village, the vilest of the vile!"

Miss Hortense had the fire of eloquence in her eyes, and it was plain there was more to follow. The bad boys of the village were her especial hobby, and since ten years back she had held a grudge against Nathan on account of her pet cat.

Marcia, cool, controlled, tried to interrupt. She was feeling very angry both on her own account and for the boy's sake, but she knew she could do nothing to pour oil on the troubled waters if she lost her temper.

"I think you have made a mistake, Aunt Hortense," she said gently, "Nathan isn't a bad boy. I've known him a good many years and he has some beautiful qualities. He has been over here playing with Rose a great deal and I have never seen him do a mean or selfish thing. I am, in fact, very fond of him, and he has made a good playmate for Rose. He is a little mischievous of course, most boys are, but there is no real badness in him I am sure."

Rose looked at her mother with shining gratitude, but the two old ladies stiffened visibly in their wrath.

"I am mistaken. Am I?" sniffed Miss Hortense. "Yes, I suppose young folks always think they know more than their experienced elders. I have to expect that, but I must do my duty. I shall feel obliged to report this to my nephew and he must deal with it as he sees fit. But whether you think I am mistaken or not, I *know* that you are, and you will sadly rue the day when you let that young emissary of Satan darken your door."

Miss Hortense retired into the folds of her handkerchief, but Miss Amelia at this juncture swelled forth in denunciation.

"You are quite wrong, Marcia, in thinking my sister mistaken," she said severely. "You forget yourself when you attempt to tell your elders that they are mistaken. However, you are excited, *you are young* [as if that were the worst offence in the category]. My sister and I have had serious cause to know of what we speak. Our fine pet cat, Matthew,—you will perhaps remember him as being still with us when you came to live here, he died about five years ago you know—who was as inoffensive and kind an animal as one could have about a house, was put to terrible torture before our very eyes by this same paragon of a boy whom you are attempting to uphold. My dear, [here she lowered her voice sepulchrally and hissed out the words vindictively with her thin lips] that dreadful boy tied a tin can filled with pebbles to our poor dear Matthew's tail: think of it! His tail! that he always kept so beautifully clean and tucked around him so tidily! We always had a silk patchwork cushion for him to lie on by the fire and he never presumed upon his privileges; and then for him to be so outraged! My dear, it was more than human nature could bear. Poor Matthew was frantic with fear and mortification. He was a dignified cat and had always been treated with consideration, and of course he did not know what to make of it. He attempted to break away from his tormentors but could not; and the tin can came after him, hitting his poor little heels. Oh, I cannot describe to you the awful scene! Poor Hortense and I stood on the stoop and fairly implored that little imp to release poor Matthew, but he went after him all the harder—the vile little wretch—and poor Matthew did not return to the house until after dark. For days he sat licking his poor disfigured tail from which the beautiful fur had all been rubbed, and looking reproachfully at us,—his best friends. He lived for four years after that, but he never was the same cat! Poor Matthew! And I always thought that was the cause of his death! Now do you understand, Marcia?"

"But Aunt Amelia," broke in Marcia gently, trying not to smile, "that was nine years ago, and Nathan has grown up now. He was only five or six years old then, and had run wild since his mother's death. He is almost sixteen now, and very much changed in a great many ways—"

The two old ladies brought severity to bear upon her at once in frowns of differing magnitudes.

"If they do these things in a green tree, what shall be done in the dry?" quoted Aunt Amelia solemnly. "No, Marcia, you are mistaken. The boy was bad from his birth. We are not the only ones who have suffered. He has tied strings across the sidewalk many a dark night to trip people. I have heard of hundreds of his pranks, and now that he is older he doubtless carries his accomplishments into deeper crime. I have heard that he does nothing but hang around the stores and post office. He is a loafer, nothing short of it, and as for honesty, there isn't an orchard in the neighborhood that is safe. If he'll steal apples, he'll do worse when he gets the chance—and he'll make the chance, you may depend upon it. Boys like that always do. You have taken a great risk in letting him into your house. You have fine old silver that has been in the family for years, and many other valuable things. He may take advantage of his knowledge of the place to rob you some dark night. And as for your child, you cannot tell what awful things he may have taught her. I have often watched his face in church and thought how utterly bad and without moral principle he looks. I should not be in the least surprised if he turned out one day to be a murderer!"

Miss Amelia's tones had been gradually rising as she came to this climax, and as she spoke the word *murderer* she threw the whole fervor of her intense and narrow nature into her speech, coming to an eloquent and dramatic pause which was well calculated to impress her audience. But suddenly, like a flash of a glittering sword in air, a piercing scream arose. As she might have screamed if some one had struck her, Rose uttered her furious young protest against injustice. Her beautiful little face, flushed with outraged innocence and glorious in its righteous wrath, shone through the gathering dusk in the room and fairly blazing at her startled aunts, who jumped as if she had been some wild animal suddenly let loose upon them. The scream cut through the space of the little room seeming to pierce every one in it, and quickly upon it came another.

"Stop! Stop!" she cried as if they were still going on, "you shall not say those things! You are bad, wicked women! You shall not say my Nathan is a murderer. You are a murderer yourself if you say so. The Bible says he that hateth his brother is a murderer and you hate him or you would not say such wicked things that are not true. You shall not speak them any more. My Nathan is a good boy and I love him. Don't you *dare* talk like that again." Another scream pointed the sentence and Rose burst into a furious fit of tears and flew across the room, fairly flinging herself into her mother's arms, and sobbing as if her heart would break.

Into this scene of tumult came a calm, strong voice:

"Why, what does all this mean?"

CHAPTER 8

THE aunts looked up from their fascinated, horrified stare at their grand-niece to see the two doors on the opposite sides of the room open and a figure standing in each. In the doorway of the front hall stood David, perplexed, dismayed, eagerly seeking an answer in his wife's face; in the doorway of the pantry stood Miranda, arms akimbo, nostrils spread, eyes blazing like a very war horse that she was, snuffing the bale from afar, and only waiting to be sure how the land lay.

For a moment nobody could say anything for Rose's sobs drowned all else. Marcia had all she could do to soothe and quiet the excited child who had been so strained up for a few minutes that she was now like a runaway team going down hill and unable stop.

David had sense enough to keep still until the air cleared, and meantime he studied the faces of each one in the room, not forgetting Miranda, and was able to get a pretty clear idea of how matters stood before anybody explained.

Presently, however, Rose subsided into low convulsive sobs smothered in her mother's arms, as Marcia drew the little girl down into her lap in the big arm chair, and laying her lips against the hot wet cheek said softly;

"There, there, mother's dear child, get calm, little girl, get calm. Get control of yourself."

The sudden lull gave opportunity for speech, and Miss Amelia, much shaken in body if not in mind, hastened to avail herself of it.

"You may well ask what this means, David," she began, gathering her forces for the combat, and reaching out to steady her trembling hand on the back of a chair.

"Sit down, Aunt Amelia," said David hastening to bring forward two chairs, one for each of the old ladies. "Sit down and don't excite yourself. There's plenty of time to explain."

"I thank you," said Miss Amelia drawing herself up to her full height, "I prefer to stand until I have explained my part in this disgraceful scene. I want you to understand that what I have said has been wholly disinterested. I have been merely trying to protect you and your child from the thoughtless folly of one whose youth must excuse her for her conduct.

Your wife, David, has been admitting to the company of your innocent daughter a person wholly unfit to mingle in respectable society. He came in tonight while we were here, a rough, ill-bred, lubberly fellow, whose familiarity was an insult to your home. I was merely informing Marcia what kind of a boy he was when Rose broke out into the most shocking screams and cries, and used the most disrespectful language toward me, showing plainly the result of her companionship with evil; and not only that but she expressed herself in terms that were unmaidenly and unseemly for a girl, almost a woman, to use. Your mother would never have allowed herself to so far forget herself as to say that she *loved*—actually loved, David,—that was the word she used,—a *boy*. And that too a boy who only needs a few more years to become a hardened criminal. I refer to that scapegrace of a son of Nathan Whitney. And she dared to call him *hers*— *my* Nathan, she said, and was most impudent in her address to me. I think that she should be punished severely and never be allowed to see that young wretch again. I am sure you will bear me out in feeling that I have been outraged—"

But now Rose's sobs dominated everything again, heartbroken and indignant, and Marcia had much ado to keep the child from breaking away from her and rushing from the room. David looked from one to another of his excited relatives and prepared to pour oil on the troubled waters.

"Just a minute, Aunt Amelia," he said coolly as soon as he could be heard. "I think there has been a little misunderstanding here—"

"No misunderstanding at all, David," said the old lady severely drawing herself up with dignity again. "I assure you there is no possible chance for misunderstanding. Your wife actually professes fondness for this young scapegrace, calls his wickedness mischief; and tries to condone his faults, when everybody knows he has been the worst boy in the town for years. I told her that I should inform you of all this and demand for the sake of the family honor that you never allow that fellow! that loafer! that low-down scoundrel!! to enter this house again or speak to our grandniece in the street."

Miss Amelia was trembling with rage and insulted pride, and purple in the face. At this juncture Miranda beat a hasty retreat to the pantry window.

"Golly!" she ejaculated softly to herself. "Golly! wouldn't that old lady make a master hand at cussin' ef she jest didn't hev so much fambly pride! Golly! she couldn't think of words 'nough to call 'im."

Miranda stood for a full minute chuckling and thinking and staring at the sky that was just beginning to redden with the sunset. Words from the other room hastened her thinking. Then with cool deliberation she approached the door again to reconnoitre and take a hand in the battle.

David was just speaking:

"Aunt Amelia, suppose we lay the subject aside for a time. I feel that I am fully capable of dealing with it. I have entire confidence in anything that Marcia has done, and I am sure you will have also when you hear her side of the matter. Rose doubtless is overwrought. She is very fond of this boy, for he has been her playmate for a long time, and has been very gallant and loyal to her in many ways—"

But Miss Amelia was not to be appeased. Two red flames of wrath stood upon her thin cheek bones, a declaration of war; and two swords glanced from her sharp black eyes. Her bony old hands grasped the back of the chair shakily, and her whole body trembled.

Her thin lips shook nervously, and caught dryly on her teeth in an agitated way as she tried to enunciate her words with extreme dignity and care.

"No, David, we will not lay the subject aside," she said, "and I shall never feel confidence in Marcia's judgment after what she has said to me about that young villain. I must insist on telling you the whole story. I cannot compromise with sin!"

And then, Miranda discreetly approached with a smile of honeyed sweetness on her freckled face.

"Miss 'Meelia, 'scuse me fer interruptin', but it wasn't your spare-bedroom winders I see open when I went by this afternoon was it? You don't happen t' r'member ef you left 'em open when you come away, do yeh? Cause I thought I sensed a thunder-storm in the air, an' I thought mebbe you'd like me to run down the street an' close 'em fer you, ef you did. Miss Clarrissa's all alone, ain't she?"

"A thunder storm!" said Miss Amelia stiffening into attention at once, alarm bristling from every loop of ribbon on her best black bonnet. "We must go home at once! I never like to be away from home in a thunder-storm; one can never tell what may happen. Come, let us make haste."

"A thunder storm!" said David incredulously, and then catching the innocent look on Miranda's face stopped suddenly. The sky was as clear as an evening bell and a single star glinted out at that moment as the two old ladies issued hastily forth from their nephew's door, but they saw it not; and David, reflecting that there was more than one kind of a thunder storm said nothing. It might be as well to let the atmosphere clear before he took a hand in affairs.

"Shall I walk down with you, Aunt Amelia?" he asked half doubtfully, glancing back toward the stairs up which Marcia had just taken the sobbing Rose.

"No indeed, David," said Miss Amelia decidedly. "Your duty is to your family at such a time as this. One never can tell what may happen, as I said before, and my sister and myself can look out for ourselves."

They closed the door and hurried away down the walk.

Miranda stood at the side gate with bland benevolence on her features.

"You got plenty o' time," she said smilingly. "You ain't got any call to hurry. It'll be quite a spell 'fore the storm gets here. I'm a pretty good weather profit."

"It is not best to take chances," said Aunt Hortense looking up nervously at the rosy sky, "appearances are often deceitful, and there are a great many windows to close for the night."

They swept on down the street and Miranda watched them a moment with satisfaction. Then she looked over at the white-pillared house across the way and frowned. The mother in her trembled at the injustice done the boy she had grown to love.

"There's some folks has a good comeuppance comin' to 'em somewheres or I miss my guess," she murmured as she turned slowly toward the kitchen door, and began to wonder what Mr. David would think of her. Mr. David was too sharp to be deceived long about a thunder storm, and she would not like to incur his disfavor for she worshipped him afar.

Miranda went into the house and made herself scarce for a little while, moving conspicuously among her pots and pans, and voicing her hilarity in a hymn the church choir had sung the day before. But David was for the present quite occupied upstairs. The trembling Rose now fully subdued and quite horrified at what she had dared to say to her aunts, toward whom she had always been taught the utmost respect, lay on her little bed with white and tear-stained face, her body now and then convulsed with a shivering sob. She had confessed her sins quite freely after her aunts had departed, and had agreed that the only thing possible was an abject apology on the morrow, but her sweet drooping mouth and long fluttering lashes betokened that her trouble was not all gone and at last she brought it out in a soft sobbing breath.

"Nathan won't come here any more. I know he won't. I saw it in his face. He'll think you don't want him, and he'll never come round again. He's always that way. He thinks people don't like him—" and she began to cry softly again.

David went and sat down beside his little girl and began to question her. Sometimes Marcia would put in a gentle word, and the eyes of the father and mother met over the child in sweet confidence, with utmost sympathy for her in her childish grief, although they had not condoned one whit the words she had spoken in her quick wrath to her aunts.

"Well, little daughter, close up the tears now," said the father. "Tomorrow you will go down to see your aunts and make it all right with them by telling them how sorry and ashamed you are that you lost your temper and spoke disrespectfully to them. But you leave Nathan to me. I want to get acquainted with him. He must be worth knowing from all you have said."

"Oh, father, you dear, dear father!" exclaimed Rose ecstatically, springing up to throw her arms about his neck. "Will you truly get acquainted with him? Oh, you are such a good dear father!"

"I surely will," said David stooping to kiss her. "Now get up and wash your face for supper, and we'll see what can be done."

A whispered conference in the hall for a moment with Marcia sent David downstairs as eagerly as a boy might have gone, and Miranda's heart was in her mouth for a full minute when she looked up from the Johnnycake she was making for supper and saw him standing in the kitchen door. She thought a reprimand must surely be forthcoming.

"Miranda, have you got a good supper cooking, and do you think there would be enough for a guest if I brought one in?"

"Loads!" said Miranda alertly drawing a deep breath of relief and beating her eggs with vigor. "How many of 'em?"

"Only one, and I'm not sure of him yet, but you might put another plate on the table," said David, and taking his hat from the hall table went out the front door.

Miranda put her dish of eggs down on the kitchen table and tiptoed softly into the dining room where the window commanded a view of the street. The candles were not yet lighted so she could not be seen from without, and curiosity was too much for her. She saw David walk across the street to the big pillared Whitney house, and just as he reached the gate she saw a dark figure that walked very much like young Nate, come swinging down the street and meet him. They stood at the gate a minute or two talking, those two shadowy figures, and then David turned and walked back to the house, and the boy scurried around to his own back door. Miranda scuttled back to her eggs with happy heart and was beating away serenely when David opened the kitchen door to say:

"Well, he'll be here in half an hour. Be sure to have plenty of jam and cake." Then David went into the library, took out the New York evening paper, and was soon deeply engrossed in the last reports of Professor Morse's new Electro-Magnetic Telegraph, in the interest of which there was a bill before Congress appropriating thirty thousand dollars for its testing. It was one of the absorbing topics of the day, and David forthwith forgot not only his guest but the unpleasant happenings that had caused him to give the invitation, and Miranda in the kitchen hurrying about to stir some tea cakes and get out a varied assortment of preserves and jams such as boys are supposed to like, need have feared no reference to thunder storms, as she sang her hymns loud and clear:

"My willing soul would stay
In such a frame as this,
And wait to hail the brighter day
Of everlasting bliss."

Rose presently came down to the kitchen, chastened and sweet, her eyes like forget-me-nots after the rain, her cheeks rosy. Miranda gave her a little hotcake just out of the pan and patted the soft cheek tenderly. She dared not openly speak against the prim aunts who had brought all this trouble on her darling, but her looks pitied and petted Rose and assured her that she did not blame her darling for anything hateful she might have said to those old spitfires. Rose took the sympathy, but did not presume upon it, and her lashes down drooped humbly over the rose in her cheeks. She knew now that she had been very sinful to speak so to poor Aunt Amelia no matter how excited she had been. Aunt Amelia of course did not know Nathan as she did and therefore could not get the right point of view. Aunt Amelia had done it all for what she thought was her good. That was what Mother Marcia had tried to make her little girl feel.

Rose, her cake eaten, walked around the pleasant dining table and noted the festive air of jams and preserves, the sprigged china, and the extra place opposite her own.

"Oh, is there going to be company?" questioned Rose half dismayed.

"Your pa said there might be," said Miranda unconcernedly, trying not to show how glad she was.

"Who?"

"Your pa didn't say who," answered Miranda, just as if she had not seen those two shadowy figures conversing outside the Whitney gate.

Rose slid into the library and sat down on the arm of her father's chair, putting a soft arm around his neck and laying her cheek against his.

"Father, Miranda says there is to be company tonight?" She laid the matter before him seriously.

"Yes," said David rousing out of his perusal of the various methods of insulating wires. "Yes, Rosy posy, Nathan Whitney is coming to supper. I though I'd like to begin to get acquainted with him at once."

"Oh, father dear! You dear, dear father!" cried Rose, hugging him with all her might.

Mother Marcia came smiling downstairs, and just as Miranda was taking up the golden brown loaves of Johnnycake Nathan presented himself, shy and awkward but with eyes that fairly danced with pleasure and anticipation. He had done his best to put himself in festive array and was good to look upon as he stood waiting beside his chair at the table with the candle light from the sconces above the mantle shining on his short chestnut curls. He seemed to Rose suddenly to have grown old and tall, all dressed up in his Sunday clothes, with his hair brushed, and his high collar and neck-cloth like a man. She gazed at him half in awe as she slipped into her chair and folded her hands for the blessing.

It was a strange sensation for Nathan, sitting there with bowed head before that dainty table loaded with tempting good things, listening to the simple strong words of the grace; the fire-light and the candle-light playing together over the hush of the room; the little girl who had been his pet and playmate in her pretty frock of blue and white with her gold curls bowed—he could just see the sheen of gold in her hair as he raised his eyes in one swift comprehensive glance; Miranda standing at the kitchen door with a steaming dish in her hand and her head bowed decorously, its waves of shining hair like burnished copper; and the gracious sweet lady mother whom he adored, there by his side. Strange thrills of hot and cold crept over his body, and his breath came slowly lest it sound too loud. This was actually the first time in his life that Nathan Whitney had ever taken a meal at any other home than his own!

Meals a-many he had eaten out of a tin pail on his old scarred desk in school, or down by the brook in summer; more meals he had gone without, or taken on the road, of cold pieces hastily purloined in absence of his aunt or stepmother, but never before had he been invited to supper and sat at a beautiful table with snowy linen, silver and china and all the good things people give to company. All this in his honor! He was almost frightened at himself. Not that he was unaccustomed to nice things, for there was plenty of fine linen, rare china, and silver in the great house across the way, but it had not been used familiarly since his mother's death; and was mostly brought out for company occasions, on which occasions it had been young Nathan's habit to absent himself, because the company always seemed to look at him as if he had no right in his father's house.

CHAPTER 9

As HE looked about the cheery table after grace was concluded, Nathan Whitney could hardly believe his own senses that he was really here and by invitation. He rubbed his eyes and almost thought he must be dreaming. For this cause he answered but briefly the opening remarks directed to him, and mainly by "Yes, ma'am," and "No, ma'am," "Yes, sir," and "No, sir."

But David with rare tact began to tell a story with a point so humorous that Nathan forgot his new surroundings and laughed. After that the ice was broken and he talked more freely, and gradually his awe melted so that he was able to do a boy's full justice to the good things that Miranda had with joy prepared.

The talk drifted to the telegraph, for David felt a deep and vital interest in the great invention, and could not keep away long from the subject. Marcia too was just as interested and ready with keen and intelligent questions to which the boy listened appreciatively. He had a boy's natural keenness for mechanical appliances, but no one had ever taken the trouble to explain the telegraph to him. David saw the boy's bright eyes watching him fascinated as he attempted to describe to Marcia the principle on which the wonderful new instrument was supposed to work, and went into detail more than he would have needed to do for Marcia, who had been following each account in the papers as eagerly as if she were a man; and who, understanding, helped along by asking questions, until the boy himself ventured one or two.

David was pleased to see in his questions a high degree of understanding and insight, and his heart warmed quickly toward the young fellow. He forgot entirely that he was putting the guest through an examination at the instigation of his maiden aunts and for the sake of protecting his young daughter. Perhaps he had never had any such idea in "getting acquainted" with Nathan, but certain it is that he did not expect the process of getting acquainted to be so altogether interesting and gratifying. He understood at once why Marcia had said he was "unusual if you could only get at his real soul." As they talked the boy's face had brightened until it fairly glowed with the pleasure of his surroundings and forgetfulness of his usual feeling that he was in some measure considered an outlaw.

David had made quite a study of the telegraph, having been present several times by special invitation when Professor Morse gave an exhibition of his instrument at work to a few scientific friends. He could therefore speak from an intimate knowledge of his subject. The boy listened in charmed silence and at last broke forth:

"Why doesn't he make a telegraph himself and start it working so everybody can use it?"

David explained how expensive it was to prepare the wire, insulate it, and make the necessary parts of the instrument. Then he told him of the bill of appropriation for testing it that was before Congress at the time. The boy's eyes shone.

"It'll be great if Congress lets him have all that money to try it, I think, don't you? It'll be sure to succeed, won't it?"

"I think so," said David with conviction. "I am firmly convinced that the telegraph has come to stay. But it is not strange that people doubt it. It is even a more wonderful invention than the railroad. Why, it is only about fifteen years since people were hooting and crying out against the idea of the steam railway and now look how many we have, and how indispensable to travel it has become."

The boy looked at the man admiringly.

"Say, you go on the railroad a lot, don't you?"

"Why, yes," said David. "My business makes it necessary for me to run up to New York very frequently. You've been on it, of course?"

The boy's face took on a look of great amusement.

"Me? Oh, no! I've never been, and never expect to have the chance, but it must be a great experience I've tried to think how it would feel going along like that without anything really pulling you. I've dreamed lots of times about taking a ride on the railroad, but I guess that's as near as I'll ever get to it."

"Well, I don't see why," said David reflectively. "Suppose you go up with me the next time I go. I'd like to have company and I can explain to you all about it. I know the engineer well and he'll show us all about the workings of the engine. Come, will you go?"

"Will I go?" exclaimed Nathan too much excited to choose his words. "Well I guess I will if I get the chance. Do you mean it, Mr. Spafford?"

"Certainly," said David smiling. "I shall be delighted to have your company. I shall probably go a week from today. Can you get away from school?"

Nathan's face darkened.

"I guess there isn't any school going to keep me out of that chance," he said threateningly.

"Would you like me to speak to your father about it?"

"Father won't care," said the boy looking up in surprise. "He never knows where I am, just so I don't bother him."

A fleeting wave of pity swept over Marcia's face as she took in what this must mean to the boy, but David, seeing this was a sore point, said pleasantly:

"I'll make that all right for you," and passed on to discuss the difference the steam railway had made in the length of time it took to go from one city to another, and the consequent ease with which business could be transacted between places at a distance from one another; and from that they went on to speculating about the changes that might come with the telegraph.

"Wouldn't it be wonderful to be able to get a message from Washington in half an hour, for instance?" said David. "Professor Morse claims it is possible. Many doubt it, but I am inclined to believe he knows what he is about and to think that it is only a question of time before we have telegraphs all over the United States, at least in the larger cities and towns."

Nathan's eyes were large.

"Say, it's a big time to be living in, isn't it?"

"It is indeed," said David, his eyes sparkling appreciatively, "but after all, have you ever thought that almost any time is a big time to be living in for a boy or a man who has a work to do in the world?"

It was beautiful to see the waves of feeling go over the boy's face in rich coloring, and deep sparkling of his eyes, and David could but admire him as he watched. What could people mean that they had let this boy remain with the mark of evil upon his reputation? Why had no one tried to pull him out of his lawless ways before? Why had he never tried? What was Mr. Whitney thinking of to let a boy like this go to ruin as everybody said he was going? David resolved that he should never go if effort of his could help save him.

While they talked the Johnnycake, biscuits, cold ham, fried potatoes, tea-cakes, jam, preserves and cake had been disappearing in large quantities, and the time seemed at last to have arrived when the boy could eat no more. Marcia made a little motion to rise.

"We'll go in the other room for worship," she said, and led the way to the parlor where Miranda had quietly preceded them and lit the candles. There was an open fire in the fireplace here too, and the room was bright and cheery with stately reflections in polished mahogany furniture and long mirrors. Nathan hung back at the door and looked about almost in awe. He had not been in this room when he came to the house at other times and it seemed like entering a new world, but almost instantly his attention was held by the pianoforte that stood at one side of the room, and he forgot for the moment his shyness over the idea of "worship," which had brought a sudden tightness around his heart when Marcia mentioned it.

Worship in the Whitney home was a dull and stately form, long drawn out and wearisome to the flesh. Nathan had escaped it of late years, and neither father's nor stepmother's reprimands had sufficed to make him even an occasional attendant, so that when David Spafford had invited him to supper it had not occurred to him that family worship would be a part of the evening's program; though if he had stopped to think he might have known, for David was an elder in the church, and it was a strange thing for any respectable family of the church to be without family worship in that day. It was a mark of respectability if nothing else.

Miranda was sitting primly in her chair by the door with her hands folded in her lap and her most seraphic look on her merry face. One might almost say she seemed glorified tonight, her satisfaction beamed so effulgently from every golden freckle and every gleaming copper wave of her hair.

Nathan dropped suddenly into the chair on the other side of the door, feeling awkward and out of place for the first time since his host had welcomed him and made him feel at home. Here in this stately "company" room, with a religious service before him, he was again keenly aware of his own shortcomings in the community. He did not belong here and he was a fool to have come. The sullen scowl involuntarily darkened his brow as Rose slipped about the room giving each one a hymn book,—for all the world like church. Nathan took the book reluctantly because she gave it, but his self-consciousness was so great that he dropped it awkwardly, and stooping to pick it up his face grew red with embarrassment.

Marcia, noticing, tried to put him at his ease.

"What hymn do you like best, Nathan?" she asked, but the boy only turned the redder and mumbled that he didn't know.

"Then we'll sing the shepherd psalm. Rose is fond of that," she said, seating herself at the pianoforte.

Nathan fumbled the leaves until he found the place, and then was suddenly entranced with the first notes of the tune as Marcia began to play it over.

Now it happened that the shepherd psalm was the one young Nathan could remember hearing his mother sing to him when he was little. She had sung it, too, to the twins and Samuel when they were babies, and it was associated in his mind with her gentle voice, her smiling eyes and the feel of her arms about him as she tucked him in at night, so when the song burst forth from the lips of the family the young guest had much ado to keep back a great lump that arose in his throat, and to control a strange moisture that stole in his eyes.

> "The Lord's my shepherd, I'll not want;
> He makes me down to lie
> In pastures green, He leadeth me
> The quiet waters by—"

Miranda's voice was high and clear while little Rose, sitting in the shelter of her father's arm, joined her bird-like treble to his bass, and Marcia sang alto blending the whole most exquisitely. Nathan stole a covert glance about, saw they were not noticing him at all, and presently he forgot his own strange situation and began to grumble out the air:

> "My table thou hast furnished
> In presence of my foes;—"

(How he wished those Spafford aunts were there to see him sitting thus!—)

> "My head thou dost with oil anoint
> And my cup overflows."

He had a faint idea that it was overflowing now.

> "Goodness and mercy all my life
> Shall surely follow me;
> And in God's house forevermore
> My dwelling place shall be."

Would it? Wouldn't that be strange? Would his enemies be surprised some day if they should find him dwelling in heaven?

They were only fleeting thoughts passing through his mind, but the psalm that David read when the hymn was done kept up the thought, "Who shall ascend into the hill of the Lord? or who shall stand in his holy place? He that hath clean hands and a pure heart; who hath not lifted up his soul unto vanity, nor sworn deceitfully. He shall receive the blessing from the Lord and righteousness from the God of his salvation."

Nathan looked down at his rough boy hands, scrubbed till they showed the lines of walnut stain from his afternoon's climbing after nuts. Clean hands and a pure heart? The hands could be got cleaner by continued washings,—but the heart?

The boy was still thinking about it when they knelt to pray, and he heard himself prayed for as "our dear young friend who is with us tonight" and a blessing asked on his "promising young life." It was almost too much for Nathan, and if the prayer had not branched off into matters of national importance in a strain of thanksgiving for "all the wonders wrought in this generation," and a petition for the President and his Cabinet that they might have light and wisdom to decide the important questions that were placed in their keeping, it is doubtful whether Nathan would have got through without disgracing himself by the shedding of a tear in his excitement.

He rose from his knees with an uplifted expression on his face and looked about on the room and these dear people as if he had suddenly found himself companying with angels.

Miranda bustled out to clear off the table. Marcia called Nathan and Rose to the piano, and they all sang a few minutes, then she played one or two gay melodies for them. After that they all went into the library and gathering around the big carved table played jackstraws until it was Rose's bedtime. When Miranda finished the dishes she too came and took a hand in the game, and kept them all laughing with her quaint remarks, talking about the jackstraws as if they were people.

When the big hall clock struck the half hour after eight Rose looked regretfully at her mother and meeting her nod and smile arose obediently, and said good night. Nathan, taking her hand awkwardly for good night, arose also to make his adieus, but David told him to sit down for a few minutes, he wanted to talk to him. So while Marcia and Rose slipped away up stairs, and Miranda went to set the buckwheat cake for breakfast, Nathan settled back half scared and faced the pleasant smile of his host, wondering if he was to be called to account for some of his numerous pranks and if, after all, the happy time had only been a ruse to get him in a corner.

But David did not leave him in uncertainty long.

"What are you going to do with your life, Nathan?" he asked kindly.

"Do with it?" asked the surprised Nathan. "*Do* with it?" Then his brow darkened. "Nothing, I s'pose."

"Oh, no, you don't mean that I'm sure. You're too bright a boy for that, and this is a great age in which to be living, you know. You've got a big man's work to do somewhere in the world. Are you getting ready for it or are you just drifting yet?"

"Just drifting, I guess," said Nathan softly after considering.

"Don't see any chance for anything else," he added apologetically. "Nobody cares what I do anyway" [fiercely].

"Oh, that's nonsense. Why—Nathan—*I* care. I like you, and I want to see you succeed."

A warm red wave of delight flowed over the boy's face and neck, and his eyes flashed one wondering, grateful glance at David. He wanted to say something but couldn't. Words would choke him.

"You're going to college, of course? " said David as a matter of course.

Nathan shook his head.

"How could I?" he asked. "Father'd never send me. He says any money spent on me is thrown away. He was going to send my halfbrother Allan to college but he ran away, and he says he'll never send any of the rest of us—"

"Well, send yourself," said David as if it were quite the expected thing to have a loving parent talk like that. "It will really be the best thing for you in the end anyway. A boy that has to pay his own way makes twice as much of college as the fellow who has everything made easy for him, and I guess you've got grit enough to do it. Get a job right away and begin to lay up money."

"Get a job! *Me* get a job!" laughed Nathan. "Why, nobody'd give me a regular job that I could earn anything much with. They don't like me well enough. They wouldn't trust me. I can get errands and little things to do, but nobody would give me anything worth while."

"Why is that?" David looked keenly but kindly at him.

The boy blushed, and dropped his eyes. At last he answered:

"My own fault, I guess," and smiled as if he were sorry.

"Oh, well, you can soon make that right by showing them you are trustworthy now, you know."

"No," said the boy decidedly, "it's too late. Nobody in this town will give me the chance."

"I will," said David. "I'll give you a job in the printing office if you would like it."

"Wouldn't I though!" said the boy springing to his feet in his excitement. "You just try me. Do you really mean it?"

"Yes, I mean it," said David smiling. "But how about the school?"

"Hang the school," said Nathan frowning. "I want to go to work."

"No, it won't do to hang the school, because then you'll never be able to hold your own working, nor reach up to the bigger things when you have learned the smaller ones. How far have you got in school? What are you studying?"

Nathan told him gloomily, and it was plain there was little interest in the boy's mind for his school.

"I been through it all before anyway," he added. "This teacher doesn't know as much as my—as—that is—as Miss Bent did." His face was very red, for he couldn't bring himself to speak of his father's wife as mother. David was quick to catch the idea.

"I see, you are merely going over the old ground and it isn't very interesting. How thoroughly did you know it before?"

Nathan shook his head.

"Don't know, guess I didn't study very hard, but what's the use? They never gave me credit anyway for what I did do."

"Had any Latin?" David thought it better to ignore a discussion of teachers. He did not think much of the present incumbent himself.

"No."

"Are you in the highest class?"

"Yes."

"What would you think of leaving school and working in the printing office daytimes, and studying Latin and mathematics with me evenings?"

The boy was dumb. He looked at David for a moment, and then dropped his eyes and swallowed hard several times. When he finally raised his eyes again they were full of tears, and this time the boy was not ashamed of them.

"What would you do it for?" he asked when he could speak, his voice utterly broken down with feeling.

"Well, just because I like you and I want to see you get on; and besides, I think I would enjoy it. I'm glad you like the idea. We'll see what can be done. I think in two years at most you might be ready for college if you put in your time well, and by that time you ought to have saved enough to at least start you. There'll be ways to earn your board when you get to college. Lots of fellows do it. Shall I see your father about it, or would you rather do it yourself?"

"Father?" said Nathan wondering again. "Why you don't need to see father. I never ask him about anything. He'd rather not be bothered."

Subsequent experience led David to believe that Nathan was right, for when he went to see Mr. Whitney that grim and unnatural parent strongly advised David to have nothing whatever to do with his scapegrace son, and declared himself unwilling to be responsible for any failure that might ensue if he went contrary to this advice. He said that Nathan was like his mother, not practical in any way, and that he had been nothing but a source of anxiety since he was born, and he had only kept him at school because he did not know what else to do with him. He never expected him to amount to a row of pins. With this encouragement David Spafford undertook the higher education of young Nathan Whitney, strongly suspecting that the father's lack of interest in the son's welfare had its source in an inherent miserliness. Mr. Whitney, however, gave a reluctant permission for his son to leave school and learn the printing business in the office of the *Clarion Call;* but vowed that he would not assist him to fool his time away and spend money pretending he was getting a college education, and if he left school now he needn't do it with any expectation of getting a penny from him for any such nonsense, for he wouldn't give it.

However, David was wise enough that night to say nothing further to the boy about consulting his father, merely telling him, as he said goodnight, that he would expect him to be ready to go to New York with him a week from that day on the early morning train, and that they then would look after purchasing some Latin books, and perhaps get time to run over to the University and find out about entrance requirements so that their work might be intelligent. In the meantime it would be well for Nathan to finish out the week at school, as it was now Wednesday. That would give time to arrange matters at the office, and with his father; then if all was satisfactory he might come to the office Monday morning. There were things he could do both in preparation for the journey and while they were away to help with business, and his salary would begin Monday morning. It wouldn't be much at first, but he might consider that his work began Monday, and that the trip to New York was all in the way of business.

With a heart almost bursting with wonder and joy, and eyes that shone as bright as any of the stars over his head, Nathan walked across the street to his home, ascended a tree to his bedroom window, for he could not bear the sight of anyone just yet, and crept to his bed, where, kneeling with his face in the pillow, he tried to express in a queer little lonely prayer his praise for the great thing that had come to him, mingled with a wistful desire for the "pure heart and clean hands" of those who had a right to the blessing of the Lord. With all his heart he meant to do his part toward making good.

Across the street, high in the side gable, there twinkled the candle of Miranda for a few minutes, and then went out while the owner sat at the window, looking out on the field of stars above her, and thinking deep, wide thoughts.

Now Miranda was the soul of honor on most occasions, but if there came a time when it was to the advantage of those she loved for her to do a little quiet eavesdropping, or to stretch the truth so it would fit a particularly trying circumstance, she generally was able to get a reprieve from her conscience long enough to do it. Therefore, while David had been talking with Nathan in the library, Miranda had had a sudden call to hunt for something in the hall closet, which was located so close to the library door that one standing in the crack of one door might easily hear whole sentences of what was spoken behind the crack of the other door. Miranda would have scorned to listen if the visitor had been a grownup on business, and she never allowed herself this indulgence unless she felt the inner call to help some one or protect them. Tonight it was her great anxiety for Nathan that caused her to look so diligently for her overshoes, which she knew very well were standing neatly in their appointed place in her own closet upstairs. But she heard a great deal of what David proposed to do for Nathan and her heart swelled with pride and joy; pride in David and his wonderful little wife whom she knew was at the bottom of the whole scheme, and joy for Nathan of whom she was grown greatly fond, and for whose reputation and uplifting she was intensely jealous.

So it was with a light heart and feet that almost danced that she took her candle-lit way to her little gable room, and after a few simple preparations for the night, put out the light and sat down under the stars to think.

CHAPTER 10

NATHAN was on hand bright and early Monday morning at the office, a look of suppressed excitement in his dark eyes, and a dawning dignity and self-respect in his whole manner.

It was new to him to be expected anywhere and greeted as if he had a right to a business-like welcome. Even in school he had felt the covert protest of the teacher against him always, and had maintained an attitude of having to fight for his rights.

"You are to use this desk for the present," said Morton Howe, the factotum of the office, "and Mr. Spafford wants you to copy those names on that list into that ledger. He'll be down in about an hour. You'll find enough to keep you busy till then, I guess," and the kindly old man pointed to a stool by a high desk, and showed Nathan where to hang his cap.

"It's a real pleasant morning," he added by way of showing the new assistant a little courtesy. "I guess you'll like it here. We all do."

Nathan's face beamed unexpectedly.

"I should say I would," he surprised himself into saying.

"Mr. Spafford's a real kind man to work for." Morton Howe was in his employer's confidence, moreover he worshipped David devotedly.

"I should say he was!" responded Nathan with more fervor than originality.

Then began a new life for Nathan. The two days that proceeded the journey to New York were one long dream of wonder and delight to the boy. There was hard work to be sure, but Nathan hadn't a lazy streak in him, and every word he copied, every errand he ran, every duty he performed was so much intense pleasure to him. To be needed, and to be able to please were so new to him that he looked on each moment of his day with awe lest it might yet prove a dream and slip away from him.

Never had worker of David's been more attentive, more punctilious in performing a task, more respectful or more worshipful—and all his employees loved him.

"I see you got that young nimshi, Nate Whitney, in your office, Dave," said old Mr. Heath the second day of Nathan's service. "You better look out fer yer money. Keep yer safe well locked. He belongs to a bad lot. He's no good himself. I don't see what you took him for."

"I've never had a better office helper in my experience," said David crisply, with a smile. "He seems to have ability."

"H'mph!" said Grandfather Heath. "Ability to be a scamp I should say. You're a dreamer David, like your father was before you, and there don't no good come of dreamin' in my opinion. You gen'ally wake up to find your nose bit off, er your goods stolen a'fore yer eyes."

"Well, I haven't found it so yet," answered David good naturedly, "and I shouldn't wonder if my boy Nathan will surprise you all some day. If I know anything at all he's going to amount to something."

"Surprise us all, will he? Wal, his brother did that a number of years ago when he made out to murder Enoch Taylor, an' then git out o' the smokehouse 'ithout unlockin' the door, an' a beam acrost it too; an' me with the key all safe in its usual place and no way of explainin' it, 'cept thet he must a carried some kind o' tools 'long with him, and then fixed the lock all right so's we wouldn't suspect very early in the mornin'. Oh, he surprised us all right, an' your fine little man'll likely turn out to s'prise you in jest some sech way."

"By the way, Mr. Heath," said David more for the sake of changing the subject than because he had much interest in the matter, "how was it that they suspected Allan Whitney of that murder? He never owned up to it, did he?"

"Oh, no, he lied about it o' course."

"But just how did you ever get an idea that Allan Whitney had anything to do with it? He didn't bring the news, did he? I've forgotten how it was, it happened so long ago."

"Not he, he didn't bring no news. He hed too much sense to bring news. No, it was Lawrence Billings brought word about findin' Enoch Taylor a moanin' by the roadside."

"Lawrence Billings!" said David. "Then where did Whitney come in? Billings didn't charge him with it, did he?"

"No, we caught Allan Whitney with a gun not a quarter of a mile away from the spot, tryin' to sneak around to git home 'thout bein' seen."

"But that wasn't exactly proof positive," said David, who had now reached his own gate and was in a hurry to get in the house.

"It was to anybody that knowed Allan," said the hard, positive old man, "an' ef it wa'n't, what more'd you want thun his runnin' away?"

"That told against him of course," said David quietly. "Well, Mr. Heath, I'm going to New York in the morning, anything I can do for you?"

"No, I gen'ally make out to do with what I ken get in our hum stores. You take a big resk when you travel on railroads. I saw in the New York paper the other day where a train of cars was runnin' west from Bawstun last Sat'day, and come in contact with a yoke of oxen near Worcester, throwing the engine off the track and renderin' it completely unfit fer use; *and killin' the oxen!* It seems turrible to encourage a thing that means such a resk to life and property. And here just a few days back there was another accident down below Wilmington. They was runnin' the train *twenty miles an hour!* an they run down a hand car and overturned their engine and *jest ruined it!* A thing like that ain't safe ner reasonable. Too much resk fer me!"

"Yes, there has to be risk in all progress, I suppose; well, goodnight, Mr. Heath," said David, and went smiling into the house to tell Marcia how far behind the times their neighbor was.

Miranda was hovering songfully back and forth between the kitchen and dining room, mindful of any items of news that she could catch, very happy over the pleasure that was to come to Nathan on the morrow and she heard the whole account of David's talk with Mr. Heath, though David thought she was engrossed with her preparations for supper. Miranda had a way like that, leaving an ear and an eye flung out on watch behind her while she did duty somewhere else and nobody suspected. It was always, however, a kindly ear and eye for those she loved.

The reference to Allan Whitney and the murder brought a serious look to her face, and she managed to get behind the door and hear the whole of it. But when mention was made of Lawrence Billings her fact blazed with sudden illumination. Lawrence Billings! It was Lawrence Billings who had committed the crime, of course! Strange that she had never thought of him before! Strange she had never overheard that he had been the one to bring the news!

Lawrence Billings, as a little boy, had followed Allan Whitney like a devoted dog. His sleek, light head, his pale, pasty countenance and faded, furtive blue eyes were always just behind wherever Allan went. No one ever understood why Allan protected him and tolerated him, for he was not of Allan's type, and his native cowardliness was a byword among the other boys. It may be his devotion touched the older boy, or else he was sorry for his widowed mother, whose graying goldish hair, frightened, tired eyes, and wistful, drooping mouth looked pitifully like her son's. However it was, it was well understood from the first day little Lawrence Billings, carrying his slate under his arm, and clinging fearfully to his mother's hand, was brought to the schoolhouse that Allan Whitney had constituted himself a defender. Miranda knew, for she had stood by the school gate when they entered, and seen the appeal of the widow's eyes toward the tall boy in the school yard as the rabble of hoodlums around her son set up a yell: "Here comes mother's pet!" Something manly in Allan's eyes had flashed forth and answered that appeal of that mother in true knightly fashion, and never again did Lawrence Billings want for a champion while Allan was about. Of course Allan had protected Lawrence Billings! It was just like Allan, even though it meant his own reputation— yes! and life!

For a moment tears of pride welled into Miranda's eyes, and behind the kitchen door she lifted her face to the gray painted wall and muttered softly: "Thanks be!" as a recognition of her boy's nobility. Then she moved thoughtfully back to her cooking, albeit with an exalted look upon her face, as if she had seen the angel of renunciation, and been blest thereby.

However, when she thought of Lawrence Billings, her face darkened. What of the fellow who would allow such sacrifice of one he professed to love? Did Lawrence know that he was exiling Allan from his home all these years? Did he realize what it had meant? Had he consented that Allan should take his crime, or was he in anywise a party to the arrest?

Lawrence Billings still lived in the little old rundown house on the edge of the village belonging to his mother, and still allowed his mother to take in sewing for a living, her living and part of his, for his inefficiency had made it hard for to get or keep any kind of a position. But Lawrence always managed to keep neatly dressed and to go out with the girls whenever they would have him. His unlimited leisure and habit of tagging made him a frequent sight at all gatherings of a social nature whether of church or town; but weak mouth and expressionless eyes had always been despised by the thorough-going Miranda, though she had tolerated him because of Allan. Now, however her mind began to stir fiercely against him. Could something be done to clear the name of Allan Whitney even if he never came back to take advantage of it? It was terrible to have a man like Lawrence Billings walking around smirking when Allan was exiled and despised.

Of course, Miranda grudgingly admitted to herself she might be mistaken about Lawrence Billings being the criminal—but she knew she was not. Now that she had thought of it every word of Allan's, every circumstance of his behavior toward Lawrence in the past even the meaningful tone of his voice when he said *"But I know who did it!"* pointed to the weaker man. Miranda felt she had a clue, yet saw as yet nothing she could do with it. The conditions were just the same as when Allan went away. Mrs. Billings, just as faded and wistful, a trifle more withered, was sewing away and coughing her little hacking apologetic cough of a Sunday; a trifle more hollow perhaps, but just as sad and unobtrusive. Who could do anything against such a puny adversary? The girl had an instant's revelation of why Allan had gone away instead of defending himself. It brooded with her through the night and while she was preparing the early breakfast which Nathan had been invited to share with David.

Fried mush and sausage and potatoes, topped off with doughnuts and coffee and applesauce! How good it all tasted to Nathan, eaten in the early candle-lighted room, with the pink dawn just flushing the sky; and Rose, shy and sweet, her eyes still cloudy with sleep, sitting opposite smiling. The boy felt as if he were transformed into another being and entering a new life where all was heaven.

Afterward there was a brief sweet worship; then Miranda stuffed his pockets with seed cakes. Rose walked beside her father, holding his hand silently, as she stole glances across at Nathan, who proudly carried the valise wherein his own insignificant bundle reposed along with David's things. The early morning light was over everything and summer had glanced back and waved a fleeting hand at the day with soft airs and lingering warmth of sunshine. The boy's heart was fairly bursting with happiness.

Oh, the glories and the wonders of that journey! At Schenectady there was a stop of several minutes and David took Nathan forward and introduced him to the engineer, who kindly showed him the engine, taking apparent pride and pleasure in explaining every detail of its working. The engineer had come to be a hero to the boys and knew his admirers when he saw them. He invited Nathan to ride to Albany in the engine with him, and the boy with shining eyes allowed David to accept the invitation for him, and climbed on board feeling as if he were about to mount up on wings and fly to the moon. David went back to his coach and his discussion of Whig versus Loco-Foco.

At Albany a new engineer came on duty and Nathan went back to his place beside David in the carriage. But there was a world of new delight to watch, with David ready to explain everything; and there were two men to whom David introduced him. One, a Mr. Burleigh, was going down to New York to lecture "In Opposition to the Punishment of Death," as the notices in the *Tribune* stated. Nathan listened with tense interest to the discussion for and against capital punishment; the more because the subject had come so near to the elder brother who had been his youthful paragon and idol. David, turning once, caught the look in the boy's eyes and wondered again at the intellectual appreciation he seemed to have, no matter what the subject.

The other gentleman was a Mr. Vail, an intimate friend of and closely associated with Professor Samuel Morse, the inventor of the Electro-Magnetic Telegraph. He had recently set up a private telegraph of his own at his home and was making interesting experiments in connection with Professor Morse. This man noticed the boy's deep interest when the subject was mentioned, and the eager questions in his eyes that dared not come to his lips. He kindly took out a pencil and paper, making numerous diagrams to explain the different parts of the instrument, and the theory upon which they worked, and as the occupants of the coach bent over the paper and listened to his story, the beauties of the strange new way were almost forgotten by the boy traveller, and his eyes glowed over the fairy tale of science.

Then as they neared the great city of New York about which he had dreamed so many dreams, the boy's heart beat high with excitement. His face went pale with suppressed emotion. He was a boy of few words, and not used to letting anyone know how he felt, but the three men in the coach could not help seeing that he was greatly stirred.

"A fine fellow that," murmured Mr. Vail to Mr. Burleigh as the train drew in at the station, and Nathan seemed engrossed in the various things which David was pointing out to him.

"Yes," assented Mr. Burleigh. "He asked some bright questions. He'll do something in the world himself one day or I'm mistaken. Has a good face."

"Yes, a very good face. I've been thinking as I watched him this morning if more boys were like that we needn't be afraid for the future of our country."

Nathan just then turned, lifting un-self-conscious eyes to the two men opposite, and perceived in a flash; by their close regarding, that the words he had just overheard were spoken concerning himself. A look of wonder, and then of deep shame crossed his face

He dropped his gaze and his long dark lashes swept like a gloomy veil over the bright eager eyes that had just glowed so finely, while a deep wave of crimson spread over his face.

They had thought that of him just seeing him once, these gentlemen! But if they knew how people regarded him at home! Ah, if they knew! He could hear even now the echo of old Squire Heath's ejaculations concerning himself: "That young Whitney's a rascal an' a scoundrel. He'll never amount to a row of pins. He ought to have his hide tanned."

Nathan's confusion was so great that it was unmistakable, and David turning toward him suddenly saw that something was wrong.

"I've just got caught in expressing my opinion of your young friend here," smilingly acknowledged Mr. Vail. "I hope he will pardon my being so personal, but I have taken a great liking to him. I hope he will find it possible to come to Philadelphia some time soon and visit me. I can then show him my instrument. If you should come down next month perhaps you will bring him with you."

The flood of color in the boy's face was illumined by a holy wonder as he looked from one gentleman to the other. Truly he had been lifted out entirely from his old life and set in a sphere where no one knew he was a worthless scoundrel not to be trusted. He heard David promising to bring him with him if possible the next time he went to Philadelphia and he managed to stumble out a few broken words of thanks to both gentlemen, feeling all the time how inadequate they were. but had he known it, words were unnecessary, for his eloquent eyes spoke volumes of gratitude.

The train came to a standstill then and there were pleasant leave-takings with their fellow travellers, after which David and Nathan took their way through the city to the hotel where David usually stopped, Nathan feeling suddenly shy and young and quite countrified.

CHAPTER 11

THE stay in New York lengthened itself into nearly two weeks, for the business on which David had come was important and proved more difficult of settlement than he had expected. In the meantime life was one long, busy, happy dream for Nathan. He was with David all day long, save when that busy man was closeted with some great men talking over business matters which were private and confidential. Even then David often took Nathan with him as his secretary, asking him to take notes of things that were said, or occasionally to copy papers. The boy was acquiring great skill in such matters and could write a neat and creditable letter quite satisfactory to his employer. He had a good, natural handwriting as well as a keen mind and willing heart, which are a great outfit in any work.

Everywhere they went David explained who and what people, places and things were. Their trip was liberal education for the boy. He met great men, and saw the sights of the whole city. Every evening when business would allow, they went to some gathering or place of entertainment. He heard a lecture of Phrenology and Magnetism which interested him, and he resolved to try some of the experiments with the boys when he got home. He went to the New York Opera House to attend the Thirty-eighth Anniversary of the Peithologian Society of Columbia College, of which David Spafford was a member, and met Mr. J. Babcock Arden, the Secretary, whose name was signed to the notice of the meeting in the *Tribune*. It seemed wonderful to meet a man whose name was printed out like that in a New York paper. Mr. Arden greeted him as if he were already a man and told him he hoped he would be one of their number some day when he came to college, and Nathan's heart swelled with the determination to fulfil that hope.

They went to several concerts, and Nathan discovered that he enjoyed music immensely. The Philharmonic Society gave its first concert during their stay in the city and it was the boy's first experience in hearing fine singing. He sat as one entranced. Another night they heard Rainer and Dempster, two popular singers who were making a great impression, especially with their rendering of "The Lament of the Irish Emigrant,"

"Locked in the Cradle of the Deep," and "The Free Country." The melodies caught in the boy's brain and kept singing themselves over and over. He also came to know "Auld Robin Gray," a new and popular ballad, "The Death of Warren," "Saw ye Johnnie Coming" and "The Blind Boy." When he was alone he sang them over bit by bit until he felt they were his own. It was thus, coming upon him unaware one day, that David discovered the boy was possessed of a wonderfully clear, flute-like voice, and resolved that he must go to singing school during the winter and must certainly sing in the choir, for such a voice would be an acquisition to the church. He decided to talk with the minister about it as soon as he got home.

Two days after their arrival in New York there came the celebration of the completion of the Croton Water Works. Heralded for days beforehand both by friends and enemies, the day dawned bright and clear and Nathan awoke as excited as if he were a little boy on General Training Day.

There was a six-mile pageant formed on Broadway and Bowling Green, marching through Broadway to Union Square, and down Bowery to Grand Street. There were twenty thousand in the procession and so great was the enthusiasm, according to the papers, that "there might have been two hundred thousand if there had been room for them."

First came the New York firemen, whose interest in the new water system was most natural, and following them in full uniform the Philadelphia firemen, their helmets and bright buttons gleaming in the sun. Then came the Irish, then the Germans, then the Masons, banners and streamers flying, a brilliant display. There was a float bearing the identical printing press on which Franklin worked, and Colonel Stone sat in Franklin's chair printing leaflets all about the Croton Water Works, which were distributed along the way as the procession moved. There was another float bearing two miniature steamboats, and next followed the gold and silver artisans. After them came the cars with models of the pipes and pieces of the machinery used in the water works and maps of the construction; then the artisans whose labor had brought into being the great system. After them came the College, Mechanical and Mercantile Library Society, and last of all the Temperance Societies, whose beautiful banners bearing noble sentiments were greeted with loud acclamation by the people.

There were speeches and singing, and Samuel Stevens gave the history of New York water, telling about the old Tea-Water Pump which gave the only drinkable water until 1825. After that there were cisterns in front of the churches, and later the city appropriated fifteen hundred dollars to a tank on Thirteenth Street.

It was a great day, with bells ringing from morning to night, and the Croton Water Works sending out beautiful jets of water from the hydrants while the procession was moving; and at night the Astor House and the Park Theatre were illuminated. Nathan felt that he had been present at the greatest event in the world's history, and he wondered as he dropped off to sleep that night what the boys at home would say if they could know all that was happening to him.

A few days later David and Nathan were walking on the Battery, talking earnestly; at least David was talking and Nathan was listening and responding eagerly now and then. They were talking about the wonderful new telegraph, and its inventor, whom they had met that day and who had invited them to watch an experiment that was to be tried publicly on the morrow. It was a beautiful moonlight night, and presently as they walked and talked, looking out across the way they saw a little boat proceeding slowly along, one man at the oars and one at the stern. Other idlers on the battery that night might have wondered what kind of fishing the two men were engaged in that took so long a line, but David and Nathan watched with deep interest for they were in the secret of the little boat. In its stern sat Professor Morse with two miles of copper wire wound on a reel, paying it out slowly. It took two hours to lay that first cable between Castle Garden and Governor's Island, and the two who watched did not remain until it was done for they had been invited to be present very early the next morning when the first test was to be made, and so they hurried back to the Astor House to get some sleep before the wonderful event should take place. Nathan was almost too much excited to sleep.

The *New York Herald* came out next morning with this statement:

MORSE'S ELECTRO-MAGNETIC TELEGRAPH.

"This important invention is to be exhibited in operation at Castle Garden between the hours of twelve and one o'clock today. One telegraph will be erected on Governor's Island, and one at the Castle, and messages will be interchanged and others transmitted during the day. Many have been incredulous as to the power this wonderful triumph of science and art. All such may now have an opportunity of fairly testing it. *It is destined to work a complete revolution in the mode of transmitting intelligence throughout the civilized world.*"

At daybreak Professor Morse was on the Battery, and was joined almost immediately by David and Nathan and two or three other friends deeply interested, and the work of preparing for the great test began. At last everything was in readiness, and the eager watchers actually witnessed the transmission of three or four characters between the termini of the line, when suddenly the communication was interrupted and it was found impossible to send any more messages through the conductor. Great was the excitement and anxiety for a few minutes, while the Professor worked with his instrument. Then looking up he pointed out on the water and a light broke into his face, for there lying along the line of the submerged cable were no less than seven vessels! A few minutes' investigation and it was found that one of these vessels in getting under way had raised the line on its anchor. The sailors, unable to understand what it meant, had hauled in about two hundred feet of the line on deck, and finding no end, cut off what they had and carried it away with them. Thus ignominiously ended the first attempt at submarine telegraphing.

A crowd had assembled on the Battery, but when they found there was to be no exhibition they began to disperse with jeers, most of them believing that they had been the victims of a hoax; and Nathan, watching the strong patient lines of the fine face of the inventor, found angry, pitying tears crowding to his own eyes as he felt the disappointment for the man who seemed to him so great a hero. How he wished in his heart that he were a man, and a rich one, that he might furnish the wherewithal for a thorough public test immediately; but he turned away with his heart full of admiration for the man who was bearing so patiently this new disappointment in his great work for the world. Nathan believed in him and in his invention with all his heart. Had he not heard the little click, click of the instrument and seen with his own eyes the strange characters produced? Others might disbelieve and jeer, but he knew, for he had seen and heard.

There were other great men to meet and hear talk, men whom in after years Nathan was to know more about and feel pride at having met, and because David knew a great many Nathan came in the way of seeing them also. There was Ralph Waldo Emerson, who wrote for the *New York Tribune*. That was all Nathan knew about him at the time, and thought that was enough because being with a journalist, he thought journalism the very highest thing in literature. In after years he learned of course to know better and to be exceedingly proud of his brief meeting with so great a man in the world of letters. Then there were Honorable Millard Fillmore and a kindly faced man named Henry Clay, and William Lloyd Garrison, all especial friends of David's and honored accordingly by the boy, who worshipped them from afar.

He heard much talk of things in general: The Indian Treaty; a man named Dickens from England who had travelled in America awhile and written some bitter criticisms of American journalists (how Nathan hated him!); a wonderful flying machine that was in process of being invented by a man named McDermott, which was a giant kite 110 feet long, 20 feet broad, tapering like the wings of a bird, under the centre of which the owner stood, the frame being eighteen feet high, and operated four wings horizontally like the oars of a boat; wings made of a series of valves like Venetian blinds which opened when moving forward and closed when the stroke was made, each blade having twenty square feet of surface and being moved by the muscles of the legs. The wood was made of canes, the braces of wire, the kite and tail of cotton cloth, and the kite had an angle of ten degrees to the horizon. Nathan had it all carefully written down in his neat hand and he entertained secret hopes of making one for himself some day when he had the time. There was another one talked about, made by a man in New Orleans, a hollow machine like the body of a bird, and wings like a bird's with a man inside and light machinery to work the wings, but this seemed not so easy to carry out and Nathan inclined to the first one. Then there was great talk about postage, and the failure to have the rates cut down. Many thought it ought to be cut to five and ten cents with fifteen for long distances, and Nathan found much to think about.

But most of all he heard talk of politics, Whigs and Loco-Focos, and he began to take a deep interest in it all. When almost at the close of their stay David announced that he meant to take in the Whig Convention on the way home the heart of the boy rose to great heights. The Convention was to be held in Goshen, Orange County, 22 miles by steamboat and 44 miles by railroad, and the journey would take five hours. There were a hundred passengers in the party; notable men, and the experience meant much to the boy in after years.

CHAPTER 12

NATHAN came home from New York a new creature. He walked the old familiar streets, and met the neighbors he had known since ever he could remember, as in a dream. It was as if years had passed and given him a new point of view. Behold the former things had passed away and all things had become new. He knew that he was new. He knew that the aspirations and desires of his life had changed, and he bore himself accordingly.

The neighbors looked at him with a puzzled, troubled expression; paused and turned again to look as he passed, and then said reflectively:

"Well, I'll be gormed! Ain't that that young Whitney?"

At least that was what Squire Heath said, as he braced himself against his own gatepost and chewed a straw while Nathan walked erectly down the street away from him. It reminded one of those people long ago who asked:

"Is not this he that sat and begged?"

In former times nobody had been wont even to look at Nathan as he passed.

The boys, his companions in wicked pranks, fell upon him uproariously on his return, inclined to treat his vacation as a joke, and then fell back from him in puzzled bewilderment. He was as if not one of them. Already he gave them the impression that he looked down upon them, although he had no such notion in his mind, and was heartily glad to see them; but his mind was in a confusion and he hardly knew how to reconcile all the new emotions that strove for precedence in his breast. These foolish, loud-voiced children once a part and parcel of himself, did not somehow appeal to him in his new mood. In his heart of hearts he was loyal to them still, and glad to see them, but he wondered just a little why they seemed so trifling to him. It was not altogether the more grownup suit of clothes that David had encouraged him to buy in New York with his advance wages. This of course made him look older; but he had seen a great deal in his short stay and carried responsibilities not a few, besides having come in contact with the great questions and some of the great people of the day. He had had a vision of what it meant to be a man, and his ideals were reaching forth to higher things. He came and went among them gravely with a new and upright bearing and gradually they left him to himself. They planned escapades and he agreed readily enough to them, but when the time arrived he didn't turn up. He always had some good excuse. There was extra work; the office or he had a lesson with Mr. Spafford. At first they regarded these interruptions sympathetically and put off their plans. But they waited in vain, for when he did happen to come he did not take the old hold on things, his thoughts seemed far away at times, and they gradually regarded his disaffection with disgust and came finally to leave him out of their calculations altogether.

When this happened Nathan walked the world singularly alone, except for his friends the Spaffords. It was an inevitable circumstance of the new order of things, of course, but it puzzled and gloomed the boy's outlook on life. Yet he would not, could not, go back.

It is true that the attitude of the town toward him had slightly, even imperceptibly, changed. Instead of ignoring him altogether, or being actually combative toward him, they assumed a righteous tolerance of his existence which to the proud young nature was perhaps just as hard to bear. There was a certain sinister quality of grimness in their eyes, too, as they watched him, which he could not help but feel, for he was sensitive as a flower in spite of his courage and strength of character. They were actually disappointed, some of them, that he was seeming to turn out so differently from their prophecies. Had they really wanted him to be bad so they could gloat over him?

Nevertheless, there were great new joys opening up to the boy that fully outbalanced these other things. His work was an intense satisfaction to him. He took pleasure in doing everything just as well as it could be done, and often stayed beyond hours to finish up some bit of writing that could just as well have waited until next day, just to see the pleased surprise in David's eyes when he found out. Also he was actually getting interested in Latin. Not that he was a great student by nature. He had always acquired knowledge too easily to have made him work very hard for it until now and he had also always had too much mischief to give him time to study. But now he desired above all this to please his teacher and stand well in his eyes.

A man could not do as much for Nathan as David had done and not win everlasting gratitude and adoration from him. So Nathan studied.

David was a good teacher, enjoying his task, great progress was made; and the winter sped by on fleet wings.

Miranda, hovering in the background with opportune cookies and hot gingerbread when the evening tasks were over, enjoyed her part in the education and transformation of the boy. He was going to college and she was going to have at least a cookie's worth credit in the matter.

Miranda, as she cooked and swept and made comfort generally for all those with whom she had to do was turning over and over in her mind a plan, and biding her time. There was something she longed do, but did not yet see her way clear to it. The more she thought the more impossible it seemed, yet more determined she became to do it one day.

CHAPTER 13

In the midst of the bitterest cold weather poor little inadequate Mrs. Billings slipped out of life as inconspicuously as she had stayed in it, and Lawrence Billings came into the property, a forlorn little house all out of repair, one cow, several neglected chickens, and an income of sixty dollars per year from some property his father had left. Lawrence could not sew as his mother had done, to work at anything he could do he was ashamed, and he could not get anything he would do; obviously the only thing he could do for himself was to marry a girl with a tidy income and a thrifty hand. This Lawrence Billings set about doing with a will.

He was good looking in a washed-out sort of way, and could drape himself elegantly about a chair in a best parlor. The girls rather liked him around, he was handy. But when it came to marrying, that was another thing! He tried several hearty farmer's daughters in vain. They flouted him openly. But just after Christmas there came to town a young cousin of the postmistress, an orphan, who, rumor said, had a fine house and farm all in her own right. The farm was rented out and she was living on the income. She was pretty and liked to go about, so she accepted Lawrence Billings's attentions with avidity. They were seen together everywhere, and it began to be commonly spoken of as "quite a match after all for poor Lawrence! What a pity his poor mother couldn't have known!"

Miranda, alert and attentive, bristled like a fine red thistle. Lawrence Billings marry a pink-cheeked girl and live on her farm comfortably, when all the time Allan Whitney was, goodness knew where, exiled from home to keep Lawrence comfortable! Not if she could help it.

She came home from church in high dudgeon with a bright spot on either cheek and her eyes snapping. She had sat behind Lawrence Billings and the pink-cheeked Julia Thatcher and had seen their soft looks. Between their heads,—his sleek one and her bonneted one,—had seemed to look down the shadowy face of young Allan, fine and stern and exalted, his sacrifice upon him as he went forth into the whiteness of the storm those long, long years ago. Miranda felt that the time had come for action.

It was late winter, the winter of 1843. The heavy snows were yet on the ground and had no notion thawing. Miranda went up to her room, carefully laid aside her heavy pelisse, her muff and silk-corded bonnet, and changed her dress. Then she went quietly down to the kitchen to place the Sunday dinner, already cooked the day before, on the table. It was a delicious dinner, with one of the best mince pies that ever was eaten, for a climax, but Miranda forgot for once to watch for David's praise and Marcia's quiet satisfaction in the fruit of her labors. She was absorbed beyond any mere immediate interests to rouse her.

"Don't you feel well, Miranda?" questioned Marcia solicitously.

"Well'z ever!" she responded briefly and slammed off to the kitchen where she could have quiet. Never since the time of Phoebe Deane's trouble, when Miranda had put more than one finger in the pie before Phoebe was free from a tyrannical sister-in-law, an undesired lover, a weak brother, and happily married to the man of her choice, had Marcia seen Miranda so abstracted. There must be something the matter. But Miranda was much like a boy. If you wanted to find out what was the matter you would better keep still and not let on that you thought anything, and then perhaps you had a chance. Never, if you kindly inquired. So Marcia, wise in her day and generation, held her peace and made things as easy for her handmaiden as possible.

All that day, the next and the next Miranda gloomed, rushed and absented herself from the family as much as was consistent with her duties. Her lips were pursed till their merry red fairly disappeared. Even to Rose she was almost short. Nathan was the only one who brought a fleeting smile, and that was followed by a look of pain. Miranda was at all times intense, and during this time she was painfully more so.

The third day David came into the dining room with the evening papers, just as Miranda was putting on the supper. He was tired and cold and the firelight looked good to him, so instead of going to the library as usual until Miranda called him for supper, he settled down in his place at the table and began to read.

When his wife came into the room he looked up exultantly:

"Hurrah for Hon. John P. Kennedy! Listen to this, Marcia! 'The Hon. John P. Kennedy submitted a resolution that the bill appropriating thirty thousand dollars, to be expended under the direction of the Secretary of the Treasury, in a series of experiments to test the expediency of the Telegraph projected by Professor Morse, should be passed.' Isn't that great? Sit down, dear, and I'll read it to you while Miranda is putting on the supper."

Marcia settled herself in her little sewing chair and took up the ever-ready knitting that always lay to hand on the small stand between the dining-room windows; while Miranda, her ears alert, tiptoed about not to interrupt the reading nor lose a single word. It was thus that Miranda, through the years in this household, had acquired a really creditable education. David, realizing fully her eagerness to hear, raised his voice pleasantly that it might reach to the kitchen, and began to read:

"On motion of Mr. Kennedy, of Maryland, the committee took up the bill to authorize a series of experiments to be made, in order to test the merits of Morse's electro-magnetic telegraph. The bill appropriates thirty thousand dollars, to be expended under the direction of the Postmaster General.

"On motion of Mr. Kennedy, the words 'Postmaster General' were stricken out and 'Secretary of the Treasury' inserted.

"Mr. Cave Johnson wished to have a word to say upon the bill. As the present had done much to encourage science, he did not wish to see the science of mesmerism neglected and overlooked. He therefore proposed that one-half of the appropriation be given to Mr. Fisk, to enable him to carry on experiments, as well as Professor Morse.

"Mr. Houston thought that Millerism should also be included in the benefits of the appropriation—"

A snort from the kitchen door brought the reading to a sudden stop and David looked up to see Miranda, hands on her hips, arms akimbo, standing indignant in the doorway. When it came to a matter of understanding Miranda was "all there."

"Who be they?" she asked, her eyes snapping blue fire.

David loved to see her in this mood, and often wished some of the people who incited her to it could meet her at such a time. He beamed at her now and asked interestedly:

"Who are who, Miranda?"

"Why them two, Mr. Millerism, and the other feller. Who be they and what rights hev they got to butt in to thet there money thet was meant fer the telegraphy?"

Marcia suppressed a hasty smile and David looked down quickly at his paper.

"They're not men, Miranda, they're 'isms.' Millerism is a belief, and mesmerism is a power."

Miranda looked puzzled.

David tried to explain.

"Millerism is the belief that a religious sect called the Millerites hold. They are followers of a man named William Miller. They believe that the end of the world is near; that the day in fact is already set. They have a paper called *The Signs of the Times*. Do you know, Marcia, I read in the *New York Tribune* the other day that they have now set May 23rd of this coming year as the time of the second coming of Christ. They make it a point to be all ready dressed in white robes awaiting the end when it comes."

"Gumps!" interpolated Miranda with scorn. " 'Z if them things made any diffrunce! When it comes to a matter o' robes I'd prefer a heavenly one, and I calc'late on it's being furnished me free o' charge. What's the other ism? Messyism? Ain't it got no more sense to 't than Millerism?"

"Mesmerism? Well, yes, it has. There is perhaps some science back of it, though it is at present very little understood. A man named Franz Mesmer started the idea. He has a theory that one person can produce in another an abnormal condition resembling sleep, during which the mind of the person sleeping is subject to the will of the operator. Mesmer says it is due to animal magnetism. There have been a good many experiments made on this theory, but to my mind it is a dangerous thing, for evil-minded people could use it for great harm to others. It is also claimed that under this power the one who is mesmerized can talk with departed spirits."

"Humph!" commented Miranda. "More gumps! Say, what'r they thinking about to put sech fool men into the governm'nt t' Washin'ton? Can't they see the diffrunce atween things like thet and the telegraphy?"

Miranda, proud in her scientific knowledge, sailed back to her kitchen and took up the muffins for tea, but she had also food for thought and the rest of the evening was silent beyond her wont. It would have been interesting if she had but been in the habit of keeping a diary and setting down her quaint philosophies, but the greater number of them were buried in her own heart, and only the fortunate intimate friend was favored with them now and then.

About a week later Marcia came in from the monthly missionary meeting, which Miranda resolutely refused to attend, declaring that she had missionary work enough in her own kitchen without wasting time hearing a lot of fairy stories about people that lived in the geography and likely weren't much worse than most folks if the real truth were told.

"Miranda," said Marcia coming into the wide pleasant kitchen to untie her bonnet, "you're going to have opportunity to find out what mesmerism is. Your cousin Hannah is going to have a man to visit at her house who understands it and he is going to mesmerize some of the young people. It is Thursday evening and we are invited. Your cousin wanted me to ask you if you would be willing to help serve and clean up afterward. She is going to have coffee and doughnuts."

Miranda tossed her chin high and sniffed, albeit there was a glitter of interest in her eyes. She was not fond of her Cousin Hannah, blonde and proud and selfish, she that had been Hannah Heath, before she married Lemuel Skinner, and had been wont to look down upon her Cousin

Miranda. Ordinarily Miranda could have sent a curt refusal to such a request and Marcia knew it, but the mesmerist was too great a bait. Miranda desired intensely to hear more of mesmerism, so she only tossed her chin and sniffed; but with her lips she condescended.

"I s'pose I kin go ef she wants me so bad," she reluctantly consented.

There was a good deal of talk about the mesmerist the next few days. Hannah Skinner had hit the popular fancy when she secured the mesmerist to come to her tea party. Everybody had read about the wonderful things that were purported to be done by mesmerism, and those who were invited to the party could talk of little else. Miranda heard it every time she went to the post office or the store. She heard it when a neighbor ran in to borrow a cup of molasses for a belated gingerbread, and when she went to her grandmother Heath's on an errand for Marcia; and the more she heard the more thoughtful she became.

"Who's Hannah going to hev to her tea party, Grandma?" she had asked the old lady. Mrs. Heath paused in her knitting, looked over her spectacles and enumerated them:

"The Spaffords, the Waites, Aaron Petrie's folks, the Van Storms, Lawrence Billings, o' course, and Julia Thatcher'n her aunt, Abe Fonda, Lyman Brown, and Elkanah Wilworth's nieces up from New York—"

But Miranda had heard no more after Lawrence Billings, and her mind was off in a tumult of plans. She could hardly wait until David came home that evening to question him.

"Say, Mr. David, wisht you'd tell me more 'bout that mesmerism thing you was readin' 'bout. D'ye say they put 'em to sleep, an' they walked around an' didn't know what they was doin' an' did what the man told 'em to?"

"Well, about that, Miranda, I think you've got the idea."

"Say, d'yu reely b'leeve it, Mr. David? 'Cause I don't b'leeve nobody could make me do all them fool things 'thout I would let 'em."

"No, of course not without your consent, Miranda. I believe they make that point. You've got to surrender your will to theirs before they can do anything. If you resist they have no power. It's a good deal like a temptation. If you stand right up to it and say no, it has no chance with you, but if you let yourself play with it, why it soon gets control."

"But d'you reely b'leeve ther is such a thin' anyway? Could anybody make you do things you didn't think out fer yerself?"

"Why, yes, Miranda, it's this way. There is in us all a power called animal magnetism which if exercised has a very strong influence over other people. You know yourself how some people can persuade others to do almost anything. The power of the eye in looking does a great deal, the touch of the hand in persuasion does more sometimes. Some people too have stronger wills and minds than others, and there is no question but that there is something to it. I have myself seen exhibitions in a small way of the power of mesmerism,—the power of one mind over another. They make people go and find some article that has been hidden, just by laying the hand on the subject and thinking of the place where the article is hidden. Such experiments as that are easy and common now. But as for talking with those who have left this world, that's another thing."

"But some folks reely b'leeve that?"

"They say they do."

"Humph! Gumps!" declared Miranda turning back to the kitchen with a satisfied sniff. Thereafter she went about her work singing at the top of her lungs and not another word did she say about mesmerism or the Skinner tea party, although she walked softly and listened intently whenever anyone else spoke of it.

Miranda went to her Cousin Hannah's early in the afternoon and meekly helped to get things ready. It was not Miranda's way to be meek and Hannah was surprised and touched.

"You can come in and watch them when the professor gets to mesmerizing, M'randy," said Hannah indulgently, noticing with satisfaction the gleam of the green and brown plaid silk beneath Miranda's ample white apron, as she stooped to dust the legs of the whatnot in the corner, and then rose rustlingly to straighten a large knit antimacassar on the back of the mahogany rocking chair.

"I might look in, but I don't take much stock in such goin's on," conceded Miranda loftily. "Did you say you was going to pass cheese with the doughnuts and coffee? I might a brang some along ef I'd knowed. I made more'n we'd reely eat afore it gets stale to our house."

Miranda kept herself well in the background during the early part of the evening, though she made one of the company at the beginning and greeted everybody with a self-respecting manner. That much she demanded as recognition of her family and her good clothes. For the rest it suited her plans to keep out of sight, and she made an excuse to slip into the kitchen, where she found a vantage point behind a door that gave her a view of the whole room and a chance to hear what was being said without being particularly observed. Once, within her range and quite near, Lawrence Billings and Julia Thatcher sat for five full minutes, and Miranda's blood boiled angrily as she saw the evident progress the young man was making in his wooing. Studying the girl's pink cheeks and laughing blue eyes she decided that she was much too good for him, and above the weak-faced young man seemed to rise in vision the strong fine face of Allan Whitney, too noble even to scorn the weak man who had let him go all these years under a crime he had not committed.

Not even Hannah Heath knew when it was that Miranda slipped back into the room and became a part of the company. The fine aroma of coffee came at the same time, however, and whetted everybody's appetite. The professor had been carrying on his experiments for some time and several members of the company had resigned themselves laughingly into his hands and been made to totter around the room to find a hidden thimble, giggling foolishly under their ample blindfolding, and groping their way uncertainly; others swaying rhythmically and stalking ahead of their mentor straight to the secret hiding of the trinket. One, a stranger, a dark young man whom the professor had brought with him, had dropped into a somnambulistic state, from which trance he delivered himself of several messages to people in the room from their departed friends. The messages were all of a general nature of greeting, and somewhat characteristic of the departed, nothing to make any undesirable cloud on the spirits of the gay company. Everybody was laughing and chattering gaily between times, telling the professor how perfectly wonderful it all was, and how queer he or she felt under his mesmeric influence.

Miranda had watched it all from her covert, and observed keenly every detail of the affair, also the gullibility of the audience. At just the right moment she entered with her great platter of doughnuts and followed it by steaming cups of coffee.

Oh, Miranda! child of loneliness and loyalty! In what school did you learn your cunning?

Just how she contrived to get around the long-haired flabby professor perhaps nobody in the room could have explained, unless it might have been Marcia, who was watching her curiously and wondering what Miranda was up to now. Miranda always had some surprise to spring on people when she went around for days like that with bright red cheeks and her eyes flashing with suppressed excitement. Marcia had warned David to be on the lookout for something interesting. But David was sitting in the corner discussing politics, the various vices and virtues of the Whigs versus the Loco-Focos. He took his coffee and doughnuts entirely unaware of what was going on in the room.

Marcia was watching with delight the arts of Miranda as she laughed and chatted with the guest of the evening, travelling back and forth to the kitchen to bring him more cream and sugar, and the largest, fattest doughnuts. Suddenly Cornelia Van Storm leaned over and began to ask about the last missionary meeting, and Marcia was forced to give attention to the Sandwich Islands for a time.

"They do say that some of those heathens that didn't used to have a thing to wear are getting so fond of clothes that they come to church in real gaudy attire so that the pastors have had to reprove and admonish them," said Cornelia, with a zest in her words as if she were retailing a rare bit of gossip. "If that's so I don't think I'll give any more money to the missionary society. I'm sure I don't see the use of our sacrificing things here at home for them to flaunt the money around there, do you?"

"Why, our money wouldn't go for their dress anyway," said Marcia smiling. "I suppose the poor things dress in what they can get and like. But anyway if we sent money to the Sandwich Islands it would likely go to pay the missionary. You know the work there is perfectly wonderful. Nearly all the children over eight can read the New Testament and they have just dedicated their new church. The King of the Islands gave the land it is built on and most of the money to build it. It is 137 feet long and 72 feet wide and cost quite a good deal."

"Well, I must say if that's so they are quite able to look after themselves, and I for one don't approve of sending any more money there. I never did approve of foreign missions anyway, and this makes me feel more so. I say charity begins at home."

But just at that moment Marcia lifted her eyes and beheld what made her forget the heathen, home and foreign, and give her attention to the other end of the room; for there was Miranda, rosy and bridling like any of the younger girls, allowing the long-haired professor to tie the bandage around her eyes. There was a smile of satisfaction on her pleasant mouth, and a set of determination on her firm shoulders. Marcia was sure the stage was set and the curtain about to rise at last.

CHAPTER 14

"THIS young woman," proclaimed the professor's nasal voice rising above the chatter of the room, "has kindly consented to allow me to try a difficult experiment upon her. From my brief conversation with her just now I feel that she is a peculiarly adaptable subject, and I have long been searching for a suitable medium on which to try an experiment of my own."

David, in the middle of a convincing sentence about Henry Clay, suddenly ceased speaking and wheeled around with a sharp glance across the room, darted first suspiciously at the professor, and then with dismay at his subject. It seemed impossible to connect Miranda with anything as occult as mesmerism. David drew his brows together in a frown. Somehow he didn't quite like the idea of Miranda lending her strong common sense to what seemed to him a foolish business. Still, Miranda generally knew what she was about, and finding a thimble of course was harmless, if that were all.

"We will first give a simple experiment to see if all goes well," went on the professor, "and then, if the lady proves herself an apt subject I will proceed to make an experiment of a deeper nature. Will some one kindly hide the thimble? Mrs. Skinner, you have it, I believe. Yes, thank you, that will do very well."

It is doubtful if anyone in the room save David, whose eyes were upon Miranda, saw the deft quick motion with which she slid the bandage up from one eye and down again in a trice as if she were merely making it easier on her head; but during that instant Miranda's one blue eye took in a good deal, as David observed, and she must have seen the thimble being hidden away in Melissa Hartshorn's luxuriant waving hair which was mounted elaborately on the top of her head. A queer little smile hovered about David Spafford's lips. Miranda was up to her tricks again, and evidently had no belief whatever in the professor's ability. She meant to carry out her part as well as the rest had done and not be thought an impossible subject. She was perhaps intending to try an experiment herself on the professor.

"Now, you must yield your will to mine absolutely," explained the professor as he had done to the others.

"How do you make out to do that?" asked the subject, standing alert and capable, her hands on her hips, her chin assertive as usual.

Marcia caught a look of annoyance on Hannah Skinner's face. She had not expected Miranda to make herself so prominent, and she meant to give her a piece of her mind after it was over, Marcia could easily see that.

"Why, you just relax your mind and your will. Be pliable, as it were, in my hands. Make your mind a blank. Try not to think your own thoughts, but open your mind to obey my slightest thought. Be quiescent. Be pliable, my dear young lady."

Miranda dropped one arm limply at her side and then the other, and managed to make her whole tidy vivid figure slump gradually into an inertness that was fairly comical in one as self-sufficient as Miranda.

"I'm pliable!" she announced in anything but a limp tone.

"Very good, very good, my dear young lady," said the oily professor laying a large moist hand on her brow, and taking one of her hands in his other one. "Now, yield yourself fully!"

Miranda stood limply for a moment and then began to sway gently as she had seen the others do, and to step timidly forth toward Melissa Hartshorn.

The professor cast a triumphant look about the circle of eagerly attentive watchers.

"Very susceptible, very susceptible indeed!" he murmured. "Just as I supposed, unusually susceptible subject!"

David stood watching amusedly, an incredulous twinkle in his eyes. Miranda with studied hesitation was going directly toward the thimble, and when she reached Melissa she stopped as if she had run up against a wall, and groped uncertainly for her hair. In a moment more she had the thimble in her hand.

"You see!" said the professor exultantly. "It is just as I said, the young lady is peculiarly susceptible, and now we will proceed to a most interesting experiment. We will ask some one in the room to step forward and think of something, anything in the room will do, and the subject will tell what he is thinking about. It will be necessary of course to inform me what the object is. Will this gentleman kindly favor us? I will remove the bandage from the subject's eyes. It is unnecessary in this experiment."

Aaron Petrie, rotund and rosy from embarrassment, stepped forward, and Miranda, relieved of her bandage, stared unseeingly straight at him with the look of a sleep walker and did not move.

"You will perceive that the subject is still under powerful influence," murmured the professor, noticing Miranda's dreamy, vacant stare. "That is well. She will be far more susceptible."

He bent his head to ask Aaron Petrie what he had chosen to think about, and Aaron, still embarrassed, cast his eyes up and down and around and located them on a plate on which a fragment of doughnut remained. A relieved look came into his face and he whispered something back. The professor's eye travelled to the plate, he bowed cheerfully, and returned to place his right hand on Miranda's quiescent forehead, and take one of her hands in his, while he looked straight into her apparently unseeing eyes. After a moment of breathless silence, during which the company leaned forward and watched with intense interest, the professor said in a commanding tone: "Now tell the company what this gentleman is thinking about."

Miranda, her eyes still fixed on space, slowly opened her mouth and spoke, but her voice was drawling and slow with an unnatural monotony:

"He—is—wishin'—he—hed—'nuther—doughnut!" she chanted.

The little assembly broke into astonished, half-awed laughter. The receptivity of Aaron Petrie toward all edibles was a matter of common joke. Even in the face of weird scientific experiments one had to laugh about Aaron Petrie's taste for doughnuts.

"Doughnuts! Doughnuts! Very good," said the professor, nervously rubbing his hands together. "The gentleman was thinking of the bit of doughnut on yonder plate, and the subject being so susceptible has doubtless reached a finer shade of thought than the young gentleman realized when he made his general statement to me."

The laugh subsided and trailed off into an exclamation of wonder as the cunning professor made Miranda's original answer a further demonstration of the mysteries of science.

"Now, will this young gentleman give us something?" The professor was still a trifle nervous. Miranda's fixed attitude puzzled him. She was not altogether like his other subjects, and he had an uneasy feeling that she might fail him at some critical point. Nevertheless, he was bound to keep on.

Abe Fonda came boldly forward with a swagger, his eyes fixed on the younger of Elkanah Wilworth's two pretty nieces. Miranda's faraway look did not change. She was having the time of her life, but the best was yet to come.

Abe whispered eagerly in the professor's ear and his eyes sought the pretty girl's again with a smile.

The professor bowed and turned to his subject as before, and Miranda, without waiting for a request, chanted out again:

"Abe's a-thinking—how—purty—Ruth-Ann—Wilworth's curl—in—the back—o'—her—neck—is."

A shout of laughter greeted this, and Abe turned red, while the professor grew still more uneasy. He saw that he was growing in favor with his audience, but the subject was most uncertain, and not at all like other subjects with whom he had experimented. He had a growing suspicion that she was doing some of the work on her own hook and not putting herself absolutely under his influence. It would be as well if he were to go further with her, that he confine his investigations to safe subjects. The dead were safer than the living.

"Well, yes, the young gentleman did mention the younger Miss Wilworth," he said apologetically. "I hope no offense is taken at the exceedingly—that is to say—direct way the subject has of stating the case."

"Oh, no offense whatever," said the sheepish Abe. "It was all quite true I assure you, Miss Wilworth," and he made a low bow toward the blushing, simpering girl.

Now the professor had one stunt which he loved to pull off in any company where he dared. He would call up the spirit of George Washington and question him concerning the coming election, which not only thrilled the audience but often had great weight with them in changing or strengthening their opinions. He knew that the ordinary subject would easily respond yes or no. according to his will, and this remarkable young woman, no matter how original her replies, could scarcely make much trouble in politics, and would not be likely to interpolate her own personality with such a subject of conversation. He decided to try it at once, and all the more because the young woman herself had expressed a desire to see an exhibition of his power to communicate with the other world.

"This young woman," began the professor in his most suave tones, "has proved herself so apt a subject that I am going to try something that I seldom dare attempt in public without first having experimented for days with the subject. It may work and it may not, I can scarcely be sure without knowing her better; but as she herself has expressed a desire to yield herself for the experiment I will endeavor to call up some one from the other world—"

David at this sat up suddenly, his eyes searching the blank ones of Miranda. It troubled him to have a member of his household put herself even for a short time under this slippery looking man's influence, and this tampering with the mysterious he did not like. There was no telling what effect it might have upon Miranda, though he had always heretofore thought her the most practical and sensible person he knew. He could not quite understand her willingness to submit to this nonsense. Ought he to interfere? He was to blame himself for having talked to her so much about the subject. He cleared his throat and almost spoke, his eyes still upon the blank expression of the girl opposite, supposed to be in a sort of trance. Suddenly, as he watched her, one eye gave a slow, solemn wink at him. The action was so comical and so wholly Miranda-like that he almost laughed aloud, and settled back in his seat to enjoy what was to be forthcoming. Miranda was not in a trance then, but was fully and wholly herself and enjoying the hoax she was playing alike on the audience and the professor. Miranda was a witch, there was no mistaking it, and an artist of her kind. David wished he were sitting next to Marcia that he might relieve her mind, for he saw she looked troubled. He tried to signal to her by a smile and was surprised to receive an answering reassurance as if Marcia too had discovered something.

The professor now stood forth making some slow rhythmical motions with his hands on the girl's forehead and in front of her face. He was just about to speak his directions to her when she rose slowly as though impelled by some unseen force, and stood staring straight ahead of her at the open kitchen door, her eyes strained and wild, her face impressive with a weird solemnity.

"I—see—a—dead—man!" she exclaimed sepulchrally, and the professor rubbed his hands and wafted a few more thought-waves toward this remarkably apt subject.

Had Miranda arranged it with the draft of the kitchen window that just at this stage of the game the kitchen door should come slowly, noisily shut? A distinct shudder went around the company, but the girl continued to gaze raptly toward the door.

"Ask him what are his politics, please," commanded the professor, endeavoring to cast a little cheer upon the occasion.

"He—says—he—was—shot—down—by—Taylor's—woods."

An audible murmur of horror went around the room and everybody sat up and took double notice.

"Twelve—years—ago—" went on the monotonous voice in a high strident key.

"Enoch Taylor, I'll be gormed!" ejaculated old Mr. Heath, resting his horny hands on his knees and leaning forward with bulging eyes.

David could not help but notice that Lawrence Billings, who was sitting opposite to him, started nervously and looked furtively around the company.

"He— says— to— tell— you— his— murderer— is— in— this— room"— chanted Miranda as though she had no personal interest in the matter whatever.

In this room! The thought flashed like lightning from face to face—
"Who is it?" David found his eyes riveted on the pale face of the young
man opposite who seemed unable to take his eyes from Miranda's but sat
white and horrified with a fascinated stare like a bird under the gaze of a
cat.

"He— must— confess— tonight— before— the— clock— strikes—
the— hour— of— midnight"— went on the voice— "or— a— curse—
will— come on— him— and— he— will— die!"

There was a tense stillness in the room that filled everybody with horror,
as if the dead man had suddenly stepped into sight and charged them all
with his murder. They looked from one to another with sudden suspicion
in their eyes. The oily professor stood aghast at the work he had wrought
unaware.

"Oh, now, see here," he began with an attempt to break the tensity of the
moment, "don't let this thing break up the good cheer. We'll just bring this
lady back to herself again and dismiss the deceased for tonight. He
doubtless died with some such thing on his mind, or else he was insane
and keeps the same notions he had when he left this mortal frame. Now
don't let this worry you in the least. There isn't anybody in this room could
commit a murder if he tried, of course; why, you're all ladies and
gentlemen."

All the time the oily anxious man was making wild passes in front of
Miranda's face and trying to press her forehead with his hands, and wake
her up, but Miranda just marched slowly, solemnly, staringly ahead toward
the kitchen door, and everybody in the room but the professor watched
her, fascinated.

She turned when she reached the kitchen door, faced the room once
more, and staring back upon them all uttered once more her curse.

"Enoch— Taylor— say— ef— you— don't— confess— tonight—
before— midnight— you'll— die— and— he ain't goin'— to— leave—
you— till— you— confess."

She jabbed her finger straight forward blindly and it went through the
roached hair on Lawrence Billings's shrinking head and pointed straight at
nothing, but Lawrence Billings jumped and shrieked. In the confusion
Miranda dropped apparently senseless in the kitchen doorway; but just
before she dropped she gave David another slow, solemn wink with one
eye.

CHAPTER 15

ALL was confusion at once, and one of the young men rushed out for Caleb Budlong, the doctor, who lived not far away. When things settled down to quiet again and Miranda had been lifted to the kitchen couch and restored with cold water and other stimulants, David had time to discover the absence of Lawrence Billings, though nobody else seemed to notice.

They all tiptoed away from the kitchen at Dr. Budlong's suggestion, and left Miranda to lie quiet and recover. He said he didn't believe in these new fangled things, they were bad for the system, and got people's nerves all stirred up, especially women. He wouldn't allow a woman to be put under mesmeric influence if he had anything to say about it. All women were hysterical, and that was doubtless the matter with Miranda.

The company looked at one another astonished. Who had ever suspected Miranda of having nerves, and going into hysterics? and yet she had proclaimed a murderer in their midst!

They turned to one another and began to converse in low mysterious tones while Miranda lay on the couch in the kitchen with closed eyelids and inward mirth. Presently, as Dr. Budlong counted her pulse and gave her another spoonful of stimulant, she drew a long sigh and turned her face to the wall; he, thinking she was dropping to sleep, tiptoed into the sitting room and closed the kitchen door gently behind him.

Miranda was on the alert at once, turning her head quickly to measure the width of the crack of the door. She held herself quiet for a full minute, and then slipped softly from her couch across the kitchen with the step of a sylph, snatched a mussed tablecloth from the shelf in the pantry where she had put it when she helped Hannah clear off the dinner table, and wrapping it quickly around her and over her head she went out of the back door.

Every movement was light and quick. She paused a second on the back stoop to get her bearings, then sped with swift light steps toward the barn door, which was open. A young moon was riding high in the heavens making weird battle with the clouds, and the light of a lantern shone from the open barn door. Miranda could see the long shadow of a man hitching up a horse with quick, nervous fingers. Lawrence Billings was preparing to take Julia Thatcher home.

Miranda approached the barn, and suddenly emerged into the light in full view of the startled horse just as Lawrence Billings stepped behind him to fasten the traces. The horse, having been roused from a peaceful slumber and not being yet fully awake, beheld the apparition with a snort, and without regard to the man or the unfastened traces reared on his hind legs and attempted to climb backwards into the carryall. There they stood, side by side, the man and the horse, open mouthed, wide nostriled, with protruding eyes; the smoky lantern by the barn door shedding a flickering light over the whole and casting grotesque shadows on the dusty floor.

Miranda, fully realizing her advantage, stood in the half-light of the moon in her fantastic drapery and waved her tableclothed arms, one forefinger wrapped tightly in the linen pointing straight at the frightened man, while she intoned in hollow sounds the words:

"Confess—tonight—or—you—will—die!"

Lawrence Billings's yellow hair rose straight on end and cold creeps went down his back. He snorted like the horse in his fright.

The white apparition moved slowly nearer, nearer to the patch of light in the barn door, and its voice wailed and rose like the wind in November, but the words it spoke were clear and distinct.

"Confess—at—once—or—misfortune—will—overtake—you! Moon—smite—you!—Dogs—bite—you!—Enoch Taylor's speerit—hant you! Yer mother's ghost pass before—you—!"

The white arms waved dismally, and the apparition took another step toward him. Then with a yell that might have been heard all the country round, Lawrence Billings made a wild dash past her to the back door.

"Food   pizen   you!—Sleep—fright—you!—Earth   swaller—you!" screamed the merciless apparition flying after him, and the horse, having reached the limit of his self-control, clattered out into the open and cavorted around the garden until his nerves were somewhat relieved.

Lawrence Billings burst in upon the assembled company in the best parlor with wild eyes and dishevelled hair, and was suddenly confronted with the fact that these people did not believe in ghosts and apparitions. In the warm, bright room with plenty of companions about, he felt the foolishness of telling what he had just seen. His nerve deserted him. He could not face them all and suggest that he had seen a ghost, and so he blurted out an incoherent sentence about his horse. It was frightened at something white in the yard and had run away.

Instantly all hands hurried out to help catch the horse, Lawrence Billings taking care to keep close to the others, and joking fearsomely about the shadowy yard as he stepped forth again from shelter.

Miranda, meantime, had slipped into the kitchen and taken to her couch most decorously, the tablecloth folded neatly close at hand in case she needed it again, and was apparently resting quietly when Hannah tip toed in to see if she needed anything.

"I guess I shan't trouble you much longer," murmured Miranda sleepily. "I don't feel near so bad now. Shouldn't wonder ef I could make out to git back home in a half hour er so. What's all the racket about, Hannah?"

"Lawrence Billings's horse got loose," said Hannah. "He's a fool anyway. He says it saw something white on the clothes line. There isn't a thing out there, you know yourself Mirandy. He's asked Dr. Budlong, to take Julia Thatcher and her aunt home in his carryall. He says his horse won't be safe to drive after all this. It's perfect nonsense; Julia could have walked with him. Mother wanted to ride with Dr. Budlong, and now she'll have to stay all night and I just got the spare bed sheets done up clean and put away. I don't see what you had to go and get into things for tonight, anyhow, Mirandy. You might have known it wasn't a thing for you to meddle with. All this fuss just because you got people worked up about that murder. Why didn't you keep your mouth shut about it? It couldn't do any good now anyway. Say, Mirandy, did you really see any one or hear them say all that stuff?"

"What stuff, Hannah? " said Miranda sleepily. "I disremember what's ben happenin'. My head feels queer. Do you s'pose 'twould hurt me to go home to my own bed?"

"No," said Hannah crossly, "it's the best place you could be. I wish I hadn't asked you to come. I might have known you'd cut up some shine,— you always did,—but I thought you were grown up enough to act like other folks out to a tea party," and with this kind and cousinly remark she slammed into her sitting room again to make what she could of her excited guests.

Miranda, meanwhile, lay still and listened, and when she made out from the sounds that Julia Thatcher and her aunt had driven off in Dr. Budlong's carryall with his family, and that all the ladies who had not already departed were in the spare room putting on their wraps and bonnets, she stole forth softly, the tablecloth hidden under her cloak,—for she had taken the precaution early in the evening to hang her own wraps behind the kitchen door,—and took her way down the street, hovering in the shadows until she saw that Lawrence Billings was coming on behind her.

He was quite near to David and Marcia when he passed where she hid behind a lilac bush on the edge of Judge Waitstill's yard.

"Moon smite yeh,—stars blight yeh," murmured Miranda under her breath, but almost in his ear, and flicked the tablecloth a time or two in the moonlight as he looked back fearfully.

Lawrence hastened his steps until he was close behind another group of homeward-bound guests. Miranda slipped from bush to bush, keeping in the shadows of the trees, until she made sure that he was about to turn off down the road to his own isolated house. Then she slid under a fence and sped across a cornfield. The night was damp and a fine mist like smoke arose from the ground in wreaths of fog and hid her as she ran, but when the young man opened his gate he saw in the changing lights and shadows of the cloud- and moon-lit night a white figure with waving arms standing on his doorstep and moving slowly, steadily down to meet him.

With a gasp of terror he turned and fled back to the main street of the village, the ghost following a short distance behind, with light, uncanny tread and waving arms like wreaths of mist. It was too much for poor Lawrence Billings. Just in front of David Spafford's house he stumbled and fell flat—and here was the ghost all but upon him! With a cry of despair he scrambled to his feet and took refuge on the Spafford stoop, clacking the door knocker loudly in his fright. This was better than Miranda could have hoped. She held her ghostly part by the gate post till David opened the door, then slipped around to a loose pantry shutter and soon made good her entrance into the house. Stepping lightly she took her station near to a crack of a door where she could hear all that went on between David and his late caller. She heard with exultation the reluctant confession, the abject humility of voice, and cringing plea for mercy. Whatever happened now somebody besides herself knew that Allan Whitney was not a murderer. Her heart swelled with triumph as she listened to the frightened voice telling how a shot had struck the old man instead of the rabbit it was intended for, and how he had run to him and done everything he knew how to resuscitate his victim but without avail. In terrible fright he had started for the road, and there met Allan Whitney, who had come back with him and worked over the old man a while, and then told him to go home and say nothing about it, that he would take the gun and if anybody made a fuss he would take the blame; that it didn't matter about him anyway, nobody cared what became of him, but Lawrence had his mother to look out for. The man declared that he hadn't wanted to do it, putting Allan in a position like that, but when he thought of his mother, of course he had to; and anyhow he had hoped Allan would get away all right, and he did. It hadn't seemed so bad for Allan. He was likely as well off somewhere else as here, and he, Lawrence, had his mother to look after.

There was no spectre in this room, and Lawrence Billings was getting back his self-confidence. All the excuses with which he had bolstered himself during the years came flocking back to comfort him as he tried to justify himself before this clear-eyed man for his cowardly hiding behind another.

Something of the contempt that Miranda felt for the weak fellow was manifest in David Spafford's tone as he asked question after question and brought out little by little the whole story of the night of the murder and Lawrence's cowardly part in it. Somehow as David talked his sin was made more manifest, and his excuses dropped away from him. He saw his own contemptible self, his lack of manliness, his wickedness in allowing another fellow being, no matter how willing, to walk all these years under the name of murderer to shield him. He lifted a blanched face and fearful eyes to his judge when David at last arose and said:

"Well, now the first thing to do is to go straight to Mr. Whitney. He ought not to be allowed to think another hour that his son has committed a crime. Then we will go to Mr. Heath—"

Lawrence Billings uttered something between a whine and a groan. His face grew whiter and his eyes seemed to fairly stand out.

"What'll we have to go to them for?" he demanded angrily. "Ain't I confessed? Ain't that enough? They can't hang me after all these years, can they? I ain't going to anybody else. I'll leave town if you say so, but I ain't going to do any more confessing."

"No, you will not leave town," said David quietly, laying a strong hand on the trembling shoulder, "and you most certainly will go and confess to those two men. It is the only possible way to make what amends you can for the past. You have put this matter in my hands by coming to me with it, and I cannot let you go until it is handed over to the proper authorities."

"I came to you because I thought you'd be just and merciful," whined the wretch.

"And so I will as far as in me lies. Justice demands that you confess this matter fully and that the whole thing be investigated. Come—!"

CHAPTER 16

MIRANDA watched through a rain of thankful tears as David escorted his guest out of the front door, and then she flew into the parlor and watched as they went arm in arm up the street and knocked at her grandfather's door. She waited with bated breath until a candle-light appeared at her grandfather's bedroom window, and slowly descended the stairs; waited again while the two went in, and another light appeared above, showing that a hasty toilet was being made; stood cold and patient by the window during an interminable time, imagining the conference that must be going on in the Heath kitchen; and finally was rewarded by seeing three men come out of the Heath door and walk slowly down the street to the big house across the way. She noted that Lawrence Billings walked between the other two. She could tell him by his slight build, and cringing attitude as he walked, and once they stopped and seemed to parley, both the other men putting strong hands upon his shoulders.

There was another delay, and she could hear the Whitney knocker sounding hollowly down the silent street. Then a head was thrust out of the upper window and a voice called loudly: "Who's there!" Miranda had opened the parlor window just a crack, and her heart beat wildly as she knelt and laid her ear beside the crack. In a few minutes a light appeared in the fan-shaped window over the front door and then the door itself was opened and the visitors let in.

Miranda waited then only to see the light appear in the front windows and the shadows of the four men against the curtain. Then she dropped on her knees by the window and let her tears have their way. "Thanks be!" she murmured softly again and again. "Thanks be!"

Whatever came now, Allan was cleared. At least three men in the town knew, and they would do the right thing. She was almost dubious about their having told Mr. Whitney. She thought he deserved to feel all the trouble that could come to him through his children for the way he had treated them; but after all it was good to have Allan cleared in the eyes of his father, too.

The conference in the Whitney house was long and Miranda did not wait until it was over. She climbed the stairs softly to her room, answered

102

Marcia's gentle, "Is that you, Miranda?" with a gruff, "Yes, I ben down in the kitchen quite a spell," and closing her door went straight to the starlit window and gazed out. There was only a star or two on duty that night, fitfully visible between the clouds, but Miranda looked up to them wistfully. Somewhere under them, if he were still on the earth, was Allan. Oh, if the stars could but give him the message that his name was cleared! Perhaps, somehow, the news would reach him. and some day he might return. Her heart leaped high with the thought.

Oh, Allan, in the wide far world! Have you ere a thought for the little girl whose heart beat true to yours, grown a woman now, and suffering for your sorrows yet? The years have been long and she has waited well; and has accomplished for you at last the thing she set her heart upon. Will the stars take the message, and will you ever come back?

She crept to her bed too excited to sleep, and lay there listening for sounds across the street. The solemn silent night paced on, and still that candle beam shone straight across the road. But at last there were voices, and the opening of a door; grave voices full of weighty matters and an awed goodnight. She went to her window to watch again. David came straight across to his own door, but Lawrence Billings went arm in arm with her grandfather to his home. Not to the smokehouse, cold and damp, where Allan had been put, but into the comfortable quiet house, with at least the carpet-covered sofa to lie upon, and the banked-up fire, and the cat for company. Grandfather Heath would never put Lawrence Billings into the smokehouse, he was too respectable. Miranda, with a lingering thought of Allan and his protection of the weakling, was almost glad that it was so. There was after all something pitifully ridiculous in the thought of Lawrence Billings huddled in the dark of the smokehouse with his fear of ghosts and spectres haunting him on every side. The fine strong Allan in all his youthful courage could not be daunted by it, but Lawrence Billings would crumple all up with the terror of it. Then Miranda went back to her bed, pulled the covers up over her head and laughed till she cried at the remembrance of Lawrence Billings frightened by a tablecloth.

The days that followed were grave and startling. After the revelation on the following morning there came a stream of visitors to the Spafford house to see Miranda. On one pretext or another they asked for her; to the back door for a cup of molasses, or to the front door to know if she would run over and stay with an ailing member of the family that evening while the others went out; anything so they could see Miranda. And always before the interview was ended they managed to bring in the mesmerizing at Hannah Skinner's.

"Say, Mirandy, did you reely see a speret? An' how did you know what to say? Did they tell you words to speak?" one would ask. And Miranda would reply:

"Well, now, Sa'r' Ann! I don' know's I ken' rightly say. You see I disremember seein' any sperets 'tall, 'r hearin' any; an' as fer what I said, I can't 'count fer it. They tell me I talked a lot o' fool nonsense, but it seems t'v all passed from my mind. It's queer how that mesmerizin' works ennyhow. I didn't b'leeve much in it when I went into it, an' I can't say 'z I think much of it now. I 'member seein' a white mist rise off'n the ground when I come home, but I don't much b'leeve sperets walks the' airth, d' you? It don't seem commonsensy, now do y' think? No, I can't rightly say 'z I remember hearin' 'r seein' anythin'. I guess ef I did it all passed off when my head stopped feelin' queer. Funny 'bout Lawrence Billings takin' it to heart that-a-way, wa'n't it? You wouldn't never uv picked him out t' commit a crime, now would you? My Mr. David says it's a c'wince'dence. Quite a c'wince'dence! them's the words he used t' the breakfast table, talkin' to Mrs. Marcia. He says: 'Thet was quite a c'wince'dence, M'randy, but don't you go to meddlin' with that there mesmerism again, f'y was you,' sez he. An' I guess he's 'bout right. Did you hear they was goin' to start up the singin' school again next week?"

And that's about all the information anybody got out of Miranda.

The next few days were marked by the sudden and hasty departure of Julia Thatcher for her home, and the resurrecting of past events in preparation for the trial of Lawrence Billings, which was set for the next week, the interval being given for Enoch Taylor's grandson and only heir to arrive from his distant home.

During this interval Miranda was twice moved to make dainty dishes and take them to Lawrence Billings, who was still in solitary confinement in her grandfather's house. Her grandmother received the dishes grudgingly, told her she was a fool, and slammed the door, but Miranda somehow felt as if she had made it even with her conscience for having put the poor creature into his present position. She knew Allan would like her to show him some little attention, and while she strongly suspected that the dainty dishes never reached the prisoner's tray, still it did her good to make them and take them. Miranda was always a queer mixture of vindictiveness and kindness. She had driven Lawrence Billings to his doom for the sake of Allan and now she felt sorry for him.

It was weeks afterward that Miranda managed to return Hannah Skinner's tablecloth, for Hannah was bitter against her cousin by reason of the notoriety that had been brought upon her. She had made that evening gathering with a mesmerist as entertainer for the sake of popularity, but to be mixed up in a murder case was much too popular even for Hannah.

The way Miranda managed the tablecloth was a simple one after all. She went to see Hannah when she knew Hannah was over at her mother's house. Slipping unobtrusively out of the Spafford house from the door on the side away from the Heath's she made a detour, going to the next neighbor's first and from there on a block or two, and finally returning to Hannah's house by a long way around another street. She was well acquainted with the hiding place of Hannah's key and had no trouble in getting in. She had laid awake nights planning a place to put that tablecloth where it would seem perfectly natural to Hannah for it to have slipped out of sight, and had hit upon the very place, down behind a high chest of drawers that Hannah kept in her dining room. It took but an instant to slide the tablecloth neatly down behind it, and Miranda was out of the house with the door locked behind her and the key in its place under the mat in a trice. There was no neighbor near enough to have noticed her entrance. The next week, just as Miranda had planned she would do pretty soon, Hannah came across the aisle to the Spafford pew and whispered:

"M'randy, whatever could you have done with my second best tablecloth the night of my party?"

And Miranda glibly responded:

"I put it on the top o' the chest in the dinin' room, Hannah; better look behind it. It might a'fell down, there was so much goin' on thet night."

"It couldn't," said Hannah, "I always move that out when I sweep." But she looked, and to her astonishment found her tablecloth.

"It seems as if there must be some magic about this house," she remarked to Lemuel that night at supper.

"Better not to meddle with such things, my dear," said Lemuel, with his little mouth pursed up like a cherry. "You know I didn't want that man to come here, but you would have him."

"Nonsense!" said Hannah sharply. "It was all Mirandy's doings. If I hadn't invited her there wouldn't have been a bit of this fuss. I thought she would know enough to keep in the kitchen and mind the coffee. I never expected her to want to be mesmerized. Such a fool! I believe she was smitten with the man!"

"Mebbe so! Mebbe so!" chirped Lemuel affably, taking a big bite of Hannah's hot biscuit and honey, and thinking of the days when he was smitten with Hannah.

When this surmise of Hannah's reached Miranda, by way of her grandmother, Miranda chuckled.

"Wal, now, I hadn't thought o' that, gran'ma, but p'raps that was what's the matter. He didn't look to me like much of a man to be smit with; but then when one's gitten' on to be a ole maid like me it ain't seemly to be too pertic'ler. Howsomenever, ef I was smit it didn't go more'n skin deep, so you needn't to worry. I ain't lookin' to disgrace this fam'bly with no greasy-lookin', long-haired jackanapes of a mesmer-man yit awhiles, not s' long 's I kin earn my keep. Want I should stir thet fire up fer yeh 'fore I go back home?"

And Miranda went singing on her way back home chuckling to herself as she went.

"Smit with him! Now ain't that real r'dic'lous? Smit with a thing like thet!"

Then her face went grave and sweet and she paused at the door stone ere she entered and stretched her hands longingly toward the thread of a young moon that was rising back of the barn.

"Oh, Allan!" she murmured softly, and "Oh Allan!" again; and the soul of the little girl that Allan had kissed stood tenderly in her eyes for an instant.

Then she was herself again and went cheerfully in to get supper for the people she loved; and nobody ever dreamed, as they looked at the strong wholesome girl going springily, joyously about her kitchen, of the exquisite youth and depth of feeling hidden away in the depths of her great loving heart. Only Marcia sometimes caught in wonder a passing reminder in Miranda's eyes of the light that glowed in the eyes of little Rose.

CHAPTER 17

THE night was wide and white and starry. The purple blue dome of the sky fitted close to the still, deep white of the earth, that glittered sharply here and there as a star beam stabbed it; or was splashed and punctured with shadowy footprints of some stealthy, furry creature wending secret way to its lair. The trees stood stark and black against the whiteness, like lonely, solemn sentinels that even in the starlight were picked out in detail against the night. On such a night it seemed the wise men must have started on their star-led way, so lonely, so longing, so crying out to be satisfied, seemed the earth.

A single trapper clad in furs walked silently like one of the creatures he trapped. He had been out all day and over his shoulder were slung several fine pelts. He had done well, and the furs he was carrying now would bring a fancy price. He had but two more traps to visit, then his day's work would be done and he could go home. He trod the aisles of the night as surely as one might walk in a familiar park of magnificent distance and note no object because all were so accustomed.

He did not whistle as he walked. He had formed the stealthy habit of the creatures of the wild, and his going was like a part of the night, a far cloud passing would have made as much stir. There was almost a majesty and rhythm in his movements.

A mile or two further on he knelt beside a deadfall trap and found a fine lynx as his reward. As easily and deftly as a lady might have stooped in her garden and plucked a rose he drew forth his knife and took the beautiful skin to add to those he already carried; made his trap ready for another victim, and passed on to the last trap.

Several times on the way he paused, alertly, listening; and then stalked on again. There were sounds enough to the uninitiated,—coyotes howling, wolves baying, the call of the wild being answered from all directions,— enough to make a stranger pause and tremble every step of the way. But it was a sound far more delicate that came to the trained ear of the trapper, and a perception of a sort of sixth sense that made him pause and gaze keenly now and again; a faint distant metallic ring, the crackle of a broken twig, the fall of a branch—they all might have been accounted for in natural ways, yet they were worth marking for what they might mean.

There was nothing in the last trap and it had the appearance of having been tampered with. The trapper was still kneeling beside it, when there came a sound like the tone of a distant organ playing an old church hymn, just a note or two. It might have been the sighing of the wind in the tall trees if there had been wind that night. The man on the ground rose suddenly to his feet and lifted his eyes to the purple-dark of the distance. Faint and far the echo repeated itself —or was it imagination?

The trapper knelt again and quickly adjusted the trap, then swung his pelts to his shoulder once more and strode forward with purpose in his whole bearing. Thrice he paused and listened, but could not be sure he still heard the sound. Just ahead was his cabin of logs. He stopped at the door again, intently listening. Then suddenly the music came again, this time sweet and clear, but far off still, and only in echoing fragments—a bit of an old tune—or was it fancy?—that used to be sung in the church at home in the East. There was only a haunting memory of familiar days in the broken strains—foolishness perhaps—a weakness that seemed to be growing on him in this loneliness.

A moment more he lingered by the door to make sure some one was riding down the trail, then he went in, swung his burden in the corner, made haste to strike a light and make a fire. If the voice he thought he had heard singing was really someone coming down the trail, he might have company to supper that night.

The strong face of the trapper was lighted with new interest as he went about his simple preparations for a guest. Double portions of venison and corn bread were put to cook before the fire, and an extra candle lighted and put in the window toward the mountain trail. When all was ready he went to the door once more and listened and now the voice came full and strong:

"Yes, my native land, I love thee."

High up and far away still, and only now and then a line or phrase distinct, but growing nearer all the time.

The trapper, standing big and strong in his cabin door that barely let his height through without stooping, listened, and his eyes glowed warmly in the starlight. There was something good in the sound of the song. It warmed his heart where it had not been warmed for many a day. He listened an instant, calculated well the distance of his approaching guest, then drew the door to and swung himself away a few paces in the dark. When he returned his arms were filled with fragrant piney boughs which he tossed down in an unoccupied corner of his cabin, not far from the fire, and spread over with a great furry skin. After placing the coffee pot in the fire he went back to the door.

There were distinct and connected words to the song now, and a familiar tune that used to be sung in the old church at home when the trapper was a little boy. He had learned the words at his mother's knee:

> "The spacious firmament on high,
>   With all the blue ethereal sky,
>   The spangled heavens, a shining frame,
>   Their great Original proclaim."

The oncomer was riding down the trail, now close at hand. The ring of his horse's footsteps on the crisp snow could be heard, and the singing suddenly stopped. He had seen the light in the window. In a moment more he came into the clearing, greetings were exchanged, and he dismounted.

The newcomer was a man of more than medium height, but he had to look up at the trapper, who towered above him in the starlight.

"I am fortunate to find you at home," he said pleasantly, "I have passed this way several times before but always there was no one here."

He was dressed in buckskin trousers, a waistcoat, and a blue English duffle coat, a material firm, closely woven and thicker than a Mackinaw blanket. Over this was a buffalo overcoat a few inches shorter than the duffle, making a fantastic dress withal. From under his fur cap keen blue eyes looked forth and one could see at a glance from his wide, firm mouth, that he was a man of strong purpose, great powers of fearless execution, reticent, and absolutely self-contained. For a moment the two stood looking quietly, steadily into each other's eyes, gathering, as it were, confidence in one another. What each saw must have been satisfactory, for their handclasp was filled with warm welcome and a degree of liking.

"I am the fortunate one," said the trapper.

"My name's Whitman, Marcus Whitman, missionary from Waiilatpu," went on the newcomer in explanation. "May I camp with you tonight? I've come a long way since daybreak and a sound sleep would be pleasant."

"You're welcome," said the host. "Supper's all ready. I heard you coming down the trail. So you are Dr. Whitman? I've heard of you of course. I'm just a trapper." He waved his hand significantly toward the heap of furs in the corner and the fine pelts hanging about the walls—"My name's Whitney. Take off your coat."

He led the stranger inside and offered him water for washing.

"Whitney is it,—and Whitman,—not much difference is there? Easy to remember. Supper sounds good. That coffee smells like nectar. So you heard singing, did you? I'm not much of a singer I own, but my wife took a lot of pleasure teaching me. She taught me on the way out here, and I try to practice now and then when I'm out in the open where I won't annoy anyone."

"It sounded good," said the trapper. "Made me think of home. Mother used to sing that when I was a little chap,—that one about the spacious firmament on high—"

There was a wistfulness in the trapper's tone to made his guest look at him keenly once again.

"Your mother is gone, then? " he ventured.

"Years ago."

"She's not at home waiting for you to come back then."

"No, she's not at home—"

It was after they were seated at the table and the meal was well under way that the conversation began again.

"You belong to the Hudson Bay Fur people?" The stranger asked the question half anxiously, as though it had been on the tip of his tongue from the first.

"I trade with them—" responded the younger man quickly, "that's all. I was with them for a while,—but there were things I didn't like. A man doesn't care to be angered too often. I'm not much of an American, perhaps you might say, but I don't like to hear my own country sneered at—"

There was deep significance in young Whitney's tone.

"How's that?" The stranger's keen eyes were searching the other's understandingly, a light of sympathy flashing into his own.

"They do not want us Americans," he said, and his voice conveyed a deeper meaning even than his words. "They want this country for England. They want undisputed sway in Oregon!"

"You have felt that, have you?" the guest's eyes were steady and his voice calm. It was impossible to tell just what he himself believed.

"Haven't you seen it? It's to your interest you should understand, if you don't. Why, sir, they don't want you and your mission! They want the Indians to remain ignorant. They don't want them to become civilized. They can make more money out of 'em ignorant!"

The doctor's eyes flashed fire now and his whole speaking face responded:

"I have seen it, yes, I have seen it. But what are the prospects? Do you think they can carry out their wishes?"

"I'm afraid they can," said the trapper half sullenly. "They have done all they can to make their hold secure. They are retiring their servants on farms and making voters of them. Every year more settlers are coming from the Red River country, and they are spreading reports among

Americans that passage over the mountains is impossible. They are alive and awake to the facts. Our government down there at Washington is asleep yet. They haven't an idea what a glorious country this is. Why, I've heard that they are talking of selling it off for the cod fisheries; and all because these Hudson Bay Fur people have had the report circulated that you can't get over the Rockies with wagons or women and children. They're wily, these fur people. They won't sell a share of their stock. They've gone about things slow, but sure. They have got everything all fixed. If they would only wait long enough and feel secure enough we might fool 'em yet, if just some more Americans could be persuaded to come this way. Somebody ought to go and tell them back at Washington. If only I—But I can't go back! Perhaps next Spring there'll be a way to send some word. I've thought of writing a letter to the President—Why don't you write a letter, Dr. Whitman? It would have weight coming from you."

"Next Spring will be too late! A letter will be too late, young man. Do you know the peril is at our door? I do not know but it is even now too late. Listen! I have just come from Fort Walla Walla, where I have heard what has stirred my soul. There was a dinner a few days ago at which were present some officers from the fort, employees of the company, and a few Jesuit priests. During the feasting a messenger came saying that immigrants from Red River had crossed the mountains, and had reached Fort Colville on the Columbia. Nearly everybody present received the news enthusiastically, and one priest stood up and shouted: 'Hurrah for Oregon! America is too late! We have got the country!' "

The log in the fireplace fell apart with a thud, and the trapper sprang forward to mend the fire, his fine, strong face showing set and indignant in the glow that blazed up.

"It is not too late yet if only we could get word to headquarters," he said as he came back to his seat, "but the snow fall has already begun. This will clear away and we'll have some good weather yet, but treacherous. No man could get across the mountains alive at this time of year."

"And yet, with so much at stake, a man who loved his country might try—" said Dr. Whitman musingly, and the other man, watching the heavy, thoughtful brow, the determined chin, the very bristling of the iron gray hair, thought that if any man could do it here was the one who would try. There was a long silence and then the trapper spoke:

"I would go in a minute. My life is not worth anything! But what would I be when I got there? No one would listen to me against the words of great men—not even if I brought messages from men who know—And—besides—there are reasons why I cannot go back East!" And he drew a long sigh that came from the depths of bitterness, hard to hear from one so young and strong and full of life.

Mr. Whitman looked at him quickly, keenly, appreciatively, but asked no question. He knew men well, and would not force a confidence.

They presently threw themselves down upon their couches of boughs and fur, with only the firelight to send weird shadows over the cabin room, but they talked on for a long time; of the country, its needs, its possibilities, its prospects; then before they slept the Doctor arose, knelt beside his couch and prayed. And such a prayer! The very gates of heaven neared and seemed opening to let the petition in. The country, the wonderful country! the people, the poor, blinded, ignorant people! That was the burden of his cry. He brought the matter of their conversation home to God in such a way that now it scarcely seemed necessary any longer to get word to Washington about the peril of Oregon, since appeal had been made to a higher authority. Then, in just a word or two the trapper felt himself acknowledged and introduced before the Most High, and he seemed to stand barefaced, looking into the eyes of God, knowing that he was known and cared for.

Overhead the silent age-old stars kept vigil, wise in their far seeing, and marvelling perhaps that the affairs of a mere nation should so stir the soul of a mortal whose life on earth was but a breath at best, since God was in high heaven and all peoples of the earth were His.

Next morning at daybreak the missionary went upon his way to Waiilatpu, and the trapper went his rounds again, yet neither was quite the same as before that long night conference.

One sentence had passed between them as they parted that had told volumes, and that neither would forget. As they looked together at the glory of the dawn, Dr. Whitman turned and gazed deeply into the trapper s eyes.

"Almost—I could ask you to go with me," he said and waited.

A light leapt forth in the other man's eyes.

"And but for one thing—I would go," was the quick reply with a sudden shadowing of his brows.

That was all. They clasped hands warmly with a quick, meaningful pressure and parted, but each was possessed of at least a portion of the other's secret.

CHAPTER 18

A FEW days before this, called by special messenger from Dr. Whitman, his four missionary associates had come from their distant stations to Waiilatpu. Quiet men, good, true, they were, with strong, courageous spirits, and bodies toughened by toil and hardship. They had come out to this far land, away from home and friends, for no selfish motive, and their hearts were in their work. They were met now, as they supposed, to consider the necessities of their work and to consult on ways and means. Each one had built his home with his own hands, tilled his land, planted fields of corn, wheat, potatoes, and melons; taught his Indian neighbors to do the same; and was maintaining, with his wife, a school for Indian children in his neighborhood, in addition to preaching and ministering to the sick for miles around. Two of them came from one hundred and fifty miles away. They were men accustomed to the difficult trail, and to the camp under the stars or stormy skies. They were expected each to bring his family expenses within three hundred dollars a year. They sometimes managed it within one hundred, for they knew the Home Board was poor.

They had known, these missionaries, that there were matters of grave import with relation to the Mission to consider; matters of which they had written to the American Board for advice; and they supposed it was for this they were brought together. But when Dr. Whitman began to talk, instead, of political matters, their faces were grave and unsympathetic.

Dr. Whitman began by laying before his colleagues a very clear statement of the way matters stood with regard to the Hudson Bay Company. He showed how they were scheming to get Oregon for England and made plain what a disastrous thing this would be for the mission, as British sovereignty would mean rule by the Hudson Bay Company, whose chief desire it was to keep away men who would teach the Indians, that they might retain the fur trade, all to the Company's advantage. He told them of the fault that had been found with the Company's agent, Dr. John McLoughlin, of Vancouver, because he had fed some starving American settlers. He made the whole thing plain, though each man already knew the main facts; and then he revealed to them that he proposed to go to Washington, tell these facts to the Government, and try to get them to do something to save Oregon, and with Oregon, the mission, of course. He had called them together to get their sanction and approval of his journey.

There was solemn silence in the great log room when he had done speaking, and the faces of the men were turned away from him. It was plain they were not deeply in sympathy with their enthusiastic colleague. At last one spoke timidly, as though feeling his way, and with his eyes down.

"It seems very commendable that Brother Whitman should be willing to undertake this great journey to save the country and the mission. I make a motion brethren, that we give him our full approval and commendation."

As if the storm of disapproval had burst with the words of good brother Spalding, the others broke forth with dissuasion, argument, condemnation and reproof.

They told him how impossible the journey was at that time of year. He would be throwing away his life, and for what? They bade him think of his mission deserted, and what might happen to his wife and his work if he left them alone for the winter. They clamored of public opinion and how it would be said he had deserted the Lord's work for earthly things. They refused absolutely to give their consent to his crazy scheme; and when he would not be turned from his purpose by all this, they told him in substance they thought he was meddling in matters that were not his concern; that he would better attend to his missionary duties and let politics alone.

Then arose Dr. Whitman from his place, faced his brethren with determined mien, and spoke:

"I was a man first before I became a missionary," he said, "and when I became a missionary I did not expatriate myself. I shall go to the States if I have to sever my connection with the mission!" He brought up his strong, firm hands that had built saw mills, planted gardens, tenderly cared for the sick, been the stay and comfort of many a despairing weary one, and dropped them forcibly again in a fine gesture that showed his mind was made up and nothing could turn it.

Dismay suddenly filled the room and sat on every face. The idea of the mission without Dr. Whitman was appalling. His withdrawal could not be entertained for a moment. At once the whole question was changed, and in a panic those who had been most opposed to his going on the perilous journey, hastened to move that his endeavor be heartily approved.

They besought him, however, to wait until the worst of the winter was over, but he would not listen to them.

The thing he had undertaken to do seemed well nigh an impossibility, a madness to attempt, yet they could not stop him. It was a ride of nearly three thousand miles that he proposed to take, and would occupy three or four months at the shortest, beginning with the first snows of the Autumn and extending through the worst of the Winter months. He would have to carry supplies to last through the whole journey, as well as provender for his horses, and blankets to sleep in upon the frozen ground, for there were no inns upon the way; and there were Indians, wild beasts, and snow storms to be encountered; yet the strong man wavered not, while for two whole days they persuaded him.

Others had taken the journey at a more favorable time of year, with a large company of companions, and a well-organized caravan of supplies and comforts, and thought it hard enough at that. He would have to go practically alone or with but one or two companions. Still, he would go: and with splendid courage his wife seconded him in his decision, though it meant months of long, weary separation and anxiety for her.

Thus, after the two days of conference, consenting unanimously at last to what they could not prevent, the missionaries went back to their stations.

Immediately upon their going Dr. Whitman set about his preparations for the journey. Two days later he took the hurried trip to Walla Walla to visit a patient in that region and also to make some quiet inquiries of Mr. McKinley of the Hudson Bay Company concerning a northern boundary treaty which he had heard was about to be made. What he learned there sent him hurrying on his way back without stopping to rest, until he came to the trapper's cabin in the clearing and found another man whose heart thrilled to the same patriotic tune as his own; and who, but for some secret shadow, would have been ready to risk his life also in this great endeavor to save Oregon.

As he rode on his faithful "cayuse" back toward the mission he did not spend his time in wondering what it could be that could prevent a fine, clear-eyed fellow like that from going back to his home again. He had been too long in that land without a past and known men too well to judge a man by one act, as they have to be judged in the heart of civilization. He knew the man he had just met was in sympathy with his deepest desires, and he trusted him fully and respected his confidence. It was a pity that he could not have gone. The way would have been better for his company. There was nothing further to be said or thought. It is a great thing to trust a man so much that you can be loyal to him even in your thoughts.

It was high noon before he came within sight of the mission: situated on a beautiful level peninsula formed by the branches of the Walla Walla River, nearly three hundred acres of land fenced in, and two hundred under cultivation, all now lying under its first Fall blanket of whiteness.

There at the left was the little adobe house, the first in which his wife and himself had lived when they came out to that country over the long toilsome trail; and off at the right was the new log house, sixty feet long and eighteen feet wide with an extension at the back, making a great T cross. Back of that was the blacksmith shop, and down by the river side the flour mill; all the work of this wonderful man's hands, and the pride and love of his heart. As he looked at it now in its setting of white with the blue ribbon of river twining it about, and the dark of the woods beyond, his heart suddenly failed him at the thought of leaving and the tears dimmed his kind, tender, far-seeing eyes. Down there in the whiteness was the tiny grave of their one little child who had been drowned in the river when scarcely more than a baby; and in the house was his wife, strong, courageous, loving, and ready to speed him on his way in whatever enterprise he undertook. He would have to leave it all and who knew whether he would ever see it again?

But Dr. Whitman was not the man to spend time in thoughts like these. Just one instant he let the pang of his going tear through his heart; the next he spurred his horse forward, knowing there was no time to be lost.

His preparations were few and simple and had been going steadily forward during his absence; yet the news he had learned made it seem necessary to cut down even the two or three days more he had hoped to spend at home and go at once, on the morrow if possible.

The people of Dr. Whitman's household were not of the sort that demurred when he spoke the word "I must." One instant his wife stood aghast at the thought of his going so soon; the next she had set her face to do everything in her power to make it possible and easy for him.

A message was sent at once to General Lovejoy, a young man who had come West that same summer and who had some time ago expressed the belief that it was entirely possible to go through the mountains at that time of year and promised to accompany Dr. Whitman.

The mission was astir far into the night.

It was a bright, clear morning, when they started. The mules stood ready with the supplies well strapped to their backs, the horses saddled, and Lovejoy and the guide already in their saddles when Dr. Whitman came out of the house.

All the Indians who lived near by had come to see the party off and a few of the most devoted proposed to ride the first day's journey with them.

In the doorway stood Mrs. Whitman with thirty or forty little Indian children of the school grouped about her.

Their goodbyes had been said in the quiet of their own room, these two who had left the whole world behind and come out West to do God's work together. They understood one another perfectly, and no selfish wishes were put in the way of the great purposes of their united lives. Each knew what a trial the succeeding months were to be to the other, and each had accepted it; and now as the missionary stood forth to take his leave his wife wore a bright, courageous smile. It was harder perhaps to stay behind than to go and fight storm, peril, wild beast and wilder man, and the man knew that she bore the harder part. His own heart was bearing her grief as he turned with a wave of his hand to her, and sprang upon his fleet and faithful cayuse; tears unbidden sprang in his eyes as he looked at her, brave and smiling among the little children.

. They rode away into the crisp, invigorating morning, strong in hope and brave of heart. The courageous woman watched them out of sight and then turned back to her long task of waiting.

All day the men rode forward, a long journey; tethered their horses, built their fire, prepared supper, ate it and slept soundly till dawn; then up and off again.

Eleven days they rode, resting on the Sabbath, and reached Fort Hall, four hundred miles from their starting place, at the rate of forty miles a day. Their Indian friends had of course turned back and there were only Whitman, Lovejoy and the guide, with the pack mules. But all along the way they had met Indians who forbade them to proceed. Dr. Whitman well knew by whose instructions they so acted, but in his wise way he held parley with each band and succeeded in going on his way.

At Fort Hall Captain Grant informed him that the Pawnees and Sioux were at war, and it would be death to go through their country, even if he succeeded in getting through the snow in the mountains, which was very deep. He was advised to either turn back or wait until Spring, but he was not the man to do either. Calmly as a mother might have picked up another toy dropped by a peevish child he adjusted his plans and added a thousand miles to his journey. Turning from the direct route he had intended to travel he took the old Spanish trail for Santa Fe. Taking a new guide from Fort Hall he pushed on across the northeast corner of Utah to Fort Uintah in the Uintah Mountains, and now the way grew white with storm, and the weather severe. The snows were deep and blinding, and greatly impeded their progress. A weaker man would have seen the folly (?) of his ways and turned back, but Dr. Whitman kept steadily on as if these things had all been a part of his plans.

They changed guides at Fort Uintah, continuing their journey across Green River over to the Valley of the Grand into what is now the State of Colorado. At Fort Uncompahgre they stopped for a brief rest, made a few purchases, changed guides, then off again.

The trail led over the highlands among the irregular spurs of the Rocky Mountains, and for four or five days more all went well. Steadily, surely, they were making their way toward the goal. It was still a long way off, but the start had been good, and the missionary gave thanks.

Then suddenly one day without warning the air grew white with storm about them. The blinding snow fell with such rapidity, and the wind blew with such violence that in a few minutes they were almost bewildered. They were forced to seek shelter at once, but though a ravine was not far away, and they turned toward it instantly when the storm surrounded them they found great difficulty in reaching it, and had to struggle through high drifts before they found it. In shelter at last with hearts profoundly thankful, they cut cottonwood trees for the animals, made themselves as comfortable in camp as was possible under the circumstances, and sat down to wait while the terrific storm raged about them three or four days.

Still whiteness all about, thick whiteness in the air, shut in from the world, they sat and waited. The strong, patient face of Whitman showed no sign of what might be going on within that eager, impatient soul of his. Off there in one direction through that whiteness was Oregon, beloved Oregon, his wife, his home, his mission, all in peril. Off there through the whiteness in the other direction, miles and miles more away, was a government unawares, toying with a possibility of possession, and knowing not the treasure they were so lightly considering. Here was he, willing and eager with the message, sitting, storm-stayed in the whiteness held by ropes of feather in this mountain fastness, while the nation perchance sold its rich birthright for a mess of pottage. What did it all mean? No hand of man had been able to stay him thus. But it was the hand of God that was holding him now; the soft, white, strong hand of God. He sat patient, submissive, not understanding, but waiting and looking up for the reason.

At last the storm subsided and the weather cleared off intensely cold. Cheerily, though with difficulty, the brave little party made its way again to the highlands, but the snow was so deep and the wind so piercing that after a brief attempt they were forced back to camp to wait for several more days till a change of weather made it safe for them to venture forth again.

At last the weather moderated, and thankfully they made their way up, but after they had wandered about for days hunting the trail the guide at last came to a halt, a sullen look upon his dark countenance and confessed he did not know where he was. He said the snow had so changed the whole look of the country that he could not get his bearings, and was completely lost. He could take them no farther.

This was of course a terrible blow to Dr. Whitman's hope, which had been rising steadily since the storm ceased; but invincible as ever he did not become downcast. Some men would have said that surely now they had done all that was possible, and would have felt thoroughly justified in turning back, and trying to find comfort and safety, at least until Spring;

not so this man. After thinking it over carefully and consulting with Lovejoy they agreed that Whitman should take the guide and try to get back to the Fort for a new guide, while Lovejoy should remain in camp with the pack mules.

No small part had Lovejoy now to play in the Winter drama. Alone with the horses and a dog in his mountain camp, with no idea whether Whitman would ever be able to find the Fort or not; and even if he succeeded in getting back to the Fort, whether he could return and be able to find Lovejoy again. It required faith and courage to stay alone with the animals and bear that week, that whole long, solemn, silent week in the snowy world.

A precious week, a wasted week it took, to go back and return, for the snow was very deep and going slow and uncertain; but Whitman braced his shoulder to the added burden, kept his good cheer, and at last the watcher in the mountains saw his companion returning.

Then slowly, like a train of snails, the little party crept its difficult way through the snow again, on and on, over the mountains, until one fair morning they could sight the winding shore of the Grand River.

Joyfully they hastened forward, as fast as possible, counting every difficulty small now that they saw the river ahead. But when they reached the shore at last despair descended upon them.

The river was from one hundred and fifty to two hundred yards wide, and frozen a third of the way across on either side. The current was so very rapid in the center that even in that bitter weather it had been kept from freezing, and what were they to do? The guide said it would be most perilous to attempt to cross. It looked as if another impossible barrier lay across their way. But Dr. Whitman was not stopping till he had to. He led the little party out upon the ice as far as it was safe, then mounted his brave cayuse and directed Lovejoy and the guide to push him off the ice into the boiling, foaming current; which, after much vain protest, they finally did.

It seemed like casting Whitman into a terrible grave; and at first man and horse completely disappeared under water; but soon came up unbaffled, master and beast appearing to be of one and the same spirit, and buffeted the waves magnificently, making their way gradually, although a long distance down stream, to the opposite shore, where the rider leaped from his horse upon the ice, and soon had the faithful animal safely by his side.

It was no easy task for Lovejoy and the guide to follow the example set, force the mules into the stream, and then to take the perilous trip themselves, but they did so. People couldn't help doing big things when they were around Dr. Whitman. His presence in their midst required it. For very shame they had in some measure to live up to the pattern set.

By the time they were all safely landed Whitman had a good fire burning, and soon they were cheerfully sitting around the blaze drying their frozen clothing, one more peril passed, and one less river between them and the goal.

It was by this time the middle of January, and all over the country the cold was so bitter that many people even in protected towns were frozen to death. Out in the open the cold seemed to be like an iron grip that enfolded one, and slowly, relentlessly grew tighter and tighter. A black stillness seemed to settle upon everything, a vast and universal cold and fear that penetrated into the very soul.

On one of these terrible mornings as the Doctor began his usual preparations for going on, the guide shook his head and protested vigorously. A blinding storm had come on through the night and the wind had made up for what moderation there was in the atmosphere. Travelling was sheer suicide that day but Dr. Whitman had already lost too much time. He laughed off fears, and cheered the others with his hearty voice, and so they set forth well muffled. They were in a deep gorge of the mountains of New Mexico and toiled on for a while in the blinding snow, but when they reached the divide and the wind rushed up from a new direction the biting snow and cold almost drove the horses mad. Whitman saw his terrible mistake, and turned at once to retrace his steps to camp, convinced that to go farther would be folly. This, however, was found to be impossible, for the driving snow had obliterated all trace of the way, and the whole country was deep and white and awful. The sky grew darker until it was almost as black as night, and the snow was falling so heavily that every step became more and more difficult.

Then suddenly hope seemed to vanish, too, and leave the world in absolute darkness. The staunch missionary saw that apparently the end had come. They could not live for more than a few minutes longer in this fearful cold and to go on was as useless as it was impossible, for they could not find their way anywhere.

With the feeling of utter failure he slipped from his saddle and stood beside his horse. Then bending his head he commended himself and his distant wife to the God in whom they both trusted; and with the bitter thought that through his own folly the cause he was serving must be lost, he gave himself up to wait for the white grave which was fast closing in about them.

Suddenly the guide noticed the ears of one of the pack mules, and said, "That mule will find the camp if he can live to get to it."

In great excitement they mounted once more and followed the mule.

He kept on down the divide for a little way, then made a square turn and plunged straight down the steep mountain side, over what seemed fearful precipices, down, down; no one to urge him or guide him; on he went just as if he knew what great things depended upon him.

At last he stopped short in the thick timber over a bare spot, and looking down they saw there was still a brand or two of the fire they had left in the morning! They were saved!

The guide was too far gone to dismount, but the missionary slipped from his saddle, and found that he had strength still left to build up the fire. With profound thankfulness he went to work and soon had the rest of the party comfortable. His own ability to withstand the cold was probably due to the heavy buffalo hides which he wore.

When the weather moderated once more and they were able to make their way out from camp, Dr. Whitman moved ahead cautiously, not willing to let his own eagerness risk the safety of his whole enterprise again.

One other narrow escape was theirs when they came to the headwaters of the Arkansas after a day in a terrible storm, and found the ice upon the river too thin to bear a man erect, and every stick of wood in the vicinity over on the other side. Dr. Whitman, taking his axe in one hand, a short willow stick in the other, spread himself upon the ice, arms and legs as far apart as possible, and thus crept across, cut the wood, shoved it over, then returned, creeping as before. That night a wolf stole the hatchet for a leather thong that had been bound around the split helve, and the rest of the journey the small comfort of an axe was denied them.

The way to Fort Taos was slow and painful, for the snows were very deep and their provisions were growing less and less, so that they were finally forced to kill and eat the mules. When they reached the Fort at last they had to stay a couple of weeks to rest.

Bent's Fort on the Arkansas River was the next destination and their route led them through Santa Fé, over a well-travelled trail, which, had the season been summer, would have made it easier for them. On the way, however, they met people who gave them word of a party about to leave Bent's Fort for St. Louis. Though there was very little likelihood of his being able to reach them before they left, Dr. Whitman, on his best horse, with a few provisions, started on ahead of his party; but was lost on the way so that Lovejoy with the guide arrived at the Fort ahead of him. Having sent a message to the St. Louis party camped forty miles ahead to wait until the Doctor joined them, Lovejoy went himself a hundred miles back to search for the lost missionary. Failing to find him he returned to the fort and waited anxiously until the doctor came at last, worn and weary, and feeling that his bewilderment and loss of time were a just punishment for his travelling on Sunday in order to make time,—the only time in all the long, toilsome, hurried journey that the good man had travelled on the Sabbath.

Lovejoy was worn out with the hardships and it was decided that he should remain at Fort Bent until Whitman should return in the Summer with a party of emigrants on his way back to Oregon. Dr. Whitman, invincible as ever, taking only one night's rest, pressed on alone to overtake the party of mountain men and go to St. Louis with them.

Four hundred miles and more the trail led him, along the banks of the Arkansas to Great Bend, across the country to Smoky Hill River, down the Kansas River till it joined the Missouri; and about the end of January he reached the little town of Westport, Missouri.

His going was like that of a sower going forth to sow good seed; for as he went, wherever he met anyone he told them of Oregon; how the way thither was open for wagons and women and children; how he had come over that long trail in the Winter snows just to tell them that it was possible, and that they were being deceived by the reports spread by the Hudson Bay Company, who wished to keep the Americans out of Oregon. Everywhere he found people who had intended going West but had been stopped by these very false reports that the way was impassable. He told them to get ready to go with him when he should return. Everywhere he went the reports of his story about Oregon went forth to all the country round about and people were stirred to take their families and go out to claim land in this rich, fertile country. The enthusiasm spread like wild fire. Lovejoy in his resting place was not idle either, but continued to tell the good story, urging all whom he met to go to Oregon and save it for themselves and for their country. It meant a great deal to them that the wonderful missionary who had so successfully crossed the mountains to tell them the story had promised to return and guide them to the promised land.

And so in his fantastic garb of "buffalo coat with a blue border," as he mockingly described his garments, Dr. Whitman went on his way to St. Louis.

In those days it was seldom that one came across the mountains in Winter from Santa Fé or the Columbia, and they gathered around him and plied him with questions. There were fur traders, trappers, adventurers, and contractors for the military posts, all eager to hear the news. They wanted to know the prospects for furs and buffalo hides the next season, but Dr. Whitman had no time for such things. He was in haste to get to Washington. He wanted to know if the Ashburton treaty was concluded, and when he found it had been signed by Webster and Ashburton the Summer before he demanded to know if it covered the Northwest, and how it affected Oregon. He asked if Oregon had been under discussion in Congress and what was being urged about it in the Senate and House. The great question with him was, could he reach Washington before Congress adjourned on the fourth of March?

Leaving his horse he took the stage at once, and one day in the last of February, he walked into the home of a minister friend in Ithaca, New York,—a friend who had once crossed the mountains with him.

"Parker," he said, the first surprise of greetings being over, "I have come on a very important errand. We must go at once to Washington or Oregon is lost, ceded to the English."

But the friend was not so easy to persuade, and thought the danger less than Dr. Whitman said, so, alone, the courageous spirit hurried to Washington. Suffering still from his frost-bitten fingers, feet, nose and ears, lacking the sympathy and enthusiasm of even his dearest friends, worn and weary, yet undaunted, he pressed on to complete his task. Arriving in Washington on the third of March, he went at once to interview Daniel Webster, the Secretary of State, to endeavor to convince him that Oregon was worth saving for America.

CHAPTER 19

DAVID SPAFFORD had been in Washington for a week on matters connected with the political situation, in which he was deeply interested, when he happened to call on Hon. Joshua Giddings, who was boarding on Capitol Hill, in what was known as "Duff Green's Row." He was deep in converse with the Honorable gentleman, when another man entered the room, a man whom he did not know but whose strong, fine face instantly attracted him. He was gaunt, almost haggard in appearance, and browned with the weather, but behind his keen blue eyes there burned a fire of earnest purpose that made David instantly feel that he was a man worth knowing. Instinctively he arose as the stranger entered the room, and he noticed that his host did also, and that he went toward the newcomer with an outstretched hand that meant a hearty sympathy with him in whatever cause for which he stood.

"Mr. Spafford, allow me the pleasure of introducing to you Dr. Whitman of Oregon!"

"Oregon!" exclaimed David, grasping the stranger's hand with a thrill of instant interest, "Oregon? Really? How long since?"

"Today," said Marcus Whitman briskly, as if it were only over in the next county, "I just arrived this morning. Left home last October and been travelling ever since."

"You don't say so!" There was wonder, amazement, delight and deep admiration in David's voice. "And how is Oregon?"

"About to be lost to us if something isn't done quickly," said the grave, earnest voice, "That's what I'm here about. I've spent all the eloquence I have on Daniel Webster this morning, but they've got him so filled with the idea that Oregon is of no use to our country because the mountains are impassable that nothing else seems to have any effect. Lord Ashburton, Sir George Simpson and their friends have done their work well."

"How is that?" asked David, keen to understand the situation.

"Why, you see they have been quietly working to impress our statesmen with the idea that the Rocky Mountains are so impassable to wagons that it cannot be peopled from the States, and therefore is of very little value to this country. They want it for themselves,—that is the Hudson Bay

Company wish to retain their control, and keep the Indians in their present state of ignorance, so they can make more advantageous deals with them."

"Sit down and tell me about Oregon," said David, "I have been deeply interested in all that was said in the papers about it. It has seemed to me a foolish thing to let it go for the cod fisheries. You think it is worth while saving, don't you, or you never would have come?"

Clearly, concisely, Whitman told, and in a few minutes the little parlor on Capitol Hill was thrilling with the story of the new land. The few who were privileged to listen were convinced.

"And have you told all this to Webster?" asked David.

"Yes," said the missionary with a sigh. "Tried my best to convince him that he was the victim of false representations about the character of the region; and told him I intended to take a train of emigrants over to Oregon this summer, but it made no impression. He thinks I am a dreamer, or a foolish enthusiast, I suppose."

"A man is not fit to be Secretary of State who has not clear vision for the future," said David rising in his excitement and striding across the room restlessly. "He ought to make sure of his facts. Your words may at least set him thinking. Perhaps he will investigate. It is the same thing they are doing to my friend, Professor Morse, and his wonderful invention of the electric telegraph. They will not pass the bill for an appropriation to try the thing out and see if it is a success. See, this session of Congress is all but over and it has only passed the House. There is little hope left for this time. Yet it has been practically proven already in a small way. Think what that will be to the country when the whole United States is able to communicate by electricity and messages can be received within a few minutes of their sending, even from great distances. Who knows, perhaps the whole earth might be girdled some day by an electric telegraph. You have heard of it?"

The tired blue eyes lighted with interest.

"Just a hint or two," said Whitman, "I heard that a man over in England had invented something that would carry messages over a few miles; but very little of the details have reached me. I heard too that some American was working at the same thing, but did not dream it had become a practical thing. It seemed to be a sort of plaything. You say it is really a success? You have seen it? What a miracle! Ah! If it had but been invented a few years sooner, and perfected, and put in working order! If there were only a telegraph over the Rockies I might have been spared this journey and all this time away from my work. I would have kept the wires hot with warnings until they had to heed me."

"Have you seen President Tyler?" asked David, suddenly wheeling and looking keenly at the missionary.

"Not yet," answered the doctor. "My friend, Senator Linn, of Missouri, is trying to arrange an interview for me. I hope to see him this afternoon or tomorrow sometime. Senator Linn is a staunch friend of Oregon. He will do all he can."

And even while they were talking there came a messenger from the Senator saying that the interview was granted.

"I shall be anxious to know how this comes out," said David, watching the kindling fires in the strong, worn face of Whitman.

"You are to be in Washington for several days yet?"

"I am not sure," said David, "I shall stay until Congress adjourns—anyway. I am interested in Professor Morse's bill and don't want to leave as long as there is a chance of doing anything for it."

"And I shall want to know how that comes out also. I shall see you again before you go. You are a man after my own heart," said Dr. Whitman with a hearty grasp of David's hand, and with that he was gone to the interview which meant so much for Oregon, and for the man who had assumed its cause.

All day long that same day, another of God's heroes, with the patience of the ages in his heart, and the perseverance of a genius, sat in the gallery of the Senate and waited; waited for other men to recognize their opportunity and set their seal upon his effort, making it possible to come to something; and all those small-great men sat and bickered about this and that and let the matters that were of world-wide moment slip unnoticed.

Ten long fruitless years had Samuel Morse labored and waited,—hoped and waited in vain for the world to do its part for his Electric Telegraph, since first he caught his vision of what it might be and knew his work in the world. And now, if this day passed without the bill coming before the Senate he would go home to New York with only the fraction of a dollar in his pocket to stand between him and starvation. As he sat and waited while petty business of a nation droned on its way his mind went back over his life; the enviable reputation as a painter he had dropped and left to die for the sake of this new love, this wary elusive maiden of electric charm and uncertainty. If this day failed to bring his finished invention to a place before the world where it could win recognition he was ruined. There was little wish in his mind to go on any farther trying to make a blind world see what he had done for its benefit. Let it go. Let the wonderful invention drop back into the obscurity it had occupied before it was born in his own struggling soul.

As the day dragged on and his friends and acquaintances came and went they spoke to him about his bill. They were sorry for him sitting there so hopelessly, so patiently. Few hoped with him, few bothered even to pity him. All told him there was little hope now that his bill would come to the front at all, with all the business there was yet on the docket, and Congress to adjourn at midnight. Some stopped to say it was a shame, and to hint that there was intention on the part of some members in the House to procure its defeat in the Senate.

Evening drew down, business dragged on, a weary session full of things in which he had no interest and at last, assured by his friends that there was no possibility now of his bill being reached that night Professor Morse, dispirited, and well-nigh heartbroken, stole from his gallery and went to his room at the hotel to lie down and sleep the sleep of utter exhaustion and disappointment.

Half an hour later, just a few minutes before midnight, his bill was reached, and wonder of wonders! passed; but the man on whose heart it had lain for the long years, whose very life had been given for it day by day, was lying asleep and did not know till morning.

They told him while he sat at breakfast the next morning, and he could scarcely believe his senses that the weary years were over and his chance to put his invention before the world had really come at last.

It was three days later that David, still in Washington but just about to go home, met Dr. Whitman on Pennsylvania Avenue, and extended his hand in greeting:

"So you are here yet!" he exclaimed eagerly, "And how did you come out with Oregon? Did you find Tyler had any better idea about things than Webster did?"

"Not a bit, not a bit," said Whitman grasping the extended hand as if he had found an old friend, "but I think—I believe he understands the situation better now. When I first began to talk I felt almost as if it were useless to try. He was firmly entrenched behind the same views that Webster held, that Oregon was useless to the United States. But I began to tell him all about it. I told that I had gone over the mountains four times, once in the dead of Winter, and that seven years ago I took a wagon over. I informed him that I intend to carry a large party back with me in the Spring, and that we, being American citizens, would claim protection from the national government. I showed him my frozen limbs and he looked in my face and believed me! Then I told him all about the climate and soil and the importance of Oregon to the nation, and he began to be convinced. At last he gave me a conditional promise of protection if my emigration plan succeeds. My last word to him was that the emigrants *would go over and would look to him for protection* when they reached their destination, and would expect the moral support of the government and the necessary legislation by Congress. In parting he wished me success in the undertaking. And now,—" and the missionary's face lit up with eager determination, "now, God giving me life and strength, I will connect the Missouri and Columbia with a wagon track so deep and plain that neither national envy nor sectional fanaticism will ever blot it out."

"God bless you in your wonderful undertaking," said David reverently. "And who knows but some day your wagon track may be a railroad."

The far-seeing eyes of the missionary rested on the other man's face in growing wonder and the light of the miracle believer shone in them as he said in a tone of awe:

"Who knows."

And then he briskly changed his tone.

"Your telegraph came out all right. I'm glad. Oh, God is in all these things. They must come out right sooner or later even though the people through whom they come are slow and hard of heart, and filled with their own devices. I wish you were going to Oregon with me."

"I wish I were," said David heartily, "Nothing would delight me more, but I guess my work is here for the present."

"You are right. We need such men as you in the East to keep things straight; level-headed, far-seeing men are scarce. I shall feel safer out in Oregon for knowing you are here at work, thinking and acting and voting, and writing,—for they tell me you have great power in that direction. Give Oregon a good word now and then."

"I will indeed," said David smiling, "You have made me an ardent supporter of the cause. I could wish that more of my party understood the matter fully. There is a general feeling among Whigs that we should stick to Abolition and not bother with Annexation. I think they are wrong in that. I shall do my little best to make a few men see. I wish I might have the pleasure of another talk with you. How soon are you leaving this part of the world? Couldn't you spend a few days with me at my home up in New York State?"

"I haven't much time," said the missionary, "But New York State,— where in New York State? Any where near Ithaca? I must go to Boston to attend a meeting of the Prudential Committee of the American Board. There are important matters connected with the Mission for me to attend to; I must have a day with my old friend Parker in Ithaca, and then I must go home for a brief visit with father and mother. If I could work it in I'd be delighted to see you in your home. It would be a memory to carry back— but you see how it is, my time is short."

"But our home is right on your way. You might at least stop over night with us. Why not go on with me tomorrow? Or do you have to stay in Washington longer?"

"No, I guess I have done about all I can here now," said the missionary, "and I ought to be on the move. I have one or two more people to see, but I hope to see them today. I'll try to do it. What time do you leave?"

"I was expecting to take the morning train, but can wait until afternoon if that will suit you better. It would be worth waiting to have your company."

"Thank you," said Whitman with fine appreciation in his eyes, "but I think I can get ready by morning. Don't change your plans. I'll be there." And with a hearty grasp of the hand he was gone.

CHAPTER 20

MIRANDA tied on a clean apron, put a finishing touch to the tea table and went to the window to watch. The afternoon train was in and it would be time for the people to be coming from it. Rose had taken her little brother and gone down the street to stand at the corner and watch for her father, for a letter had come that morning saying he hoped to get home that day.

Miranda had made rusk for supper and there was chicken with gravy and applesauce and a custard pie. Mrs. Marcia was sitting by the dining room window where she could see a long distance down the street. Her knitting was in her hands, but her eyes were down the street with a light of welcome in them and the pink flush of her soft cheek told the keen-eyed Miranda how eagerly she watched for her husband's coming. Miranda at the pantry window where she could see the street as well without obstructing Marcia's view, exulted in the joy of the household whom she served, and watched as eagerly for the home coming of the master as if he had been her own. Having none of her own she loved these dear people whole heartedly and devotedly.

"Well, he's comin'," she said bustling into the dining room, "an' he's got a queer lookin' pusson with him. 'Spose he's bringin' him to supper? It beats all how Mr. David does pick up queer lookin' pussons that has a his'try to 'em. This one looks like he'd killed a bear and put on his skin. Well, there's plenty o' chicken an' rusks, an' there's three pumpkin pies an' a mince down cellar ef the custard ain't 'nuff. Do you 'spose he's bringin' him in?"

Miranda patted the fresh napkins and slipped up behind Marcia for another view of the street.

"It looks like it," said Mrs. Marcia. "Yes, they're turning in at the gate. Better put another plate on and fill the spare room pitcher. He'll likely want to wash."

"Spare room pitcher's full," said Miranda triumphantly, " 'spose I wouldn't keep that ready when Mr. David was a comin' an' might bring comp'ney? Guess I'll put on a dish o' plum jam too—" and Miranda hastened happily and importantly away. There was nothing she delighted

130

in more than to be ready for the unexpected; and company was her joy and opportunity.

In a moment more Rose and her little brother came dancing into the kitchen shouting: "Father's come! Father's come, and brought company! A nice, funny man with a big fur coat. Get the supper on, Miranda, Father's here, and he's brought us each an orange, and mother a new silk dress, all silvery with pink flowers over it, and a lace collar just like a spider's web. Hurry Miranda, we're so hungry!"

It was while they were eating supper that Nathan came to the door with a bundle of letters from the office and the light of a great welcome in his eyes for his beloved chief.

"Come right in my boy and have supper with us," said David heartily. "Miranda, have you another plate handy? Nathan, I want you to know this great man and hear him talk. This is Dr. Whitman of Oregon and he has ridden three thousand miles across the Rocky Mountains to save Oregon for the United States. Mr. Whitman, this is my right hand man, Nathan Whitney. Some day when he gets through his college education he'll be coming out to be a Senator or Governor or something."

Dr. Whitman, with the human, eager look in his face that made him interested at once in all mankind, rose from his seat and stretched out a hand to the shy boy, looking searchingly in his face.

"Whitney! Whitney! Where have I heard that name recently? Ah, yes, I remember, out in Oregon just the night before I left. He was a young trapper, and I noticed the name because it was so like my own. We had supper together in his cabin and I stayed all night with him. I took a great liking to him. He was in thorough sympathy with me in my undertaking. I would have liked to bring him with me, but he said there were reasons why he could not come East, so I did not urge him. But he certainly was a fine fellow, and I am looking forward to seeing him again when I go home. Who knows but he is a relative of yours? I'll have to tell him about the boy I saw of his name, when I get back, and how you are coming out to us when you are through with your education."

Nathan's eyes shone over this hearty greeting, and he managed to stammer out a few words in answer, and drop into the seat Miranda had prepared for him, his eyes fixed on the keen, worn face of the visitor.

They all settled back into their seats once more going on with their supper, and no one noticed Miranda, who during the introduction had stood stock still in the kitchen doorway, her face as white as a ghost, and the tea towel which she had held in her hand lying unheeded on the spotless floor at her feet, while she grasped the door frame with one hand and involuntarily pressed the other hand to her fluttering heart.

"You must have a good many fine young fellows out there," said David, as he helped Nathan generously to chicken and mashed potato.

"Well, not so many,—not so many! A good many are pretty rough specimens. They almost have to be, you know, for it's a hard life,—a rough, hard, lonely life out there. But this man was unusual. I knew it the minute I laid eyes on him. I was riding down the mountain trail singing hymns to while away the time. I sing occasionally when I'm out where no one can hear me; my wife likes me to do it for practice you know—" he smiled his rare whimsical smile—"and when I reached the clearing and the little cabin that stood there, I saw a light in the window, and at the door stood a great, tall giant of a fellow waiting to welcome me. He said he had heard me singing and the song was one his mother used to sing when he was a little shaver. Well, I went in and found he had supper all ready for me, and a good supper, too. Perhaps you don't know how good corn bread and venison can taste after a long day on the trail. He had a nice little cabin with a cheery fire going, and the table spread for two. All around the walls pelts were hung, and there were fresh pine branches in the corner for a bed, with a great buffalo hide spread over, the finest bed you ever lay upon. We talked way into the night, and he told me a lot of things about the Hudson Bay Company. He was an unusually fine fellow—"

Miranda stood spellbound still in the doorway, and the coffee obviously boiled over on the fire. Marcia had to speak to her twice before she turned with a jump and a bright wave of color over her face and went to her neglected task. When she brought the coffee pot to the table her hand was trembling so that she could scarcely set it down.

The table talk was very interesting. Stories of the trail, anecdotes of the mission, descriptions of the Indians and their way of life; incidents of the long, long pilgrimage East, and details of the stay in Washington and Whitman's work there. Nathan sat with red cheeks and shining eyes, forgetting to eat; Rose, round-eyed and eager, watched him and listened too; Marcia, noting Miranda, absorbed in the doorway gathered little David into her arms and let his sleepy head fall on her shoulder, rather than disturb the conversation by slipping away to put him to bed, or send Miranda away to do it.

At last Nathan mustered courage to ask a question.

"How did you come to go out there in the first place?"

Whitman turned his keen blue eyes on the boy and smiled.

"I think it was reading the pathetic story of the Indians who came East in search of the Book of Heaven. Did you ever happen to hear it?"

Nathan shook his head, and David seeing his eager look urged: "Tell it to us, won't you, Doctor?"

"A few years ago," began the missionary, "a white man was present at some of the Indian religious ceremonies and he told them that that was not the way to worship the Great Spirit, that the white men had a Book of Heaven that would show them how to worship acceptably, so that they would enjoy his favor during life and at their death would be received into the country where He resides to be with Him forever. When the Indians heard this they held a council and decided that if it were true they ought to get that book right away and find out how to worship the Great Spirit acceptably. So they appointed four of their chiefs to go to St. Louis to see their great father, General Clark. He was the first American officer they had ever known and they felt confident that he would tell them the truth, help them to find the book and send teachers to teach them.

"These four Indians arrived at St. Louis after a long, hard journey on foot over the mountains and finally presented themselves before General Clark and told him what they had come for. General Clark was puzzled and perhaps not a little troubled at this responsibility thrust upon him, but he received the Indians courteously and tried to explain to them about the Book of Heaven. He said there was such a book and he told them the story of man from the creation as well as the story of the Saviour, and tried to explain to them all the moral precepts and commandments laid down in the Bible. Then, feeling perhaps that he had done his duty, he tried to make the visit of these four men a pleasant time to them. He took them all over the city and showed them everything; and they of course were greatly pleased and delighted with much that they saw, especially with riding around in a carriage on wheels, which pleased them more than anything else they saw.

"But the hard journey and the change of food was too much for two of the men and they died while in St. Louis. The other two, dismayed and sorrowing, and not feeling very well themselves, prepared to go back to their homes. Before they left the city, however, General Clark gave them a banquet, at the close of which one of the Indian chiefs made a farewell speech, through an interpreter of course, and one of the men present wrote it down. It got into the papers and it was the reading of this speech, perhaps, more than anything else, that determined me to go if possible to preach the gospel to the Indians. He said:

" 'I came to you over a trail of many moons from the setting sun. You were the friend of my fathers, who have all gone the long way. I came with one eye partly opened, for more light for my people who sit in darkness. I go back with both eyes closed. How can I go back blind to my blind people? I made my way to you with strong arms, through many enemies and strange lands, that I might carry back much to them. I go back with both arms broken and empty. The two fathers who came with me—the braves of many winters and wars—we leave asleep here by your great water. They were tired in many moons and their moccasins wore out. My people sent me to get the white man's Book from Heaven. You took me where you allow your women to dance as we do not ours, and the Book was not there. You took me where they worship the Great Spirit with candles, and the Book was not there. You showed me the images of good spirits and pictures of the good land beyond, but the Book was not among them. I am going back the long, sad trail, to my people of the dark land. You make my feet heavy with burdens of gifts, and my moccasins will grow old in carrying them, but the Book is not among them. When I tell my poor, blind people, after one more snow, in the big council, that I did not bring the Book, no word will be spoken by our old men or by our young braves. One by one they will rise up and go out in silence. My people will die in darkness, and they will go on the long path to the other hunting grounds. No white man will go with them, and no white man's Book to make the way plain. I have no more words.'

"It is among the people of that tribe that sent those chiefs after the Book of Heaven, that I am now working."

It was late when they arose from the supper table and went into the parlor for worship. Miranda roused from her absorption finally, and tiptoed around softly removing dishes from the table and putting everything in order in the kitchen for morning, but she kept the kitchen door open wide and handled each dish gently that she might hear every word the great man spoke; and all the while her heart throbbed loudly under her ruffled white bib apron, and her thoughts were busy as her fingers, while on her lips there grew and grew that steady look of determination.

Nathan did not go home until after ten o'clock, a most unearthly hour for people to sit up in those days, and when he took his leave the missionary grasped his hand again and looked steadily into his clear, brown eyes:

"Boy, don't forget that you are coming out to Oregon some day to help us make a great country of it. We need such men as you are going to be. Get good ready and then come, but don't be too long about it. It is strange—" and he turned to David smiling—"but this boy has taken a great hold on me. His eyes are like the eyes of that young trapper I told you about, young Whitney. Perhaps you'll find a distant relative in him when you get there, lad. I must tell him about you. Goodnight."

The front door closed and Nathan went home under the stars feeling as though in some subtle way a great honor had been bestowed upon him. Miranda, in the back hall, turned and fled up the stairs with her candle, but she had heard every word, and her heart was beating so hard she could scarcely get her breath when she reached her room.

She put down her candle on the bureau and went and sat down on the edge of her bed with her eyes shining and her hand on her heart. After a minute she went softly over to her mirror and stood looking into it.

"Oh, Allan, Allan!" she breathed softly; and slowly the look of determination that had been growing in her face crystallized into purpose, and she turned swiftly from her mirror and went down stairs.

David, having just finished locking up, and banking the library fire, was surprised to see her descending the stairs again.

"You're not sick, are you, Miranda?" he asked anxiously. "Shall I call my wife?"

"No, thank you, Mr. David," said Miranda briskly, "I jest wanted to borry the loan of a quill. Ther's somethin' I made out I'd write an' I disremember where I left mine the las' time I wrote a letter."

David, rather surprised, found her a pen, ink and paper, and Miranda went happily back to her room, taking the precaution to stop in the kitchen and procure a couple of extra candles.

Through the long night watches Miranda sat oblivious of cold or weariness, and wrote; and then laboriously rewrote.

"Now what do you suppose Miranda is up to this time," said David to his wife upstairs. "She's just borrowed writing materials. Is she inspired to literature do you suppose? Or does she want to set down some of the wonderful tales she heard this evening?"

"There's no telling," said Marcia smiling, "she's just the oddest, dearest thing that ever was made. What ever we should do without her I don't know. She would make a wonderful wife for some man, if one could be found who was good enough for her, which I very much doubt—that is one who knew enough to appreciate her—but it's lucky for us that she doesn't seem inclined that way. Oh—David! It's so good to have you back again. The time has been so long!"

And straightway these two married lovers forgot Miranda and her concerns in their own deep joy of each other.

CHAPTER 21

In the early dawn of the morning, when the candle flickered with a sickly light against the rosy gleam that came from the East, Miranda finished, signed and sealed her letter. On her bureau lay a goodly pile of little bits of paper, torn very fine, the debris of her night's work.

Fine feelings had Miranda, and very conscious was she of the Allan who had left her with the promise of return some day. As if his kiss were still fresh upon her lips, she shrank from any hint that he was bound to come back to her. Not for worlds would she have him think she held him responsible for that kiss, or that it meant anything else but the only gratitude he could then show for the release she gave him to go from his prison and trial into the world of freedom. He must not think this letter had any personal interest for her at all. The years had gone by and she was no fool. The kiss and his last words had been precious experiences that she had treasured through all this while, but to which of course she really had no right in any sense such as kisses usually meant. The possibility that Allan was still alive and might some day get her letter brought her face to face with the practical side of life, and she felt that after sending that letter she could not cheat herself into believing that he belonged to her any longer. She would have to surrender what had come to be the sweetest thing in her soul; but it was right of course, and she was odd enough to give up such foolishness. This one night she would exult in speaking to him once more, feeling that he was hers and that his fate hung yet in her hands. Then after she had done her best to give him the truth, his fate would be in his own hands and she could do nothing more for him. And so she wrote and smiled, and tore up her letters, though they were all of them matter of fact and none of them foolish; and at last with a sigh and a glance at the advancing morning she finished and sealed one; knowing that her time of delight was over, and she must return to the plain sordid world, the jolly old-maid life that was ahead of her.

The letter when it was finished read:

"Mr. Allan Whitney, Esq.

"Dear sir:—I now take my pen in hand to let you know that I am well and hope you are the same—"

So much had all her efforts in common; a brave beginning culled from "The Young Ladies Friend and Complete Guide to Polite Letter Writing," a neat volume in red and gold that Grandmother Heath had bestowed upon her the day she wrote a composition that was considered by the teacher good enough to be read aloud. Miranda kept the book wrapped in tissue paper in the bottom of her little hair trunk, from whence she had brought it in triumph to help on with this night's work; and earnestly, laboriously had she consulted it, but having got her brave beginning she searched in vain for further sentences that would be applicable to the occasion, and at last in desperation plunged into her own original language.

"And if you are really Allan Whitney I guess you'll know who you are an why I'm writin. Ef you ain't the right one no harm's done. But I felt like if 'twas really you I'd ought to let you know. I wouldn't uv thought it was you, only this misshunery man said your name was Whitney, an said you was tall with brown eyes an couldn't come East, so I sensed it might be you. And I'd uv left you know sooner ef I'd knowed where to write, only it only happened a couple o' weeks past ennyhow, and maybe the man won't ever get back with this ennyhow cause he says its a powerful long way, an he most died comin, an it seems to me you run a turrible resk with Injuns out there, only I spose you didn't want to come back till you knowed. And I hope I ain't speakin too plain ef this should fall into the hands of any Injuns who could read, but ennyhow its all over now. And so I perseed to give you the noos.

"Bout three weeks ago come last Wednesday Lawrence Billings got scared at a mezmerizin that Hannah Heath got up, with a long haired man to do the mezmerizin who said he could call the dead. So on the way home Lawrence Billings got scarder and scarder an he stopped at Mr. David Spaffords and owned up to what he'd done, an they hed a trial an found him guilty, but they let him off cause he said he didn't go to do it, an Enoch Taylor's grandson didn't hev time to come to the trial, but everybody knows he done it now, an so I thought you would feel better to know too, and Mr. David Spafford he says there hed been injustice done an so they put a advertisement in the New York papers ennybody knowin the whereabouts of the one they'd thought done it—you know who I mean—I wont write out names count o' the Injuns might get this—they would get a reward, an the town passed a lot of resolutions about how sorry they was them doin an injustice. So I thought you'd ought to know. So I wont write enny more as it's late an I hev to get breakfast fer that misshunery. He's visitin my Mr. David and Mrs. Marcia where I live now an he told us stories about the Injuns.

"And you might like to know that your brother Nathan is growed tall an fine an he's goin to colledge in the Fall. Mr. David's' ben teachin him. He's real smart an looks a lot like you.

"The misshunery man says you don't hev bedclothes fer your beds, only wild animals skins. I could send you a quilt I pieced all myself, risin sun pattern, real bright an pretty, red an yellow an green, ef you'd like it. If you'll jest let me know it's really you I'll send it the first chancet I get. So no more at present. Your humble servant,

                                                            Randa Griscom."

The reverting to the childish name by which he had called her, and her mention of the bed quilt were her only concessions to sentiment, and she sealed the letter liberally and quickly, that her conscience should not rebuke her for those; then freshening up her toilet she crept down to the kitchen to get a breakfast fit for a king for the "misshunery man."

Fortune favored her. Dr. Whitman came down to breakfast five whole minutes before the rest of the family appeared and sat down in the pleasant bay window of the dining room to read a paper that lay there. After brightly peering at his kindly face through the crack of the kitchen door Miranda ventured forth, her letter in her hand carefully hidden in the folds of her ample kitchen apron.

"Pleasant mornin'," she addressed him briskly. "Real springy. Guess the snow'll soon be gone."

Dr. Whitman laid down the paper and smiled his good morning pleasantly.

"Them was real enterestin' stories you was tellin' us last night," she went on; and he perceived she had an object in her conversation and waited for her to lead up to it.

"I was takin' notice of what you said 'bout that trapper," she glided on easily, "and wonderin' ef it might be a Whitney I used to know in school. He went off West somewheres—" Miranda was never hampered for lack of facts when she needed them. If they were not there at hand she invented them. "I couldn't say 'g'zactly where, n'whiles he was gone his mother died; an' there ain't much of ennybody left that cares; an' there was some things 'twould be to his 'dvantage to know. I'd a wrote an' told him long ago only I didn't know where to send it, an' I jest was wonderin' ef you'd mind takin' a letter to him. 'Course it mightn't be the same man, an' then agin it might. It can't do no harm to try. You didn't happen to know what his fust name was, did you? Cause that might help a lot."

"Why no, I'm afraid I don't," said Dr. Whitman interestedly. "I have only met him the once you know but I shall be glad to carry the letter to him. If he isn't the right man I can return the letter to you, you know."

"Now that's real kind of you," said Miranda; with relief in her voice, and her dimple beginning to show themselves after her hard night's vigil. "Mebbe you could tell me what sort of a lookin' man he was."

"Tall and splendidly built," said the Doctor, "With large brown eyes and heavy dark hair. There was a look about that lad last night that reminded me of him. He was your—*friend?*"

"Oh, not specially," said Miranda with a nonchalant toss of her ruddy head, "I jest was intres'ted when you spoke about him 'cause I thought he might like to know a few things 'bout his home I ben hearin lately. I jest writ him a short letter, an' ef he turned out to be Allan Whitney you might give it to him ef you'll be so kind. 'Taint likely he'll remember me, it's ben some years sence I seen him. I'm jest M'randy Griscom, an' he's likely hed lots o' friends sence me."

"Not out there, Miss Griscom, I can vouch for that. You know there are very few ladies out in that region, that is, *white* ladies of course. My wife was the first white woman the Indians around our mission had ever seen, and they couldn't do enough for her when she first came. A man out there gets lonely, Miss Griscom, and doesn't easily forget his lady friends."

The way he said "lady" made Miranda feel as though she had on her best plaid silk, and her china crepe shawl and was going to a wedding at Judge Waitstill's. She grew rosy with pleasure, dimpling and smiling consciously. The missionary's eyes were upon her and he was thinking what a wholesome, handsome young woman this was, and what a fine thing it would be for a man like that handsome young trapper to have a wife like her coming out to keep him company. He was conscious of a half wish that he might be the bearer of some pleasant message to the young man who had impressed him so deeply.

"A man might be proud to call you his friend," added the kindly doctor with a frank smile.

Miranda ducked a sudden little courtesy in acknowledgment of the compliment, when she heard footsteps coming down the stairs, and in a panic produced her letter and held it out.

"Thank you," she said breathlessly, and "Here's the letter. You won't tell anybody I spoke about it, will you? Cause nobody knows anythin' about it."

"Of course not, of course not," said the missionary, putting the letter in his inside pocket, you may rely on me to keep your secrets safely, and I'm sure I hope the young man appreciates what a fine girl is waiting at home for him. I'd like to see you out there brightening his lonely cabin for him. The West needs such women as you are—"

But Miranda, blushing to the roots of her copper gold hair had fled to the kitchen shed where she fanned her burning cheeks with her kitchen apron and struggled with some astonishing tears that had come upon the scene.

She never remembered how she got that breakfast on the table, nor whether the buckwheats were right or not that morning. Her thoughts were in a flutter and her heart was wildly pounding in her breast, the words the kindly missionary had spoken had stirred up all the latent hopes and desires of her whole well-controlled nature, and put her in a state of perturbation which bordered on hysteria.

"Golly!" she said to herself once when she fled to the harbor of the kitchen shed for the fifth time that morning. "My golly! To think he'd say those things to me—*me*! A real old maid, that's what I be. And he talkin' like that. He ought to get hisself some spectacles. He can't see straight. My golly! I hope he won't say nothin' like that to Allan ef it's reely him I'd die of shame. Now you wouldn't think a sensible misshunery man like him with a fur coat an' all would talk like that to a hombley red-haired thing like me. Golly! You wouldn't!"

Late that afternoon Whitman went on his way, with many a "thank you" for the pleasant visit he had enjoyed, and many a last word about Oregon, but before he left the house he stepped into the kitchen and shook hands with Miranda.

"I shall carry your letter safely, and I hope my man is the right one. Keep a soft spot in your heart for Oregon, my dear young lady, and if ever you get a chance to come out and brighten the home of some good man out there, don't fail to come." And Miranda, giggling and blushing, took her moist hands out of the dish water, wiped them on her apron, and shook hands heartily with him. She went to the pantry window and watched him through a furtive tear as he went down the street, carrying her letter under that buffalo coat, and walking away so sturdily into the great world where perhaps Allan was waiting for him. Then she murmured half under her breath:

"Golly! What ef I should!"

CHAPTER 22

As David Spafford and Dr. Whitman went out the gate together David said to his guest:

"I've started you a little earlier than was necessary because there is a famous Whig speaker in town and I thought it might interest you to get a few minutes of his speech. It's just a stump speech, and the gathering will be held in front of the tavern. It's on our way to the train, and if you get tired of it we can stop in the office until train time."

The guest's eyes sparkled.

"Good! I'm glad to get a touch of modern home politics. You don't know how hard it seems sometimes not to get word who has been elected for a whole year after election. What chance do you think there is for the election of Clay?"

"It's hard to say yet," answered David. "There is a great deal of speculating and betting going on, of course. One man, a Loco-Foco, has made a great parade of betting $10,000 on the choice of president. But how does he do it? He picks out the twenty States that he thinks least likely to go for Clay and offers to bet five hundred on each, leaving the six strongest Whig States out of the question."

"Just what are Clay's cards for the presidency? I really haven't been paying much attention to the matter since I came. You know my mind has been full of other matters."

"Well, the Abolitionists of course, first, then the Liberty Men and Manufacturers of the North, the Native Americans, and those who are for Bank and Internal Improvements—"

"Just how do the Whigs stand with regard to annexation?"

"The opposite party is trying to force the Whigs into standing *against* annexation but their leaders do not come out openly on the subject. There is a great divergence of opinion on the subject. Of course one of the great hobbies of the Whigs is tariff. We believe in home production."

At that moment they came in sight of the tavern, and saw the crowd gathered and the speaker already in the midst of his speech. The farmers had come in from all the country round, and their teams were hitched at the side of the road up the street as far as one could see, while the men

141

themselves were listening eagerly to the words of the orator who stood in their midst on a temporary platform in front of the tavern. It was an interesting spectacle.

The speaker's voice was big and clear and almost as soon as they turned the corner they could catch the drift of his words.

"Suppose," he was saying, "that New Jersey should be able to produce bread more cheaply than to buy it elsewhere. Then of course you would say they ought not to import it. But suppose also that hemp grew in New Jersey in such abundance that people could make a dollar a day more from hemp than bread, by giving all their time to the production of hemp and buying their bread. Should they not then buy their bread?

"Now it is easy to suppose that bread, well-baked, should grow in spontaneous profusion in a country, while hemp, ready rotted and cleaned, should insist on obscuring the entire surface of another country, but Nature has ordered differently—"

An audible smile rippled over the surface of the audience, who were visibly moved by the argument, although their faces had a grim, set look as if they had taken counsel before they came with their inner consciousness not to be too easily led.

"It's a strange and curious thing to watch a crowd like that swayed by one man's eloquence, isn't it? What a great power one human being has over another! And what tremendous responsibilities a man takes when he undertakes to decide these great questions for his neighbors!" said Whitman in a low tone as they turned off the sidewalk and went to stand under a great tree nearer to the speaker.

"They do indeed!" said David seriously. "A man ought not to speak like that until he knows absolutely what he is talking about. I sometimes think more harm is done by careless eloquence than in any other way. I wish you were going to stay longer. We would have a meeting like this for you to tell people about Oregon. Everybody ought to hear from the lips of one who really knows—"

But the sentence was suddenly arrested by the loud tones of the speaker who had reached another point in his address:

"Next, as to Oregon—" he was saying. "It is more than twenty years since we made a compact that the people of each nation should occupy that wild and distant region, being governed by their respective laws and magistrates. Not a whisper of dissatisfaction was heard during our opponents' administration, but now when election time draws near they desire to cover up important issues with this foolish and rash talk of forcing the country into war, and with Great Britain—"

David drew his watch softly from his pocket and glanced at it, then started in surprise.

"I'm afraid, Dr. Whitman," he whispered, "that we ought to be going if you wish to get a comfortable seat in the train. I must have looked at my watch wrong before, for it is ten minutes later than I thought."

"Let us go at once," said the Doctor wheeling away from the speaker and walking rapidly beside his host, "I am sorry I cannot stay to the end. I'd like to tell that good brother a few things about Oregon and England's state of mind. But I must go. It can't be helped. Other duties call, and after all, I don't suppose he can do much harm. I shall look to you to write us a good editorial in answer to that man and all the others. I am glad we have so strong an advocate for Oregon."

"I shall do my best," smiled David. "I cannot tell you how glad I am that I have met you and had this good talk with you. Perhaps when you get the wagon route established, or at least when the railroad is running out your way, my wife and I will visit you. Wouldn't that be great? And we may be able to send you a telegram before that comes. Think of that? Ah! There is Nathan with your bag looking for us. I fancy he has secured you a seat already. I might have thought of that and let you stay five minutes longer at the meeting."

"It's just as well," said the missionary smiling, "for if I had stayed much longer I might have had to speak. I couldn't hold in many more minutes, and then my train would have gone and left me. That's a fine boy you have. I'll be proud and glad to see him coming out West some day. Well, I suppose the time has come to part—I am so glad I have had this delightful visit at your home, and shall think of you often when I get back, and tell my wife about you. Don't forget Oregon!"

The good man climbed into the seat Nathan had reserved for him and gave the boy's hand a hearty grasp and a few kind words of encouragement, then amid a big noise of shouting trainmen the train moved out of the station.

Nathan, as he walked slowly beside David toward the office, suddenly looked up and said:

"I'd like to go out there some day and help make that country. Do you think I could?"

"I surely do," said David, "if we can spare you from the East. Get your education and then we'll see what your work in the world is to be. You are doing good work now, and I look to see you come through your examinations this Spring with flying colors and enter college in the Fall."

"I shall do my best," was all Nathan said in reply, but his eyes shone with gratitude and wonder over the way life was opening up for him.

It was the next week that Miranda went to her first missionary meeting. It came about in this way.

Mrs. Marcia had twisted her ankle slipping down the last three steps of the cellar stairs, and she had a paper to read in the meeting.

"I suppose I could manage to get there in the carryall," she said looking troubled, when David came home at noon and bent over her couch in great distress, while Miranda prepared a tempting tray and brought it to her side.

"No indeed!" said David emphatically. "We'll not take any risks with a thing like that. You'll stay right here on the couch till Dr. Budlong says you're able to go out."

"But my paper! They were depending on me to tell about the North American Indians. I promised to take the whole time."

"Well, you have your paper all clearly written out. Let Rose carry it over to Mrs. Judge Waitstill's. She's the president, and she's a good reader. Run over right away with it, Rose, so she can look it over beforehand. Is this it, here on the desk?"

Marcia subsided, content to be taken care of, and Rose started down the street on her errand. But in a few minutes she returned, the paper still in her hand.

"Mrs. Waitstill's gone out in the country to her cousin's for dinner and won't be back till she goes straight to the church for missionary meeting. Sarah Ann said she wasn't going herself today because she had to fry doughnuts, so she couldn't take it."

"Now, you see I must go, David," said Marcia half rising from her couch.

"Now, Marcia, surely there is some one else. Why I can take it over to the meeting myself if necessary, or couldn't Rose run down to the church—"

"I'll take it, Mr. David," said Miranda grimly, "and read it too ef thur ain't no one else by to do it better."

"Would you really, Miranda?" said Marcia, wondering what kind of fate her paper would meet in Miranda's original handling, "I didn't ask you because you're so set against missionary meetings."

"Well, I don't know's I've changed my 'pinion of missionary meetin's, but ef they've got to be why they sha'n't go wantin' your paper, not ef I hev to lay all my 'pinions on the floor an' walk on 'em. I use 'ter be a tol'ble good reader. Gimme a try at it. Ef I don't hit it right on all them Injun names I heerd you reelin' off to Mr. David th' other evenin' there's one thing, no one'll know the diffrunce."

"Oh, I can tell you how to pronounce them. There's only one that's important and that's Waiilatpu. It's pronounced Wy-ee-lat-poo. I think you can get through all right. It's good of you to go, Miranda, and I presume Mrs. Waitstill will be willing to read the paper."

So Miranda, attired in her best plaid silk and her handsome pelisse and bonnet, sallied forth to her first missionary meeting; serene with confidence in her own ability as a reader, she breezily entered the sacred precincts of the "lecture room"—as they called the place where they held the missionary meetings,—and announced that she had come "to take Mis' Spafford's place 'count o' her havin' sprained her ankle."

The good ladies looked at one another apprehensively, but settled back demurely to listen, and Miranda, after the opening exercises, unfolded her paper with a flourish and began to read.

Now strange to say, Miranda, in spite of her quaint speech, was a good reader. To be sure she left off her g's and was rather free in her translations into common vernacular, but she had a dramatic quality of naturalness about her reading which made you presently forget her rare English; and before she had finished reading the first page of Mrs. Marcia's fine clear handwriting she had the attention of her audience to a woman. Even her Grandmother Heath leaned over with one hand up to her deaf ear, and her sharp eye suspiciously fixed on her granddaughter whom from her cradle she had learned to regard with suspicion. Miranda had always been up to some prank, and it was impossible for Mrs. Heath to think that her sudden appearance at the missionary meeting bode any good.

But the reading went steadily on, Miranda sailing glibly over the two or three Indian names as though she had lived in Oregon all her life; and the reader like any public performer under like circumstances became aware that her audience was spellbound. The knowledge went to her head, and she threw in comments as she went along, facts that Dr. Whitman had told in her hearing, which made the story all the more dramatic. Marcia would have been much amused if she could have heard how her paper had grown. Miranda, among other things, dilated somewhat freely upon the fact that the missionaries were obliged often to live mainly upon horse meat. At which her grandmother gasped and adjusted her spectacles, trying to look over the girl's shoulder to see if such revolting things were really in the original text. Miranda went volubly on however, and when the paper had drawn to a close she folded it reluctantly and looked calmly around upon her audience.

"They say they ain't got any bedcloes," she announced spicily, "jest hev to use furs, an' I shouldn't think that would be a bit healthy. Don't you think 'twould be a good idea ef we was to make a few bed quilts an' send to 'em? They might hev good scriptur patterns an' be real elevatin'. I was thinkin' o' beginin' one all red and white an' black hearts. I ain't got any black caliker, but I got some chocolate brown with sprigs onto it. I don't 'spose the Injuns would know the diffrunce."

Miranda's suggestion did not meet with marked enthusiasm from the ladies, who sat with folded hands and disapproving expressions. After an impressive silence, Mrs. Waitstill spoke:

"It was real good of you, M'randy, to come and read Mrs. Spafford's paper for us, and I'm sure we all appreciate hearing these strange and wonderful things about the savages. We might consult the Board about sending a quilt if that seems advisable to the ladies. I should think one quilt would be enough for our society to send in case it seems advisable. Of course there are a great many other societies to help the cause along. I am sure we all ought to be thankful that we are born in a civilized land. Mrs. Budlong, will you lead us in a closing prayer?"

During the long, quavering, inaudible prayer which followed, Miranda sat in her importance with decorously bowed head, and heart that beat high with excitement; and when she caught a sentence of petition for "the nation that sits in darkness," there swept over her a sudden wild desire to pray, too. But her prayer was not for the heathen in his ignorance and sin. "Oh, God, take care o' Allan! Oh, God, keep him safe from the Injuns, and make it be him, make it be reely him out there, please!" This was her silent prayer over and over.

"M'randy Griscom! Lemme see that paper," demanded her irate Grandmother the minute the closing hymn was sung, "I don't b'leeve Mis' Spafford ever wrote that stuff about their eatin' horse flesh. Why 'taint decent! Why,—they'd be cannibals! Where is that place, M'randy? I don't b'leeve there's any sech writin' there!"

Miranda pointed in triumph to the sentence: "During the first years the principal meat of the missionaries was horse flesh."

"Wal, I swan!" said Grandmother Heath quite forgetting herself, "Jest look here, Mis' Waitstill, it's really here."

Miranda with a look of injured innocence and a glitter of the conqueror in her eye received the manuscript back and rolled it up ostentatiously. She took her lofty way home feeling quite a pioneer in the cause of missions, and hugging a secret delight that she had been permitted to be even so close to Allan as to have read about the place where he might possibly be living.

That night at the supper tables of the village there was grave discussion concerning the morality of missionaries who for their own carnal pleasure would kill and eat a horse.

"And it wasn't as if they didn't have corn and potatoes and parsnips and beans and things," declared Mrs. Eliphalet Scripture, "the paper said they had taken seed there and planted good gardens. Seems 'zif they might 'a gone without meat, or taken a good supply o' ham with 'em. Think of killing and eating our Dobbin!"

"Well, Patience, I don't know's that's any worse than killing and eating our cow Sukey, and we don't think anything of eating cows," responded Eliphalet while taking a comfortable mouthful of his excellent pork chop.

"That's very different," said Mrs. Scripture convincingly, "I'm sure I don't feel like upholding such doings and I for one shall not make any bed quilts for the Injuns."

Over at the Heath house another discussion was in progress.

"They're jest spilin' M'randy over to Spafford's, hand over hand," said Grandmother Heath pouring her tea out into her saucer and balancing it on the palm of her hand comfortably. "Ef they should ever git tired of her an' send her packin' there wouldn't be no livin' with her. She's that high headed now she thinks she can even tell Mis' Waitstill what to do. I d'clare 'twas r'dic'lous. I was 'shamed o' her b'longin' to me this afternoon."

"Wal, I told you 'twould be jest so ef you let her go over thar to live. I 'spose it's too late to undo it now, but I allus did think David Spafford was an unpractical man. He 'ncourages all sorts o' new fangled things. You know he was hot an' heavy fer the railroad, an' now they've got it, what hev they got? Why, I read in the paper tonight how a farmer lost his barn an' all his winter crop he hed stored in it through a spark from the engine lightin' on the roof, an' burnin' it up root an' branch. An' now he's all took up with this telegraphy they wasted thirty thousand dollars on in Congress. Fool nonsense I call it! Allus' gettin' up som'thin' new, as ef the good ole things our fathers hed wasn't good nuf fer enny of us. As fur as this missionary business goes it don't strike me. I take it ef th' Almighty hedn't a wanted them Injuns off there by themsel's He wouldn't 'a put 'em thar, an' it's meddlin' with Providence to interfere. Tryin' to Christianize 'em! If Providence hed a wanted 'em Christianized do you guess He'd a put 'em off thousands o' miles in an' outlandish place where they git so demoralized that they eat horse meat? No, I say ef they choose to live way off there let 'em stay savages an' kill 'emselves off. I heard the other day how some big Senator 'r other said that every country needed a place where they could send all their scallawags to, and this here Oregon was just the very thing fer that, 'twas the mos' God fersaken land you ever see, nothin' growin' there, and no way to git to it, an' the mountains so high you couldn't git a wagon ner a woman acrost 'em. An' here comes David Spafford spoutin' a lot o' nonsense 'bout Oregon, how it's a gardin of roses an' potatoes, an' a great place to live, an' the comin' country, an' all that sort of stuff; an' citin' that thar queer lookin' missionary Whitman he hed t'other day visitin' him. In my 'pinion thet man was a liar an' a hypocrite. Why, M'lissy, what 'd'e want to come rigged out like that ef he wa'n't? He might a put on cloes like any Christian. He was just a pertendin' he was a missionary so's to git Dave Spafford to write one of his nice, pretty pieces 'bout Oregon so he could git rid of the land he hez out thar at a big price. Take my word fer it, M'lissy, that man was jest a wolf in sheep's clothin'—an' that thar buffalo hide he wore was jest stuck on fer effect. Oh, Dave Spafford's turrible easy took in. You jest better tell M'randy ef she 'spects to stay round thar hob-nobbin' with those Spaffords she needn't to expect to lean back on us when they git sick o' her."

The old lady, nodding her agreement, took a long satisfying draught from her tea saucer, and Grandfather Heath having delivered himself as the head of the house cut a large, thick slice of bread from the loaf, spread it liberally with apple butter, and took a huge bite.

"An' I ain't goin' to waste no bed quilts on the Injuns," reiterated Mrs. Heath.

"Wal, I suttenly shouldn't," agreed her husband." I don't hold much with these missions anyhow. Let them as does support 'em, I say. Eatin' good horse flesh! Hump! They might better stay to hum an' do some *real work*, I say!"

CHAPTER 23

SPRING crept slowly into the world again and one day late in May there came a letter from Dr. Whitman to David saying that he was just about to start from St. Louis to join the emigration which would rendezvous at a place called Independence, a few miles beyond the Missouri line. There were nearly a thousand in the company and this would tell greatly for the occupation of Oregon. He said that a great many cattle were going but no sheep. The next year would tell for sheep.

"You will be the best judge of what can be done, how far you can exert yourself in these matters and whether the secret service fund can be obtained—" he wrote. "As now decided in my mind, this Oregon will be occupied by American citizens. Those who go will only open the way for more another year. Wagons will go all the way, I have no doubt, this year. But remember that sheep and cattle are indispensable for Oregon. I mean to try to impress on the Secretary of War that sheep are more important to Oregon interest than soldiers. We want to get sheep and stock from the Government for Indians, instead of money for their lands. I have written him on the main interests of the Indian country, but I mean to write him again.

"I shall not be surprised to see some of you on our side of the mountains in the near future—"

David was reading the letter, and Miranda, according to her usual custom when anything of interest was going on in the other room, was hovering near the door working as silently as possible. When he had read this sentence a sudden queer choking noise, half giggle, half cough, from the kitchen door caused him to look up; but Miranda had disappeared and was clattering some pans in the closet noisily, so David, thinking nothing more of it, read on to the end.

Miranda thumped her pots and pans that night as usual, but she went around with a dreamy expression, and every now and again it seemed to her a sheep's head peered pathetically at her from a corner, or blinked across the room from space, and the gentle insistent "ba-a-a" of some little woolly creature from the meadow behind her grandfather's barn would make her heart strings tighten and the smile grow in her eyes. The days

149

went by, and the slow caravan wound its two hundred wagons, cattle and horses, and at their head the man whose untiring energy, strong spirit, and undaunted courage had brought him thousands of perilous miles to gather them together for this great endeavor. Safely in his keeping went the letter, and with it travelled Miranda's spirit.

Well had she listened to the missionary's story of his experiences, and stored them in her heart. There were wide rivers to cross where quicksand and strong currents vied with one another for their destruction. There were fearful heights to climb and sudden perilous precipices to avoid. There were hostile tribes, hunger, heartache, cold and sickness to be met, and the days would be long and hard before they came to the promised land. Miranda knew it all and followed them day by day.

Night after night she crept to her window, gazed up at the stars and prayed: "Oh, God, make it really him and let him get the letter!" Then she went to her bed and dreamed of a strange place of wonderful beauty and wildness, inhabited by a savage folk, and infested with shadowy forms of skulking furry creatures; who were always preventing her as she searched, searched for Allan—just to tell him there was a letter coming.

Miranda's interest in missionary meetings increased and she took great pride in putting her mite into the collection which was taken at each meeting.

During these days there grew a sweetness in Miranda's life. She had always been bright, cheery, and ready to lend a hand to anybody in need; but there had been about some of her remarks a hardness, almost bitterness, that sometimes gave a sharp edge to her tongue, and a gleam of relish to her eyes. Now these faults seemed to fade, and though she still made her quaint sarcastic remarks about the people she disliked, it was as though something had softened and gentled all her outlook on life, and she had found out how to look with leniency on slack, shiftless people, and even on those who were "hard as nails," which was one of her favorite phrases.

She seemed to grow prettier, too, as the Spring came on and deepened into Summer. Naturally of a slender build, she had taken on a plumpness that enhanced her beauty without giving her an appearance of stoutness. She glowed with health, and her color came and went with the freshness and coloring of a child. Her years sat lightly upon her, so that most people looked upon her as still a young girl in spite of the fact that they had known her since she was a baby and could count the time, upon occasion, shaking their heads and saying:

"Mirandy's gettin' on in years, it's high time she was gettin' settled if she's ever goin' to be. She'll soon be an old maid."

Miranda's contemporaries grew up, married, brought their babies to be baptized in the church, and took on matronly ways; the next younger set grew up and did the same; and still Miranda kept the bloom of youth. Her twenty-seven years might have been but seventeen; and the strength that had grown in her face with the years, had been sweetened and softened. There had been pain of loneliness and disappointment in her little unloved days of childhood, but her happy philosophy had taken it all sweetly, and the merriment danced in her eyes more brightly now than when she had been ten.

Her friends gave up expecting her to grow up and act like other people. Only her relatives paid much heed to it, and were mortified that she should so shamelessly override all rules and insist on being the irresponsible merry girl she had always been. They hadn't expected her to marry, somehow, but they did think she should grow into a silent background and begin to recede into maturity as other girls did. Grandmother Heath and Hannah felt it most, and bewailed it openly in Miranda's hearing, which only served to make her delight the more in shocking them by some of her youthful pranks.

But that summer a quiet, unconscious difference grew in her, that made even those who disapproved of her doings turn and look after her curiously when she passed, as at a vision. It seemed almost as if she were growing beautiful, and those who had known her long and classified her as red haired, freckled and homely, couldn't understand why there was now something unfamiliar in her face. In truth, she seemed like some late lovely bud unfolding slowly into a most unexpected bloom of startling sweetness. Grandmother Heath looked at her sometimes with a pang of conscience and thought she saw resemblance to the girl's dead mother, whose beauty had been more ethereal than was common in the Heath family. Hannah looked at her in church and resented the change without in the least realizing or recognizing it.

There was a kind of expectancy growing in Miranda's eyes, and a quick trick of the color in her cheek that added piquancy to her ways. One evening after watching the girl's changing countenance during a glowing recital of one of her own escapades in which as usual she had worsted some grumpy old sinner and set some poor innocent struggling one free from a petty thraldom, Marcia said to her husband:

"I declare, David, I can't understand why it is that Miranda has been left to give us comfort all these years. She seems to me far more attractive than most of the younger girls in town. Isn't it strange some man doesn't find it out?"

"Miranda has prickles on the outside," said David laughing, "she doesn't let any but her friends see her real worth. I fancy her sharp tongue keeps many away who might come after her, and so they never learn what they are losing. I doubt if there are very many men in town who would know enough to appreciate her. There are not very many good enough for her."

"That's true," Marcia heartily agreed, "but sometimes, although I should miss her very much, I can't bear to think she will never have a home of her own and some one to love her and take care of her, as I have—"

"Dear little unselfish woman," and David stooping touched her forehead with his lips, "there is no other like you in the whole world."

Meantime the caravan with the letter wound its long, slow way over the hundreds of miles, crossing rivers which hindered them for days, making skin boats of buffalo hides to carry their goods; and again, with the wagons chained together and driving at a tremendous rate over a ford to escape being mired in the quicksands; discouraged, disheartened and weary; out of provisions, many of them sick and worn out, they kept on. Always at their head, in their midst, everywhere he was needed, that sturdy indomitable figure of Whitman, swimming a river on his horse again and again, back and forth, to find the best ford and encourage those who were crossing, planning for their comfort, finding out ways to get the wagons through when everyone said there was no passage; quietly adopting three daughters of a family whose father and mother died on the journey; and finally late in August, bringing the company safely to Fort Hall.

Here they were met with the information given them by the trading people of the Hudson Bay Company that it was foolish and impossible for them to attempt to take their wagons through to Columbia—they could never accomplish it.

Dr. Whitman had been absent from the company for a few hours and when he returned he found them in a state of terrible distress.

But when he discovered the cause of their anxiety he came cheerfully forward and said: "My countrymen, you have trusted me thus far. Believe me now and I will take your wagons to the Columbia River."

The pilot who had brought them so far left them and went back to Missouri, and Whitman took charge of the company. So, with many misgivings, and amid the repeated warnings and coldly given advice of the Hudson Bay people, they started on once more.

It was late in August and the new trail over the Blue Mountains was rocky and steep, often obstructed by a thick growth of sage two or three feet high. The only wagon that had ever before gone farther than Fort Hall was Dr. Whitman's, but with strong faith in their leader and a firm determination to overcome all obstacles they pressed on their way. They forded more rivers, passed through narrow, difficult valleys filled with timber, and again through fertile valleys lying between snowclad mountains; encountered severe snow storms in the mountains, losing their cattle in the timber and finding the road terribly rough and almost impassable at times, yet pressing on, ever on, until at last on the tenth of October they reached Whitman's Mission station where were rest and abundance!

Dr. Whitman had hurried on ahead at the last stage of the journey, on account of the severe illness of one of the other missionaries who had sent a message for him, leaving the company to be guided by an Indian friend. By the time they reached the station he had repaired his gristmill, which had been burned by hostile Indians during his absence. When the emigrants arrived it was possible for grinding to be done. Dr. Whitman sold the travellers flour, potatoes, corn, peas and other fresh vegetables. For a few days they rested and feasted after the hard fare of the journey, and then went on to the Williamette Valley south of the Columbia, where most of them intended to remain.

It was some time before Dr. Whitman had matters at the mission in such shape that he could go out himself to deliver Miranda's letter, but as soon as possible he took a trip to Fort Walla Walla and timed his coming to the cabin in the clearing so that he might hope to find his friend. But no cheerful light shone out across the darkness and no friendly form was waiting at the door to greet him this time. The cabin was closed and dark, and when he succeeded in opening the door he found no sign of the owner's recent occupancy.

With a feeling of deep regret he lighted a candle that stood on the table and looked the place over carefully. There were clothes hanging on the wall, and a few pelts, but there were few eatables and the fire had been dead for days. Well, at least the owner had not moved away. But what terrible fate might have been his in this land of wide wastes, fierce hates, evil beasts, great silences, who could know? Time only could tell, and even time might not choose to reveal.

With a sigh the faithful messenger sat down at the rough table and wrote a note:

"Friend Whitney: I have just returned from the East with a large emigration. I have a letter which I think is for you from an old friend, and which I think has good news. I am much disappointed not to find you at home. Come over and see me as soon as you return and get the letter. It is important.

Yours truly,
MARCUS WHITMAN,
Waiilatpu."

With another regretful look around he put the note where it would be safe and attract attention at once when the owner came back, then fastening up the door he mounted his horse and rode away, the letter still in his pocket.

Inquiry by the way and when he reached home brought no information concerning the absent trapper. There was nothing to do but keep the letter safely, and hope and wonder.

There were matters enough to keep the mind of the missionary busy at the mission. During his absence there had been a quiet influence of enemies at work poisoning the minds of the Indians. One of the results of this had been the burning of the gristmill, together with a large portion of his store of grain. There was much to be done to get things in running order again, for the passing of the emigrants had depleted his stores greatly. Then there had been a good deal of sickness among the missionaries and he had several trips to make in his capacity as physician. Most of all he was anxious about his beloved wife, who had been ill during his absence and who had been away part of the time with friends at another mission. As soon as things were made comfortable at Waiilatpu he hurried after her, rejoicing to find her much better.

While Whitman had been East a provisional government had been organized, an Executive Committee being elected and a body of laws adopted, but the number of Americans and English were so equally divided that little else had been done, each side moving cautiously because of the other, until more settlers should arrive. Now, however, all was changed, for the majority of voters were Americans! There were matters about the government which demanded his attention.

In addition to all this the growing alienation of the Indians was a matter for constant anxiety. There was one comfort, however, in the fact that his own Indians about him were never kinder nor more docile, and those whom he had left in charge of his crops had done their work well, cultivating the land almost as well as if he had been there himself.

The Winter drew on and the Indians came back from their wanderings to the station as usual. Dr. Whitman's Sabbath services in February had an attendance of two or three hundred, and his work grew heavier all the time.

Some of the emigrants wintered at the mission, expecting to be able to get work breaking land for the Indians, taking their pay in horses, or planting some land for themselves; but the Indians were most of them in such a state of mind that they would not pay for breaking land because it was *their own*, and they would not plant it for themselves because they had been told that the Americans were going to overrun the country and would benefit by it. They also annoyed Whitman and attempted to prevent him and his men from breaking a new field lest he should sell his crops to the emigrants and make money out of *their lands*. Constant daily annoyances began to be felt, and disaffections grew.

It was all too evident that an enemy was at work. An important thing to be done was to impress the Home Board with the fact that a grant of land for the mission must be obtained from Congress or the mission itself would be without a home before long.

Everywhere there was agitation among the Indians, and strange unfriendly stirring evident. Two murders of reputed sorcerers among them had occurred not far from Waiilatpu. There was much suspicion of the Americans. The Indians were like children, wishing to have their lands cultivated, yet unwilling to do anything much toward that end, or to pay for having it done. They complained that they had taught their language to the white men but the white men had not taught them theirs. They wished to have everything the white man had, and to be civilized, yet wished to have it without trouble to themselves.

Through all the Winter, though many others came and went, the young trapper Whitney, from the cabin in the clearing on the way to the Fort, came not, nor was he heard from by any, though Dr. Whitman inquired often and several times took journeys that way to see if he had returned. So still the letter waited.

Back in the East as Spring came on, one evening David Spafford was reading the paper aloud as usual, with Marcia knitting by his side, while Miranda cleared off the supper table.

He read a brief item down at the bottom of the column:

"Another expedition is said to be about to start to go to the Rocky Mountains. This will rendezvous at Independence. There are ten women in the company."

A strange sense of quiet in the room made both David and Marcia look up suddenly, and they beheld Miranda, standing wistful in the doorway unconscious of their gaze, with a strange, far away look in her eyes, the hungry appeal of a woman's soul for all that life was meant to be to her. One would never think of the word "fragile" in describing Miranda, yet Marcia thinking it over afterward, almost thought she had seen a hint of fragility about her, but decided that it was instead a growing refinement of the spirit. They both looked away at once and David went on reading, so Miranda never knew they had seen that glimpse of her secret soul, understanding and sympathizing because they themselves knew love. They never connected her look with the item in the paper, not even for an instant, and they could not have understood of course why that should have brought the heart hunger into her eyes; but they grew more careful and tender of her from day to day, if that could be possible, because of that they had seen.

The great excitement that Spring was the going of Nathan down to New York to take his examinations, and great was the rejoicing and the feast prepared by Miranda the day word came that he had passed in everything and might enter college in the Autumn.

Politics in the East were at high pressure all that Summer. Stump speeches and mass meetings were the order of the day and night. Banners were flying everywhere, some with pictures of the presidential candidates, others with talismanic inscriptions that set the people's imagination on fire as they passed. Everywhere were bulletin boards setting forth reasons why men should vote for this candidate or that. The name of Clay was on the lips of some, with praise and loud acclaim, while others told of all that Polk stood for, and were just as enthusiastic in his praise. Those who thought and wrought and *cared* spent anxious days and nights; then talked and wrought the harder.

Now the time began to draw near when messengers from the far country might be expected. Dr. Whitman had said that he hoped there might be a chance of sending back word of his safe arrival before the Winter had set in, and Miranda naturally had hoped, a little, that her letter might have reached its destination and perhaps have brought some recognition then, yet no word had come from Dr. Whitman; but now the Winter was passed and it was time to hope again.

Miranda began to peruse the *Tribune* every night, and no word of Oregon or Indians escaped her, but neither did she find anything to make her hope that travellers had arrived from over the Rockies. She had heard them tell how the missionaries were often a year and a half getting a letter from Massachusetts, and she had set her faith and her patience for a long wait, so her courage did not fail; but as the warm weather came on, that spirit look came oftener in her eyes, as if patience were trying her soul almost too far; and Marcia, noticing it, suggested a trip to New York and a few days at the sea. She even hinted that she and Rose and little David would go along, but to her surprise Miranda seemed almost panic-stricken and declared she didn't care for journeyings.

"You and Mr. David go, honey," she said indulgently, "an' I'll stay home an' clean house. It's jest the chance I ben watchin' fer to get all slicked up 'thout nobody knowin' it. I don't keer fer the big cities much, an' oncet in a lifetime's nuf fer me. As fer the o'shn, I kinda think 'twould give me the creeps, so much water all goin' to waste, jest settin' thar ar gettin' in the way when folks wants to go acrost. Guess I'll jest stay t' hum an' clean house, Mrs. Marcia ef it's all the same t' you."

And stay she did, as cheery and sturdy as ever except now and again when the far away spirit look came into her eyes. Nights now when she crept up to her starry window she prayed:

"God, I reckon it wa'n't him after all, but I guess you'll jest hev to tell 'im yerse'f, ef it's all right he should know."

Sometimes her head went heavily down on the casement sill, and she slept so till dawning.

Miranda had evinced a strong interest in the coming of the mails since early Spring, and seemed to enjoy going down to the post office in the late afternoons. But no letter had come for her, nor indeed did she really much expect one. She had told herself again and again that there was no obligation on his part to write, and men didn't write letters unless they had to. He might perhaps sometime write and say he thanked her for letting him know, that was all her hope; for that the color came and went in her cheeks; her eyes grew bright and her breath grew short whenever she went to the post office.

The summer waned, the far-away look grew in Miranda's eyes, the wrangling about politics went on to its climax and at last the morning of election day came.

CHAPTER 24

THE morning train came in bringing a few wanderers from home who had come back to vote. They hurried down the street which seemed to have a cleared-up, holiday look, almost like Sunday, save that groups of men were standing about laughing, gesticulating, talking, with anything but their Sunday attitude.

None of them had time to notice a stranger who got off the train with them and stood a moment looking about him as if to get his bearings.

He was a tall, broad-shouldered fellow, well dressed and well groomed. His handsome face was bronzed as if he had been out in all weathers, but he was clean shaven and his hair cut in the way they were wearing it in New York. All his garments were new and fine, and the carpet bag he carried was of the best. There was about him, moreover, an air of being entirely superior to his clothes which gave him a commanding presence. The station agent turned to look curiously after him as he stepped off the platform, starting down the street. He half ran after the stranger, begrudging someone else the right to direct him, and wondering why the man had not stopped to inquire the way of him, for a stranger he certainly must be.

But the stranger did not appear to see him so the agent stood and watched till he turned the corner by the court house into the main street. Then he went reluctantly back to his work. It was hard luck on a day like this to have to stay around the station all day instead of being about the polls with the other men.

Passing the courthouse the stranger crossed over in front of the Presbyterian Church, walked down the street slowly and surveyed each well-known place as he came to it. There was the bank with its great white pillars and its stone steps where he had played marbles twenty years or more ago. Next stood the old house where Elkanah Wilworth lived and from whose small attic windows he and young Elkanah of the third generation had fired peas on the heads of the unsuspecting passers below.

Eleazer Peck lived next door. They had tied a cat to his front door and left her scratching and howling one evening while they enjoyed the view of Eleazer, candle in hand, come to see what it was all about. There was the store kept by Cornelius Van Storm and John Doubleday, with its delightful collection of calico, coffee, nails, eggs, plows, etc., in exciting confusion. How he had loved that store! The hours he had spent in a nail keg behind the stove listening to the tales the men had to tell! Ah, he could match those wonderful fairy stories of his youth now with stories a hundred times more thrilling!

Dr. Budlong's office came next in the same old house where his father had been doctor before him, and beside it was the blacksmith's shop, where 'twas handy to get a loose shoe tightened before driving out to the country on a bad day. There in the doorway stood the same old blacksmith, Sylvanus Sweet, gazing idly out into the street, and staring at the stranger curiously; never knowing him for the bad little boy who used to tickle the horse's hind legs while he was setting a fore shoe, in the days of his apprenticeship.

Across the street was the post office; next, the two taverns, one on either side of the street, and here the groups were assembled and the interest was centred, for the voting place was close by.

The stranger paused and looked about him.

Just at the edge of the road stood David Spafford, a trifle older, with a touch of gray in his hair, but the same kindly, hearty expression he remembered when he was a little boy. David was evidently waiting for the return of a slender young fellow with dark hair and an oddly familiar back who had run out to speak to some men in a wagon. Two excited fellows were arguing loudly in the road. Could one of them be Silas Waite? He wasn't sure. And that must be Lyman Rutherford with his hat off pushing his hair back. He couldn't quite see his face, but was sure it was his attitude. He was talking with Eliphalet Scripture. Tough old Eliphalet Scripture alive yet and not a day older to all appearances! That man behind him with the gray beaver hat couldn't be anybody else but old Mr. Heath, and he was talking with Lemuel Skinner. H'm! Lemuel Skinner used to go with Hannah Heath! Did he win her finally, the stranger wondered?

Ah! There went old Caleb Budlong across the street as hale and chipper as ever, and his doctor's carryall was hitched near at hand in front of the opposite tavern.

How unchanged and natural it all looked, and only he was strange—a stranger in his own home. No one knew him.

He looked about with a great loneliness upon him, and his eyes fell upon a single figure standing in front of a billboard on which "HENRY CLAY" stood out in large letters under a poising eagle. It was his own father, grave, silent, severe-looking as ever—among men, yet not of them! Not ten feet away, yet with no thought that his own son was so close at hand!

For an instant the young man started as if to go to him, then drew back in the shadow of the tavern again, and after a moment more passed on down the street. No, he would not speak to him, would not let anybody know yet who he was. There was just one human being in all his home village who had the right to recognize him first and greet him, and to her he was going.

His passing had been so quiet that few had seemed to notice him, though a stranger of such fine presence could scarcely walk through town and not turn many curious eyes his way; but no one knew who he might be.

A group of small boys playing at marbles on the side walk looked impudently up at him and warned him not to spoil their game. He stepped obligingly round it, and almost felt as if one of them might be his former self.

On down the pleasant street he passed till he came to his own old home, standing white pillared and stately behind its high hedges, and holding out no more friendly welcome now than it had done to him in childhood. He hesitated and looked toward it a moment, a rush of old loneliness and sorrows coming over him, then deliberately turned toward David Spafford's house, walked into the front gate, and knocked at the door.

Now Miranda had the house to herself for the day, for Marcia and the children had gone to the aunts for dinner, and David was to go there at noon. Miranda had taken the day to bake pumpkin pies and fry doughnuts. When the knocker sounded through the house she was deep in the business with her sleeves rolled above her plump elbows and a dust of flour on her cheek and chin. She waited to cut the round hole in another doughnut before answering the knock.

The morning sunshine was bright, but the hall was slightly dark, and when she opened the door her eyes were blinded for a moment. She could see only a figure standing on the stoop, the tall fine figure of a stranger with a travelling bag in his hand.

In haste to get back to her doughnuts she did not wait for him to speak but curtly told him:

"Mr. Spafford is out. He won't be in till evening."

But the stranger stepped calmly in as he replied:

"I didn't want to see Mr. Spafford, I came to see you."

Miranda caught her breath and stepped back surveying him aghast. In all the years she had guarded Mr. Spafford's front door, and back door, never had she met such effrontery as this, actually getting in the door in spite of her! Who could this be who dared to say he had come to see her? He did not look like a person who would be rude, and yet rude he certainly was. She drew the door wider open that the light might fall on his face, and turned to look at him, but he put out one hand and pushed it gently shut.

"Randa, don't you know me?" he said softly, and somehow in an instant she was carried back to the old smoke-house and the dark snowy night when the one love of her heart went from her.

"Allan!" she breathed. "Oh, Allan!" and her voice was as when she talked to God under the stars—as no human being had ever before heard her speak.

The tall stranger put his travelling bag down on the floor, pushed the door shut with a click and folded her in his arms.

"Randa!" And stooping, he laid his lips upon hers.

"Oh!" gasped Miranda, and her cheek, flour and all, went down upon the breast of the immaculate overcoat.

For a full minute joy and confusion rolled over her, and then she struggled to her senses.

"But, oh!" she gasped again, drawing away from him. "Come in, won't you?"

She led him into the parlor where it was bright with Autumn sunshine and the reflection of yellow leaves from the trees outside. But when she turned to look upon him she beheld a stranger, tall, handsome, with the garments of a fashionable gentleman, and a lot of fineness and nobleness which seemed to set him miles above her. She drew back abashed.

"Oh, Allan! Is it really you?" she cried half fearfully. "You look so grown up an' diffrunt!"

A great light was shining in Allan's eyes as he looked at her.

"It's really me, Randa, only it's been a good many years, and maybe I'm a little taller. And it's really you! I'd have known you anywhere—those eyes,—and that hair—" he passed his hand softly over Miranda's copper locks that were ruffled into little rings and sprangles all over her head, though they had been neatly piled in place early in the morning. "Why, Randa, I knew you the minute my eyes lit on you—only, Randa, I didn't expect you'd be so—so *beautiful*!" A frightened look came into Miranda's eyes.

"Beautiful! *Me?*" she cried aghast. "Oh, what makes you talk like that?" She turned her head away and great tears welled into her eyes. He had come, the Allan she had waited for so long, and he was making fun of her! It was more than she could bear!

"Randa!" His arms were about her again, and he lifted her face. "Look up, Randa! Look into my eyes, I mean it. You *are* beautiful! How could you help knowing it? You're the most beautiful woman I ever saw! Look into my eyes and see I mean it."

Miranda looked, and what she saw there filled her with wonder and joy, satisfying all the hunger and longing which had for years filled her eyes with that yearning look.

"Why, Randa, don't you know I've dreamed about you? I've always meant to come back when I could and when your letter came saying it was all right I hurried off as soon as possible. I've dreamed you all out as you used to be, and then tried to think how you looked grown up. Those eyes all full of sparkle like sunshine on the water where it sifted through the chestnut leaves into the depths of the pool down by the old swimming hole, do you remember? That dimple in the corner of your mouth when you laughed, and the other one in your other cheek that played at hide and seek with it, and made you look so wicked and so innocent both at the same time. That sweet mouth that used to look like crying whenever I got whipped at school. The white, soft, roundness under your chin. How often I've wished I could hold it in my hand this way! And the little curl in the back of your neck where your hair was parted! Why, Randa, I've spent hours dreaming it all out; and it's just as I thought, only better—much, *much* more *beautiful*!"

But all this was too much for Miranda. The strong-minded, the courageous-hearted, the irrepressible, the indomitable! She who had borne loneliness and lovelessness and hardness unflinchingly, melted as wax under this loving admiration, buried her face in the strong arms around her and wept.

"Why, Randa, little Randa! Have I hurt you?" he whispered softly. "Have I perhaps made a mistake and spoken too soon? Maybe there is some one else ahead of me and I had no right—!"

But here Miranda's face like a Summer thundercloud lifted fiercely:

" 'Z if thur c'd *ever* be anybody else!" she sobbed.

"Then what you crying about, child?"

" 'Cause—you—come-n-n-n—look so fine—an' say all them po'try things just like I was one o' the Waitstill girls, an' I'm only me—jest plain, hombly, turn-up-nose, freckle-faced, red-haired M'randy Griscom! An' you ain't looked at me real good yet ur you'd know. You ben dreamin' an' you got things all halo'd up like them ugly saints in pictures they paint a ring o' light over thur heads an' call 'em a saint,—but it don't make 'em no prettier 'z I c'n see. Mrs. Marcia's got one she says is painted by a great man, but thur ain't no ring o' light round my head, an' when you look at me good you'll see thur ain't. An' then you won't think that way any more. Only I ain't ever hed nobody talk thet way to me afore, an' it real kinda hurt thet it don't b'long t' me. Guess I'm gettin' nervous though I ain't sensed it afore. You see I never knowed what I'd missed till you spoke thet way, an' 'tain't so easy to think o' givin' it up 'cause it don't b'long to me." Miranda struggled to wipe away the tears with her kitchen apron, but Allan put it from her hand, wiping them on his own fine clean handkerchief; taking her soft chin in his hand and holding her face up to his just as he had dreamed he would do.

"But it does belong, Randa, it *all* belongs. Why, Randa, don't you know I love you? Don't you know I've loved you all these years an' come thousands o' miles after you? And now I've got here you look better to me than I've dreamed. Randa, haven't you ever dreamed about me? Maybe this has all been one-sided—"

"Lots o' times," cut in Miranda sniffing.

"Maybe you don't love me, Randa, but I sort of thought—you see when you were just a little girl you always took my part, and slipped me apples and gingerbread out of your dinner pail—I was a great hog to eat them away from you, but boys are selfish beasts when they're young and I guess they take it for granted the world was made for 'em till they get a little sense in their heads, and some of 'em never get it;—and then you fixed that cream so it'd pour over the teacher and stop his whipping me; and you saved my life—Miranda, you know you saved my life at great risk to yourself. You needn't tell me. I know your hard old grandfather and what he might have done to you if he'd found out. Miranda, I've loved you ever since. I didn't know it just at first, when I stole out of the smokehouse that night in the snow and got away into the world. I was all excited and glad to go, and you were only a little part of it that I was grateful for. Something made me want to kiss you when I left, but I didn't think much about it then.

"I got through the woods to the river by the next night, and found a haystack to sleep under till the snow let up. I was so tired I fell asleep, but after I'd slept a little while I woke up and thought they were after me, your grandfather and the officers; and I put my hand outside the haystack into the snow and remembered where I was, and knew I must keep still till morning. I lay very still and thought it all over, how you'd done—how you'd always done for me all my life, and what a sweet little thing you'd always been to me, so quiet and out-of-sight except when you were needed. So smart and saucy to other folks, so keen to find ways to help me when I was in trouble; and I thought of the curl in your neck, too, and the way you turned your head on the side when you used to sit in front of me in school, and the shine on the waves in your hair. Then I thought of the kiss, how warm and soft your lips felt when they touched mine out there in the falling snow, and all of a sudden I knew I loved you and that I should come back some day and get you if it was thousands of miles I had to go.

But somehow, it never came to me to think that some other fellow might have got you before I came. You always seemed so to belong to me. You see, I didn't realize how beautiful you would have grown, and how you might have forgotten me—me off working in a wilderness and growing like a wild creature—"

"You!" cried Miranda, drawing back and looking at him. "You, Allan Whitney, *wild!* Why, you're a—why, you're a—why, you're a *real gentleman!* an' me? I'm jest—M'randy!"

"You're just what I want!" said Allan stooping to kiss her again. And just at that inopportune moment a smell loud and virulent made itself felt in the house.

"Oh, *my golly!* That's my fat burnin'!" said Miranda, struggling from the arms of her lover and fleeing to the kitchen. "Jest to think I'd git so overcome thet I'd fergit them doughnuts!"

But Allan Whitney had not come three thousand miles to be left in the parlor while his lady fried doughnuts, and he followed her precipitately to the kitchen and proceeded to hinder her at every turn of her hand.

CHAPTER 25

"I DIDN'T get your letter until February," began Allan, sitting down beside the table, to watch Miranda's deft fingers cutting out the puffy dough, and thinking how firm and round her arm was from wrist to floury elbow.

"You didn't!"

Miranda stopped operations to look at him in wonder.

"Now, ain't that great! All that time! Why, the misshunery man said he 'spected to git home afore the Summer was over."

"He did get home," said Allan watching the sunshine on her hair as it shone through the window and thinking how dear and good her quaint speech sounded to him. "He got home in October and came right up to my cabin, but I wasn't there, I'd gone to Vancouver. I had a good chance to make a lot of money—I'll tell you all about it later when we have more time—so I went, and thought I'd probably get back in a week or so, but things went slick and I stayed till I'd got the thing through that I went for, and that wasn't till February. Then I had things in shape so I could work 'em from anywhere and I went back to my cabin; and there I found a note from Whitman saying he had a letter for me, at least he thought it was for me, from a friend in the East, and it was important.

"Well, I knew he must be mistaken, because there wasn't any way any of my friends could know where I was. But I took a great notion to Whitman one night when he stayed with me, and I wanted to see him again and hear all about his trip East in the Winter time. I knew he was back for the settlers in the Williamette had brought the news, but I wanted to see him and hear all about it from his own lips. So as soon as I could get my cabin straightened up a bit I went down to Waiilatpu to see him.

"He gave me a hearty welcome and hurried me right into the house. Then he left me for a minute, going into another room, but came back at once with your letter which he laid in my hand.

" 'Is that your letter?' he asked, and looked me through with his kind eyes. You know how sharp and pleasant they are, Randa. I looked at the letter and then I looked up into his face.

"It was a long time since I'd been afraid of anybody finding me away out there. At first, after I went away from home I used to start awake at night thinking old Mr. Heath was after me, and many's the time I've dodged around corners in New York to get away from people I thought looked at me suspiciously. But after I went out to Oregon and got used to the bigness of it all, and the farawayness of everything else, I sort of forgot that anybody could think they had a right to arrest me and shut me up away from the sky and the trees and the living creatures. I forgot there was such a thing as hanging, and I got strong and able to defend myself. Somehow when you've neighbored alongside of the wild things and the fierce beasts you don't get afraid of just men any more.

"But that morning, for a minute, when Whitman asked me if my name was Allan, and looked at me that way, it kind of came to me all suddenly, that he'd been East and maybe mentioned me, or heard some one say I'd killed a man. Then I looked up into his eyes and I knew I could trust him. I knew whatever he believed he'd not go back on me; and I determined to make a clean breast of it if I had to—not mentioning any names of course, for I hadn't protected poor Larry all these years just to go back on him now. And anyhow, I didn't seem much to care. I'd made some money, enough to be comfortable on, and yet life didn't look very interesting to me; just living on and making more money and hoarding it up with nobody to enjoy it with me. If I'd had a real home and a family it would have been different. I'd have cared then. But I couldn't ask any girl to marry me and have her find out some day that folks thought I was a murderer. And anyhow I hadn't seen any girl I wanted to marry. There weren't many out there and what there were I didn't train with. It just always seemed to me I'd kind of been left out of life somehow, and what was the use of living? At least, that's the way it seemed after I'd begun to succeed and didn't have to work so-dog-weary hard just to get food to keep me alive.

"So when I looked in Whitman's eyes I never turned away, nor flinched. I just owned up I was Allan Whitney all right, no matter what he knew. Then I waited to see how he would take it, but there didn't any severe look come in his face. Instead he just kind of smiled all through his eyes as if he were real glad, but he'd known it was so all along.

" 'Well, I just felt it in my bones you were,' he said, gripping hold of my hand real hard. 'And I'm mighty glad of it. You're good enough for her I guess, and she's one of the salt of the earth or I miss my guess. You're to be congratulated that you have a woman like that somewhere in the world that cares enough to hunt you up and write to you. She's a fine friend for anybody to have. Now read your letter!' And with that he went off and left me alone.

"You'd better believe I opened that letter pretty quick then for something told me there must be something wonderful in it, and when I looked at the name, 'Randa Griscom,' signed at the bottom just as you used to write it on your slate when you'd done your spelling lesson, I saw your little slender white neck again with the bright curl where the hair parted, and I saw your little straight shoulders braced stiff when the teacher called me up to the desk—and a great big longing swept over me to get right out on the trail and come back to you, Randa! And I've come. I started just as soon as I could fix up things so I wouldn't lose all I'd gained down at Vancouver, because I didn't want to come home penniless."

Miranda's comprehensive eye swept his fine new garments with a shy smile of pride, but she said nothing.

"I had to go back to Vancouver to see to some things, and when I finally got on my way I found one of the fellows in my train was sick and wasn't fit to travel fast. He hadn't let me know because he was afraid I wouldn't take him along, knowing I was in a hurry, and he was anxious to get home to his mother. Of course I couldn't leave him to come along alone behind—he wasn't fit to travel at all, really, and some days we just had to stay in camp if the weather wasn't good,—just on his account. At last when we got about a third of the way he broke down completely and was real downright sick, and we had to camp out and take care of him. Then the guide got ugly and went back on us; said he wouldn't go with us unless we went off and left the fellow with an Indian for his nurse and a few provisions but of course I couldn't do a thing like that—"

"Of course not!" snapped Miranda sympathetically.

"Well, it was some six weeks before we got under way again with the fellow on a sort of swinging bed between two horses, and then it was most two weeks before we could do more than crawl three or four miles a day. But he got a little strength after a bit, and we finally made out to reach the next fort.

"The rest of the party hurried on from there, but the poor fellow who'd been sick begged so hard for me not to leave him that I couldn't see my way clear to do it, so I put by for a couple of weeks more till he got real rested and we got together a guide, some more outfit, and a wagon, and started on again. The wagon was one some emigrants had left behind when they'd gone West, having been told they couldn't possibly get it over the mountains—fool nonsense by the way, plenty of wagons have been over now—but this one did us a good turn. It was hard going sometimes though, but we jogged on slowly, and at last got to St. Louis, where I left my man with his mother, the happiest soul I ever hope to see on this earth. I felt impatient a good many times at the long delay when I was in such a hurry to get back and see if you were really here yet, but I can't say I regretted getting that fellow to his mother alive. I tell you she was real glad to see him!"

Miranda, her eyes like two stars, her rolling pin in one hand and a velvety circle of dough in the other, came and stood before him.

"Oh, Allan, that was jest like you! Why, I couldn't no more think o' your goin' off on your own pleasurin' leavin' a poor dyin' weaklin' alone, then I c'd think o' God not lightin' the stars nights, an' lettin' His airth go dark. Why, it was jest that in you made me —"

Miranda stopped in confusion, and regardless of rolling pin and dough Allan wrapped her in his arms again, stooping and whispering in her ear: "Made you what, Randa?"

But Miranda would not tell, and presently the doughnuts in the frying fat cried out to be attended to, and Miranda flew back to her duty.

It was a long beautiful day. Sometime before late afternoon these two who took no note of time sat down to a delicious lunch together, cold biscuits, ham, apple pie, fresh doughnuts and milk; but they might as well have feasted on sawdust for all they knew how it tasted, they were so absorbed in one another.

They talked of all the years that were passed, and the experiences they had been through. Allan had actually gone abroad for a year and worked his way here and there seeing the sights in the old world. Miranda told him of the item she had heard read from the *Tribune*, and they smiled together over the littleness of the world after all. It appeared, too, that there were stars in Oregon whose friendly faithfulness had often cheered the exile from his home. Stars were queer things, knowing the secrets of the ages, looking down from a height so great that petty details were sublimated by the vastness of the comprehension, yet shining with such calm assurance that it would all be right in the end. These two had both felt it, only they didn't quite express it that way.

"I mostly waited till I got a glimpse of the stars when I got discombobulated," declared Miranda naively. "They, bein' up so high, an' so sot an' shiny, kinda seemed to steady me. They musta kinda seemt t' say, 'M'randy, M'randy! You jest never you mind. We ben up here hunderds an' hunderds o' years jest doin' our duty shinin' where we was put, an' we hed to shine jest th' same when 'twas stormin' an' no folks down thar c'd see us 'n appreciate us, an' when 'twas the darkest night we did our best shinin' 'cause folks could see us better then; an' M'randy, the things what makes you feel bad down thar ain't much more'n little thin storm clouds passin' over yer head, and pourin' down a few drops o' rain an' a stab er two o' lightnin' jest to kinda give yeh somepin' to think 'bout, so M'randy, don't you mind, you jest keep a shinin' an' they'll all pass by, an' some these days thur won't be no more storms 'tall. An' M'randy, you jest look out when thet time comes t' it finds you shinin'!' So, I get kinda set up agin, an' come downstairs next mornin' tryin' to shine my very shiniest, only my way o' shinin' was bakin' buckwheats an' sweepin' and puttin' up pickles and jells, an' that kinda thing—an' when I'd go back agin at night, hevin' shun my best, them stars would always kinda wink at me, an' say somepin'—Wanta know what they'd say? They say, 'M'randy, *you're a little brick*!' 'Member how you wrote that oncet fer me? Well—that's what they'd say. An' then nights when I hadn't done so good they'd jest put on a far-away, ain't-to-hum look, like they'd pulled their curtings down an' didn't want 'em pulled up that night."

"Strange," said Allan, musing and putting out a hand tenderly to touch the edge of the girl's rolled up sleeve. "The stars meant a lot to me too. Nights when I'd be out alone with my traps they seemed to kind of travel with me from place to place and somehow I fancied sometimes there were voices whispering around them, friendly voices—I used almost to think I was getting daffy. The voices seemed to speak about me as if they cared!"

"I reckon them was the prayers," said Miranda with a strangely softened look on her face, pausing in her wiping of a dish to look meditatively at him. "I prayed a lot. I do' kno's it done much good. I s'pose most of 'em didn't get much higher'n the stars ef they got that fur, an' there they stuck, but it done me good ennyhow, even ef God wouldn't care fer prayers sech ez mine. Landsakes!"

Miranda broke off suddenly and dropping her dishtowel began to roll down her sleeves. "Ef thar ain't my Mrs. Marcia an' Mr. David coming down the street an' you in the kitchen! Not a stroke done fer supper neither! What'll they think? Come, you'd best go in the parlor. They'll say I hedn't any manners to bring a gentleman like you into the kitchen."

But the guest arose in a panic.

"No, Randa, jest let me get my bag before they come in and I'll slip out the back door now. I don't want to see anybody yet. I'll come over right after supper and make a formal call. I must go home and see father and the children—now. Do you guess they'll be glad or sorry to see me?"

He strode through to the hall, seized his bag and made good his escape out the back door just as the front door was being opened by the householders, but Miranda slipped out after him into the evening dusk.

"Allan!" she called softly, and Allan stepped back to the door stone. "Allan, I forgot to tell yeh, did you know yer pa was married again?"

"Gosh! Is he? Who did he marry, Randa, anybody I know?"

"M'ria Bent," said Miranda, "she taught school after you left fer 'bout five years an' then she married him. Don't you r'member her?"

"Yes, Randa, I remember her," said Allan, making a wry face, "but I shan't trouble her if she doesn't trouble me. Good-bye, I'll be back this evening," and he caught her hand and pressed it tenderly.

Miranda hustled back into the kitchen and began a tremendous clatter among the pans, her cheeks as red as roses, just as Marcia came into the kitchen.

"So you got back a'ready!" she exclaimed in well feigned surprise. "Well, I got some belated, but I'll hev supper in three jerks of a lamb's tail now. I thought you wouldn't be hungry early, hevin' a big comp'ney dinner, like you always do up to Mis' Spaffordzes. Did you hev a good time?"

"Very pleasant," said Marcia gently, "and you,—were you lonely, Miranda?"

"Not pertick'ilarly," was Miranda's indifferent reply, with her head in the pantry. "I hed callers. Say, did you know Mis' Frisbee's goin' to give up tailorin' an' go'n live with her dotter over to Fundy? S'r' Ann says she told her so herself."

The inference was that Sarah Ann had been the caller.

"Why, no, I hadn't heard it," said Marcia carefully rolling her bonnet strings. "She'll be greatly missed by the people she's always sewed for. Did Sarah Ann say how Mrs. Waitstill was today?"

"No, she didn't say," answered Miranda after a moment's pause while she cut the cake. It did go against the grain for Miranda to deceive Mrs. Marcia, but this was an emergency and couldn't be helped.

CHAPTER 26

WHEN Allan Whitney dawned on the village there was a stir such as had not been seen since the Waitstill girls had brought a fine young Canadian officer to church and feted him for a week afterwards.

Allan Whitney, the town scapegrace, stealing forth from his smoke house prison in the thick of a winter's snow storm with the stigma of murderer upon him, and his own father's anathema added to that of the village fathers, was one person; this fine bronzed handsome gentleman attired in New York's latest fashion, walking with the free swing of one who had ranged the western vastnesses, haloed with the romance of the wild and unknown distance where heroes are bred, reconciled to his family, acquitted from all his past crimes, and spending money like a prince, was entirely another. The village fathers welcomed him, the village mothers feasted him, the village daughters courted him, and the village sons were jealous of him.

The young man had not been in the town twenty-four hours before the invitations began to pour in, and Maria Whitney held her head a full inch higher and prepared to take on reflected glory. There was only one bitter pill about it all. She had discovered that the house in which they lived was Allan's, willed to him by his own mother in case his father died before he did. If Maria survived her husband she could not hope to live in the stately old mansion and rule it as she chose. However, Allan's father was not dead yet, and it was worth while making friends with Allan. There was no telling what might happen to him out there in the wilds where he lived and seemed to intend to live.

The Waitstills were the first to make a tea party, as was becoming that they should, and they were closely followed by the Van Storms, the Rutherfords and all the other notables of the town.

For a couple of weeks Allan accepted these civilities amiably, taking them as a sign that the town was repenting for all its past misjudgment of himself. He went agreeably to all the tea parties, calmly unaware of the marked attention paid him by the ladies, and devoted himself to earnest conversation about Oregon with the men. But strange to say his indifference only made the ladies more assiduous in their attentions, and one evening after supper Allan suddenly awoke to the fact that he was surrounded by a circle of them and the one woman in all the world for him was not present. He turned his attention from Lyman Rutllerford's last remarks about the annexation of Texas and looked from one woman to another keenly, questioningly. Why was Miranda not among them? Now that he thought of it she had not been present at any gathering since his return. What was the meaning of it? Did they not know that she was his friend? But of course not. He must attend to letting them know at once. He would speak to Miranda about it the very next day.

In the morning early Allan was going, down the street to the post office as he had done every morning since his return home, for he had sent a very important letter to Washington and was daily expecting an answer. As he passed the Van Storm's, Cornelia Van Storm came radiantly out of the house door and joined him, gushing over the beauty of the morning and the happy chance (?) that made him her companion down the street. She professed to have deep interest in Oregon and to desire above all things to have more information concerning it. She asked numerous questions and Allan answered them briefly. He had keen memories of Cornelia Van Storm's snicker in the schoolroom years ago when he was called up for a whipping. Up to that time he had thought her pretty, but that snicker he had never forgiven, and not all her blandishments could cover her mistake of the past. In truth his mind was a little distraught, for he was sure he saw a slim, alert figure coming toward him up the street, and his whole attention was riveted upon it.

Miranda was returning in haste from an errand for Mrs. Marcia, for it was high time the bread was put in the pans, and if she delayed it would get too light. Miranda hated bread with big holes in it.

Allan watched her light footsteps, with their long, easy swing, and the spring of the whole little figure, his heart filling with pride that she loved him. The woman beside him had pink cheeks and blue eyes that languished on occasion—they were languishing now, but in vain—she wore handsome garments and cast ravishing glances at him, but it was as if a wall of iron rose between them, and he could only see Miranda.

A moment more and Miranda was passing them. Cornelia Van Storm looked up to get her reward for the compliment she had been giving, and saw her companion's eyes were not upon her. With vexation she looked to see who might be distracting his attention, and to her amazement saw only Miranda Griscom. She stiffened haughtily and flung an angry stare at Miranda, then turning back to Allan beheld him bowing most deferentially to her, "exactly as if she were a real lady," Cornelia declared to her mother on returning, "the impudent thing!"

Miranda was never one to be cowed by a situation. She smiled her merriest, and called out:

"Mornin'!"

But Cornelia only raised her chin a shade higher and her eyebrows arched haughtily. She paid not the slightest heed to the other woman and went on talking affectedly to Allan:

"It's been so pleasant, Mistah Whitney, hearing all about youah chosen country. I've enjoyed it immensely. I'd *love* to heah moah about it. Couldn't you come ovah this evening? Mothah would love to have you come to suppah, and then we two could have a nice cosy time aftahwahds talking ovah old times."

Her voice was loud and clear, intended for Miranda's ear.

"I'm afraid not, Miss Van Storm," said Allan curtly. "I—ah—shall be very busy this evening. Good morning, I must step in here and see Mr. Spafford," and Allan abruptly left her, pausing, however on the steps of the newspaper office to look down the street after Miranda, an act which was not lost on the observing Cornelia.

"The idea!" she said indignantly to her mother afterwards. "The very idea of his looking after *her*. It was odious!"

But Allan was getting his eyes open. He remained in the office only a moment, not even waiting to find out if David was there, and then forgetting his important letter, he went back down the street after Miranda.

She was not in sight any more. Wings had taken her feet, and she was in the kitchen thumping away at her batch of dough, kneading it as if she had all the Van Storms and Rutherfords and Waitstills and the rest of the female population of the town done up in the mass and was having her way with them, while down her cheeks rolled tears of bitterness and humiliation, so that she had to turn her face away from her work, and wipe it on her sleeve to keep them from dropping on her work. Then the overwhelming hurt came upon her so forcefully, that, secure in the fact that Marcia was upstairs sewing and the children were off at school, she turned and hid her face in her crossed arms and sobbed.

Allan was wise enough not to go to the front door and rouse the house. He went straight to the kitchen, and lifting the latch half dubiously, peered in; then strode across the threshold and folded the sobbing woman in his arms.

"Randa," he said. "Randa, tell me why she did that and why you haven't been asked to any of the parties? I've looked for you every time and you neve came." But Miranda only sobbed the harder.

"Randa," he kept on tenderly, "dear little girl, don't cry Randa! Why are you crying?"

"I ain't," sobbed Miranda trying to draw away from him, her head still hidden in her arms, her voice all trembly and unlike her, "I guess what broke me up was jest seein' the truth all sudden like when I be havin' sech a lovely dream. Don't Allan, you mustn't put yer arms round me, it ain't the right thin'. You'd oughta go court one o' them other girls what'd give their eye teeth to git yeh. You kin git anybody in town now, an' I see it. I ain't fit fer yeh. I'm jes M'randy Griscom, an' nobody thinks I'm any 'count. You'r a fine gentleman, an' you ought to hev somebody thet is like yeh. You ben real kind an' good teh me, but you hedn't seen them others when you fust come home, an' it stan's to reason you'd like 'em better'n me. It's all right, an' I want you to know I don't grudge yeh, only it come on me kinda suddent, me not ever havin' hed anythin' lovin' in my life afore. I'd oughta hed better sense n't 'a let yeh think I was any 'count, I—"

But a big gentle hand softly covered her trembling lips that were bravely trying to send him away; and Allan's face came down close to her wet burning cheeks.

"Little girl—Randa—darling, don't you know I *love you*?" he said. "What'd you think I came three thousand miles for? Just to be invited to Waitstill's to supper, and walk simpering down the street with that smirking Cornelia Van Storm? Why, Randa, she can't hold a candle to you,—they can't any of them. You're just the only woman in all the world for me. If I can't have you I'll go back to Oregon and live in my log cabin all alone. I'll sit by my fire nights and think about how you wouldn't have me, and what it would have been if you would. But there's nobody else for me, for Randa, you're all the world to me! As for the rest of this hanged old town, if they can't appreciate you I've no use for them, and I'll not go to another one of their stiff old parties unless they invite you. Why, Randa, I love you, and I'm going to have our banns published next Sunday! We'll just be married right away and show 'em where we stand."

But at that Miranda rose up in her might and protested, the tears and smiles chasing each other down her cheeks. Indeed she couldn't be married yet, she hadn't her things ready, and she couldn't and wouldn't be married without being ready. Neither would she have him tell the community yet. If he felt that way she was content. Let them keep their secret a little longer, and not have the whole town staring and gossiping.

He held her in his arms and kissed the tears away, bringing out the dimples; then he made her sit down and tell him just what she would do. He must go back in the spring at the latest, for he had promised Dr. Whitman he would come with answers from the government at Washington, and also to accompany and advise some more emigrants who were going to Oregon. Would she go with him?

This question happily settled, they came to their senses after a time, and Miranda went on with her kneading, while Allan hurried after his belated mail.

Miranda began that very night to work at her trousseau, and before she slept she broke the news of her engagement to Marcia, who laughed and cried over her, and then set to work to help her in earnest; the while sorrowfully contemplating a future without her.

Allan went to Washington the very next day on diplomatic business for Oregon, not knowing how long he must stay, but promising to return soon.

In truth he did not come back until the middle of March except for a few days at Christmas, which he spent mainly at the Spafford home; and it was rumored through the town that he and David Spafford were working together for some mysterious political affairs pertaining to annexation. The girls admired Allan all the more because of his abstracted manner and distant ways, and strove the harder to gain his attention; but none of them, not even the keen-eyed Cornelia, suspected that the main part of his visit was not in the Spafford library with David, but in the dining room with Miranda; whose strong sense of the fitness of things would not permit her to take possession of any higher room in the house than the dining room.

In those days Miranda sang about her work like a bird and day by day grew younger and more beautiful. Her eyes shone like the stars that had taught her so many years; her cheeks were pink and white like the little blush roses that grew around the front stoop trellis. She set fine stitches in her garments, finished a wonderful quilt she was piecing, and dreamed her beautiful dreams. Whenever she went about the village and met any of the girls who were interested in Allan, she looked at them half pityingly. No more did their haughty ways and silly airs about him hurt her. She knew in her heart that he was hers, by all the rights of God and man. He had loved her long as she had loved him, and he wanted no other. She could afford to pity and be kind.

So she answered their questions about him, they little thinking that they were talking to his future wife.

"Yes, Mr. Whitney's goin' back t' Oregon," she told a group of them at the apple paring, when they gathered around her to ply her with questions, while they let her do the most of the work. "I herd 'im say he couldn't stay away from thar very long. He misses th' animals an' Injuns a lot. Gettin' use t'em thet way makes it hard yeh know. It's real good of you all to be so kinda nice to him now when he went away from here in disgrace. I was thinkin' thet over t' myse'f th' other night, an' I sez to myse'f, 'M'randy, jest see what a diffrunce!' Why, I kin remember when Allan Whitney wasn't thought much of in this town. He was shut up in my gran'pa's smoke-house fer murder, an' everybody couldn't say too much agin 'im, an' now here he comes back, hevin' travelled, an' made a lot o' money, and fit ba'rs an' coyotties, an' wil' cats an' things, an' ev'ybody's ez nice ez pie an' ready to fergive 'im. It does beat all what a diffrunce a bit o' money makes, an' a han'some face. He's the same Allan Whitney, why didn't you make a fuss over him afore?"

"Mirandy Griscom, I think you're perfectly dreadful, mentioning things like that about a respectable young man; bringing up things he did when he was a child, and horribly exaggerating them anyway. They didn't shut him up for murder at all, they only arrested him because he had a gun and they wanted to find out where he got it and trace the murderer."

"Well, now, *is thet* so?" said Miranda innocently. "Why ain't it real strange I ain't never heard thet afore? Me livin' in Gran'pa's house all thet time too. Well, now, I'm pleased to know it. H'm! Well, beats all what time will do. There might be some more things come out some day, who knows. C'r'neelyah, ain't yeh cuttin' them apples pretty thick?"

"Cut them yourself then," said Cornelia vexedly, throwing down her knife. "I'm sure such work never was very agreeable to me anyway. I suppose you've had more experience."

"P'raps I hev," said Miranda cheerfully.

"But I advise you," snapped Cornelia as she turned away, "not to talk about things you don't know anything about, or you'll get into trouble. It's never wise to talk about things you're not acquainted with."

"No," said Miranda, "thet's a fact, it ain't! I wouldn't ef I was you."

"What do you mean?"

"Oh, nothin'," said Miranda. "don't git riled. P'raps you'll onderstand one o' these days."

The matter that detained Allan Whitney in Washington had to do with the passage of a bill in behalf of Oregon, and his quiet vigilance and convincing words did much to further the interests of Oregon.

It did him good to be in touch with things at their fountain-head. His heart thrilled when he met great men, recognizing the things they stood for, and the questions that were going to stir the country in the coming years. He felt also deep hope for his own adopted territory in the far West, and his young, strong enthusiasm moved many great minds to look into matters and to put the weight of their influence on his side.

Letters passed between him and Miranda, many and often, but by reason of the precaution the lovers took to send all their letters enclosed to or from David Spafford, no word of the correspondence leaked out, though the postmistress knew the affairs of the neighborhood. Miranda had a shrinking from having her sweet secret bandied about the town, which had given both herself and Allan such rough handling and unkind judgment; and Allan understood and agreed with her.

They were not always long letters, for the two writers were more than busy, but they were wonderful in a way, for they breathed a deep and abiding confidence in one another, and a wide revealing each of his own soul for the other to see; and thus they grew to know one another better, and to bridge the years of their separation by a knowledge of each other in preparation for the long road they hoped to travel together.

The very day before Allan came back finally from Washington a wonderful event came to pass, in which both for its own sake, and because Dr. Whitman and David Spafford were so enthusiastic about it, Allan took deep interest. This event was the flashing of the first message sent by Professor Morse's electric telegraph on the new test line that had just been completed from Baltimore to Washington. Allan always counted himself most fortunate to have been among those who witnessed the sending of that first message, "What hath God wrought," over the wires, and when he returned he had a great story to tell to those who gathered that night around David Spafford's supper table.

Nathan was there, home from college for a few days, and sitting at the feet of his elder brother with worshipful eyes, listening to the wonders of his experiences. Miranda, bringing in hot muffins as fast as the plate was emptied, listened too, and her heart swelled with pride that Allan had been present at that great event, taking his place in the world of great men, higher than her highest dreams for him.

Grandfather Heath dropped in to bring David a town report that had to be published in the paper, and listened to the account. He set his ugly, stubborn lip that had objected to every new thing under heaven ever since he was born, and fixed his cold eye on Allan while he talked. When Allan at last looked up he faced the same glitter of two steely orbs that had met him that night so many years ago when he had shouldered the gun of a murderer to save him for his mother's sake. It was all there just the same, Phariseeism, blindness, unreasonableness and stolid stubbornness. Grandfather Heath had not changed an iota through the years and would not on this side the grave. He had fought every improvement since he was old enough to fight and would with his dying breath.

"H'm!" he said to Allan's final sentence. "How did yeh *know* they *wa'n't foolin'* yeh? As fur as I'm consarned I *don't believe* no sech fool nonsense, an' ef *'twas* true it would be mighty dangerous an' a mighty *blasphemous* undertakin' to persume to use the lightnin' fer writin' messages. You don't ketch me hevin' anythin' to do with sech goin's on. I say let well 'nough alone, thet's what I say. Writin' letters is good enough fer me. Better take my 'dvice an' not fool with the lightnin'; besides, you'll find out ther ain't nothin' in it. It's all a big swindle to git money out of folks, an' you'll find it out some day to yer sorrow. I never git took in by them things. Wal, goodnight."

Allan had much to say to David that night, of all that had befallen him in Washington and all he had been able to do for Oregon; and when Miranda had finished the dishes she brought her sewing, and sat shyly down at Marcia's request in the library.

But presently Rose went upstairs to bed, and Marcia went to see if young David's hoarseness was better, and in a few minutes David the father made an excuse to go out so that Allan and Miranda were left alone Then Allan turned to Miranda with a smile and said:

"Well, Randa, my work is done, and now how soon will you be ready to take the trail with me?"

CHAPTER 27

VERY decorously they walked to church next morning, Miranda with Marcia, David and Allan just behind, Rose with her young brother bringing up the rear.

Nobody thought much of it when they all filed into the Spafford pew, though it would have been more according to common custom if Allan had sat in his father's seat. Everybody knew of Allan's friendship and somewhat mysterious business relations with David. No one thought anything at all of Miranda, except, perhaps, Cornelia Van Storm.

It was David who managed that Allan should go into the seat next to Miranda, and Marcia should sit next to himself.

The service went on as usual, until toward the close, when the minister stood up and published the banns of Miss Miranda Griscom and Mr. Allan Whitney.

A stillness and astonishment that could be felt swept over the congregation in its decorous closing stir. The women who had been fastening their fur collars around their necks paused in the act; the small children whose hoods and coats had been quietly applied were suddenly left to their own devices, while all eyes were fixed upon the minister, and then furtively turned toward the Spafford pew where sat Miranda inwardly trembling but outwardly calm. Her face was as sweet and demure with its long down-drooped lashes as any bride-to-be could desire. Her white, soft neck showed beneath the cape of her green silk bonnet, and one small ruddy curl just glimpsed below willfully. Her hands were folded over her handkerchief, and her cheeks were very pink.

Allan sat tall and proud beside her. Just when the strain of the silence in the church was at its tensest he looked down at Miranda and smiled tenderly, and she by some occult power was drawn to look up with starry eyes and smile back the most lovely smile that woman's face could wear, full of adoring trust, and selflessness but with a kind of power of self-reliance, and strength to suffer too, if need be, yet be glad.

As their eyes met a kind of glory came into their faces, and all the congregation looking on saw and were profoundly moved, even in the midst of the astonishment and disapproval.

It was only a flash, passed in an instant of time, and neither of the actors in the little scene was aware that they had plighted their troth in the eyes of the world and given a sacred vision of their love that had stirred hearts to their depths. Such brief fleeting visions of what life and love may be, are little glimpsings into what heaven is and earth might become, if only hearts were pure and purged from selfishness.

Grandmother Heath saw, and remembered her own wooing, with a strange forgotten thrill; recalled the look on the face of Miranda's mother when she married "that scallawag of a Griscom," and felt a sudden pang for her own harshness toward her suffering child. For the first time since the baby Miranda was placed in her unloving arms she saw a beauty and a nobleness in her, for gratified pride had done for her what natural affection had never done. Grandmother Heath was unmitigatedly pleased. She had never thought Miranda would marry at all, and here she had surprised them all and taken a prize. The Whitney family was an old and wealthy one, and this Allan had wiped out old scores and made himself not only respected but highly approved and quite run after by the whole village. Grandmother Heath drew a long breath and swelled up satisfiedly in her pew.

Hannah Heath dropped her pretty lower lip in almost childish amazement for a moment, then preened herself and tried to look as if she had known of the engagement for years, and was enjoying the surprise of everybody now.

Cornelia Van Storm, her admiring eyes glued to Allan's handsome shoulders during the whole service, had the full benefit of the smile that passed between the lovers, and cast angry, jealous eyes at Miranda, biting her lips to keep back the mortified tears. Yet she knew in her heart that the love between those two was unusual, and that there was little likelihood that any man would ever look at her like that. It was a revelation to poor spoiled Cornelia, both of her own selfish heart, incapable of loving anybody as Miranda did; and of the fact that there was such love in the world.

Nathan Whitney, senior, at the end of his pew across the aisle, beside his sharp, unpleasant wife, lifted his expressionless countenance like a metal mask that had no power to show the inner man, and with his cold eyes saw the delicate face of Miranda gloried with that smile. No one could have told what he was thinking as he dropped his gaze emotionlessly, and meditated on the irony of a fate that gave the prize he so much coveted to his own son.

But to Maria, his wife, no kindly mask was given to veil her chagrin from prying eyes. Maria had always been jealous and scornful of Miranda, for she had learned of her husband's attentions before his marriage to herself, and had been mortified that she had been a second choice with such a rival as Miranda Griscom. She despised Miranda for her father's sake and because she occupied the position of helper in David Spafford's home. Maria could not conceal her vexation. The appalling fact that if her husband died she might have to contend with Miranda for the home she now occupied, confronted her, and she had never been an adept at self-control. She felt that her only revenge lay in letting Miranda see that she resented her boldness in setting up to be good enough for Allan.

However, for the most part the congregation, when they recovered from their first astonishment, made out to realize that the match was a good one from both sides, although so unexpected. At the church door they crowded around to congratulate the two, expressing their astonishment in hushed Sabbath tones.

It was almost pitiful to see the pride with which Grandmother Heath and Hannah pressed complacently up to share in the glory of the occasion. Miranda took her grandmother's newly developed affection gently, as if love were too precious a thing to be scorned, even when it came too late; but her old mischievousness returned upon her when she saw Hannah, and she could not forbear calling out clearly, so that those around could hear:

"Mornin', Hannah, kinda took you by s'prise, didn't I?"

Then with a smile at the discomfited Hannah, and a sly wink at Nathan, who stood grinning appreciatively by with Rose, she took Allan's arm and walked proudly-humble down the street, her time of recognition come at last. Yet it had not brought the triumphant elation she had expected, only deep, deep joy.

Grandmother Heath did not stop at anything when she got started, and during the next two weeks Marcia thought she understood where Miranda got her tendency to stretch the truth upon occasion. For somehow Grandmother Heath gave out the impression that her "beloved Granddaughter Miranda" was going as a missionary, and she actually set the missionary society to sewing on that quilt that Miranda had suggested for the Indians, only the quilt was now destined for Miranda instead of the Indians.

There were many extra sessions of the missionary society in the houses of the different members, and the interest in the North American Indians grew visibly. An actual missionary in their midst was a wonderful incentive.

When Marcia heard that Miranda was supposed to be going as a missionary she tried pleasantly to make plain that this was a mistake, but was met with such indignant replies on every hand that she refrained from further enlightenment. After all, what was the harm in their thinking so, when old Mrs. Heath seemed so set on it? Miranda would undoubtedly be a missionary wherever she went, though not perhaps the kind the American Board usually sent out.

When Miranda heard of it she sat down weakly in the big rocking chair and laughed till she cried.

"Oh, Mrs. Marcia! Now ain't that the very funniest you ever heard tell 'bout! Me teachin' the Injuns! Golly! I never thought they'd think I was even good enough to be scalped by a Injun. *Ain't* that the very funniest you ever heard? And *Gran'ma!* did you ever see the beat of her? She'll be havin' horse flesh on the dinner table next, jest to kinda get uset to bein' related to a misshunery! Golly! I never thought I'd git thar! A misshunery! Wal, I *am* beat!"

Both Miranda and Allan wished to have the wedding a very quiet affair, for they had planned to take the stage coach immediately, as soon as the ceremony was over, and cut across the country to join the emigration party. Allan had already arranged for their outfit and had everything in readiness for their comfort on the way.

But when the missionary idea took hold of the town there was no having things quiet. The people had determined to make as much of the occasion as possible. So there was a large wedding and by reason of the interest the missionary society took in the affair, the suggestion was made that the ceremony be in the church.

When this idea was first suggested to Miranda she looked startled and then a sudden softened glory grew in her eyes. Wasn't it just like the God of the stars to lend her His house to be married in when she hadn't any earthly father's house of her own? And then, it sort of seemed to set the seal of respectability and forgiveness on her and Allan, and sanctify their union,—they two who had been so long left outside the pale as it were. And so it was arranged.

Maria Bent did not like it, it took all the glory away from her, whose school-house wedding was still talked of in the annals of the village gossip.

Some of the girls who had been ignored by Allan Whitney did not like it. They said they did not see what right Miranda Griscom had to be married in the church just because she was going to be a missionary; and Cornelia Van Storm tossed her head and put in with:

"You know she isn't really a missionary. That's all poppycock! Allan Whitney is nothing but a common fur trader after all."

It was a beautiful, solemn, simple wedding. The wedding breakfast was prepared by the bride herself and eaten by the relatives and intimate friends of both families at high noon. They went away early so that the bride might have plenty of time to get ready for the journey. Then, late in the afternoon, when the Spring shadows were beginning to lengthen on the new grass, and the fresh young leaves on the trees to wave their yellow greenery sleepily as if they were tired of the day, they heard the silvery sound of the horn, and saw the old red stage coming down the street.

Miranda was all ready, seated on the front stoop with her bandbox beside her, but the last minute was all confusion after all, for Allan and the children rushed back into the house for something that had been forgotten, and Miranda, everything done that could be done, turned and looked back at the house that had been her dear home for so many years, finding unexpected tears in her eyes and throat. Then, before she could realize what was happening, she found herself enfolded in Marcia's arms, and Marcia was kissing her and whispering in her ear:

"Oh, Miranda, Miranda! My dear, dear sister! How ever am I going to do without you!"

Then indeed did Miranda give way and cry on Marcia's shoulder for the space of half a second.

"I guess it's me'll be askin' thet about you, many times," she sniffed, trying to straighten up and smile as Allan came hurrying down the steps with David, and the children rushing behind, their hands full of violets they had picked for her to take along.

Then they all said goodbye again, the horn sounded, and they were seated in the old stage, Miranda and Allan, riding off together out into the great world of life.

Everywhere along the way were friendly faces, waving handkerchiefs, and cheery words of well wishing. There was Grandmother Heath at her gate, actually a smile on her wrinkled old face, and Grandfather Heath at the door behind her waving a stiff old hand.

"Seems like't was jest some fool dream I was dreamin' an' I'd wake up purty soon an' find 'twasn't me 'tall," whispered Miranda through the happy tears.

"No, it's a blessed reality," reassured Allan in a low tone so that their fellow travellers could not hear.

Then they went around the curve and down the hill on the old corduroy road and were lost to the sight of the village.

CHAPTER 28

A FEW days later, out on the trail they started; quite a company of them, men, women, and children, with Allan as captain of the party, and Miranda,—her new role of missionary already begun,—as comforter-in-chief to all of them.

The tears were all forgotten now in the joy that had dawned upon her. To love and to be loved, to be with her beloved all the time, to be able to plan and look ahead to their home together, that was happiness enough for Miranda. The journey, hard and laborious to some, was one grand, continuous picnic to her. Not much of play had come to her childhood, save as she stole it by the way and suffered for it afterwards in hard words, cold looks and deprivations. The fun she had wrenched from life had been of her own manufacture. The flowers, the birds, the trees she loved had often been too far away from duty for her to enjoy, and the adventures she had experienced had all been in rescuing those she loved from unhappiness.

But now all this was changed.

Here was sky wide and limitless. Here were trees in profusion and birds in the poetry of their existence setting up new homes on every hand, lofty branch or humble bushes. Here were carpets of bloom in their passing. Here were rivers deep and wide and difficult to be forded with all the excitement and delight that any child could wish.

Miranda did not shrink from the crossings, no matter what the peril. She rode her horse like a man, on occasion, and scorned the wagons if she might ride by her husband's side. To ride and swim her horse across a river became one of her great ambitions. For Miranda had returned to her childhood and was sipping all the innocent delights and excitements her untamed nature craved. And Allan was proud of her.

Like two children they rode together, taking the perils and the hardships. Never once did Miranda's heart turn back with longing to the East. She was a true pioneer and looked forward with joy to the cabin in the clearing. What need had she to be homesick? She had her beloved with her, and the same stars were overhead. She carried her home where she went. Behind her in the wagon and on the pack mules were her treasures—

gifts of the dear ones at home; and not the least among them was a bundle of quilts wrought in many colors and curious designs; one highly prized from the missionary society was curiously fashioned in flaming red and yellow in the famous rising sun pattern. But the one she loved the best was pink and white in wild rose pattern, with many prickings of the finger, the work of little Rose Spafford's childish days.

At night, as often as she could, she slept in the open, and lay long looking up at the starry dome above her, murmuring softly now and then, with folded hands and reverent look. "Thanks be! Thanks be! Thanks be!"

Slowly the days and weeks crept by, and the caravan wound its difficult snail-like way along the trail. Sickness came to some, weariness and weakness. Buffaloes were not found as soon as hoped and the provisions grew short; so that hunger stalked beside them in the way. Rivers were swollen and disputed their passing; untimely snow storms overtook them in the mountains; wagons broke down and had to be mended or abandoned; Indians with hostile men appeared and shadowed them for a distance; death even entered their ranks and took a little child and its mother; discouragements were flung at them by unfriendly ones along the way; yet never in all the long weeks did Miranda lose courage or grow faint-hearted. She was riding upon the high places of the earth and she knew it and was glad.

She was writing a letter to send home to Marcia, a long diary letter such as Marcia had suggested. It would not be finished till she reached her destination, and it might not get back home for a year or two, there was no telling, but it gave Miranda a cheery, happy feeling around her heart to write it, as if she were looking in upon the dear ones at home for a little while.

That letter was worth reading. It reached Marcia almost a year and a half from the day of the wedding, and brought tears and smiles and much delight to all who read it. It was so absolutely Mirandaish.

"Dear Mrs. Marcia in pertickiler, an' Mr. David ef he cares, an' o' course Rose, an' little Davy; an' then anybody else you want.

"Wal, we're started, an' you'd laugh to kill ef you could see us. A long line o' wagguns with white piller cases over 'em, looks fer all the world like a big washday hung out to dry. I wouldn't ride inside one of 'em fer anythin', but I s'pose they're all right fer them as likes 'em. I don't think much of the women in this set. They don't hev much manners ur else they got too much, an' ain't got no strength. You gotta hev a pretty good mixture of manners an' strength ef you want to git on in this world. There's one real pretty little thin' she's mos' cried her eyes out a'ready. I donno what she come fer, n' else she hed to, her husband's so sot on goin'. An' a lot of 'em jerk they're chil'ren roun' like they was a bag o' meal. Poor little souls! I'm doin' what I kin to make up fer it. I'm dretful glad you put in all them sugar plums. They come in handy now. I don't guess the Injun's'll hev many lef' when I git thar.

"We passed a river this mornin', great shinin' thin' like a silver ribbon windin' round amongst the green valley. God musta hed a good time makin' thin's. I sensed it some today when I was lookin' at thet river, an' thet valley all laying there so pretty. Seemed he must a felt most like I do when I'd git a hull row o' pies an' cakes an' thin's made fer the minister's donation party, plum, an' mince, an' punkin', an' apple, an' custard, an' fruit, real black, an' a big fine marble cake! D'you s'pose it cud seem thet' way t' Him? . . . We crossed a river with quicksands yesterday, an' hed to lock the wagguns together with chains. Dr. Whitman taught 'em how to do it, they say. He's a great man. You'd oughta see us, it's real enterestin'. I'll tell you how it is. Every night there's five men on guard and five more 'n th' day time. At night the wagguns is ranged in a round circle, an' the mules an' horses tied inside, Early mornin' they let 'em outside awhile to feed. Then they hev to be cotched an' saddled. It takes a while. Every man hes so many things to do, an' knows his work. They hev to put on a powder flask, an' knife in their belt an' their gun afore 'em when they start each day. Oncet we rode nine hours without stoppin'. We gen'aly take two hours noonin', turn out the animals, get dinner, wash dishes an' thet like. At night we pitch tents, spread buffalo skins on the ground, then oilcloth fer a floor, an' fix yur thin's around out o' the hay, leavin' a place in the middle to eat. Thur was some Injuns came around and most o' the wimmen got scared. I didn't see much to 'em to be scared 'bout. They look dirty to me, an' don't hev nouf cloes to their backs...."

The letter went on to tell the daily occurrences of the way, noting the places, and the incidents, and one notable extract touched Marcia's heart more than all the rest:

"Wal, we come to a mounting this mornin', a real live mounting! It's thar yet right in front o' me. I got my dishes all washed an' I'm restin' an' lookin' at it by spells. You don't never need to go eny further to wonder, ef you oncet see a mounting. It's the biggest, comfortablest, settledest thin' you ever could a 'thought of. It jest sets right thar, never stirs, never seems to mind what happens round it, ur what goes over it; can't disturb him, he's a mounting! Might cut down all his forests, he wouldn't care, he'd grow some more. Might walk over him all day'n annoy him a lot, he jest sets thar an' looks up, an' by an' by all them thet annoys passes on an' *thars the mounting yit* jes' same, and he knew 'twould be so, 'cause he's a mounting. He can't die. They can't nobody move him, he's too big. 'Cept mebbe God might. But God made him, so he don't care 'bout thet, 'cause ef God could make him God wouldn't spoil him, 'n ef He moved him He'd jest put him in a better place, so what's thet? Men might cut a hole in him, but 'twould take s'long, an' be s'little 'twouldn't 'mount to much. Mounting's thar jes' same. He's a mounting, an' he looks like he knowed it, an' yet 'tain't huht him none, he's jes' es kind 'n consid'rate, 'n comf't'ble,—'n, yes,—real purty like, all soft fringes of trees at the bottom, and all sharp points, ur white frostin' of snow up top 'gainst the sky; shinin' silver in the mornin' an' the moon, towerin' up over yeh kinda big, an' growin' soft an' purpley with a wreath o' haze round his feet at night. He's a mounting! An' God musta been real pleased when He got him done. He musta been most best pleased of all when He made a mounting. I'm real glad He made 'em, and glad I lived to see one. When you come you must come this way, an' see my mounting. They say thur's goin' to be some more 'fore we git through, but I don't b'leeve none of 'em'll be so pretty as this."

The rest of the letter told of the further experiences and the homecoming, first to Waiilatpu, where they were welcomed with open arms by the missionaries, and kept and rested a while; and then to the cabin where they had a beautiful time beginning to keep house, and here Miranda's descriptions of the house and her attempts to fix it up to her mind were laughable.

Marcia, after they had enjoyed the letter thoroughly at home, took it with her in her pocket wherever she went, and let Miranda's many friends enjoy it also. She carried it first with her when David took them out on a drive, Marcia on the back seat with her daughter Rose, who was grown suddenly into young womanhood and young David with his father in the front of the carryall.

They drove straight to the house of Hannah Skinner, where Grandma Heath had come to live, after the sudden death of old Mr. Heath, which occurred a few weeks after Miranda left home.

Hannah and the old lady, both pleased at the sight of the Spafford carriage at their door, came out to welcome their guests, the cat following amiably behind.

"I've got a letter from Miranda and I thought you'd like to read it," said Marcia, leaning out of the carriage and smiling.

The old lady's face brightened.

"A letter from M'randy! Now you don't say. Well, ain't thet real interestin'? How does she git on missunaryin'? Seems sorta like gettin' word from another world, don't it? Do get out and come in."

And so the letter was read to the two women who listened in great wonder, and boasted around for many a day with "M'randy says this" an' "My Cousin M'randy says so and so," until the village smiled and wondered, and Miranda's record of discreditable scrapes was all forgotten under the halo of a missionary.

In due time the letter travelled to Nathan at college firing him with a deep desire to go out West, and when he came home in the Spring he was full of it, till finally David said:

"Well, my boy, go try it. Allan said it would do you good and you could earn something out there. We'll see if there are some people going, and you go out for a year or two and then come back and finish your college course. A rest and a little touch of nature will do you good."

As suddenly as that it came, and a few weeks later, Nathan bade them all an excited, happy farewell, and started out into the great far country also.

Rose, like a sweet, frightened flower, looked after the coach that bore him away, and fled to the window in Miranda's room, to stay alone until night fell and the stars came out to comfort her and help her understand.

Poor little Rose with your astonished feet taking the first steps into the path of sorrow and loss! How long the way lies before you beaten hard by many feet, yet you, too, will one day reach the higher ground and see your mountain!

CHAPTER 29

FOR every big bridge built or massive building reared many stones must lie under ground. No marvelous work is accomplished without destruction and sacrifice, and the greatest movements are often those baptized with blood.

Slowly, stealthily, out of the West there arose a menacing cloud. Shadowy it was at first, like a mote that one tries to brush away from a tired eye, still floating and insisting upon being seen.

Low stirrings in the grass, and sounds like the hiss of some moving, poisonous serpent; forms phantom-like and vanishing when search is made—gone, always gone, when you look—yet there, convincingly there, but elusive; stealthy footsteps in the night; prying, peering, breathless; these things were in the very atmosphere.

There had been a growing uneasiness among the Indians ever since Dr. Whitman's return with the emigrants. An enemy was at work, that was plain to be seen. Strange rumors were abroad; silent, subtle impressions, averted glances, muttered gutturals.

Still, Whitman and his workers went steadily on, omitting no one of their arduous tasks, not hesitating to visit the sick among known enemies, withholding no kindness even from the stolid and ungrateful.

Several times contagious diseases raged among the Indians with fearful fatality. The missionaries were faithful and indefatigable, giving themselves night and day with medicine and nursing to save as many as possible.

Finally an epidemic of measles broke out among them, sweeping away large numbers.

Frantic and fearful they sent for the missionary doctor, though they often omitted to follow directions afterward, or sent for their own medicine man with his incantations and weird ceremonies. Death stalked among them and the story went forth, from what source who could quite be sure?—that the missionary was poisoning them to clear the country of Indians and take their lands for the white people.

The faint cloud on the horizon now grew large and dark with portent. Ominous thunders threatened in the distance, drawing nearer and more certain. The mission knew its peril. Dr. Whitman was thoroughly convinced that a plot to murder the missionaries was nearly completed, yet he kept steadily on with his work. Day after day he told his wife and friends all that he saw and what the appearances led him to fear. Carefully and prayerfully he walked, with the light of another world on his face, knowing not at what moment he would be called away from this.

He visited the Indian camp, on the Umatilla River; called on the Bishop and the vicar general who had just arrived at the place, and had brief interviews; then rode out to where a fellow missionary was encamped, reaching there about sunset. They talked the situation over calmly, discussing the possibilities and probabilities.

"My death may do as much good to Oregon as my life can do," said the man who had crossed the Rockies and a continent in midwinter to save Oregon.

Though weary and worn, he did not stay to rest, for there was severe sickness at his home, and he started late that night on his lonely ride of forty miles back to the mission, reaching there at dawn. Then a hurried interview with his wife, a few words and tears of tenderness, cut short by calls to attend the sick.

"Greater love hath no man than this, that a man lay down his life!"

Ever had this man taken the lead in all the hard things; sacrificing, never thinking of himself; plunging into the icy river first; not asking others to go where he was unwilling to lead;—like his Master whom he served.

It was as if God would not take from him the eternal right of leadership, for which he had formed him and called him; and so arranged that even in death he should still lead.

While the sun was shining high in the heavens, stealthily, like evil shadows, the Indians gathered around the mission that once had been a happy home, and where the work was still going steadily on as if no menace in the air were felt.

Suddenly the shadows sprang from covert hiding on every side! Evil faces, stealthy steppings, flashing knives, and the deed was done! Dr. Whitman was the first to fall, a tomahawk plunged twice into his head; then the carnage began, and continued for eight days.

The first news was brought to Miranda as she stood at her cabin door watching for Allan.

He did not come with his usual cheery whistle, but striding into the clearing with deep sorrow in his eyes, and an ominous look of threatening about his mouth. His wife knew at once that something terrible had happened.

"Is it them pesky Injuns?" she asked in a voice she had taught to be low and guarded. "Drat 'em! They's ben two of 'em round the house this very mornin', an' they looked like they was up to som'pin'. What hev they ben doin'?"

"They have killed Dr. Whitman!"

"In the name o' sense what'd they do thet fur? Did they want to bite their own nose off to spite their face? How they goin' to live 'thout him? Ain't he ben doin' an' doin' an' doin' himself jest to death fer 'em? The lazy, miserable, no-count, naked creeters! I know they ain't much but naughty childern, but ain't they got no sense at all? Kill Dr. Whitman!"

"It was not their fault. Their minds have been poisoned by the enemy—"

"I know," broke in Miranda as if that didn't matter in the least, "but ennyhow I never could stomick them pesky Injuns, misshunery ur no misshunery. Kill Dr. Whitman! 'Z if they *could* kill him! *Tomy*hawks couldn't do thet! *Men* couldn't do thet! Why, a man like thet'll live ferever, yeh *can't stop him*! He ain't ben jest a livin' body, he's a livin' soul! He'll go on livin' long 'z the world stan's, 'n longer! He'll live ferever! He's like a mounting! Can't tech him! Kill *him*? Wal, I guess not!"

Miranda whirled her back abruptly round and let the tears course down her cheeks. But in an instant she had herself in hand and turned back, her face wet, her eyes snapping fire.

"Wal, what we goin' to do 'bout it?"

"Do about it?" asked Allan half astonished, then a grim look settling about his mouth, he said decidedly:

"We're going to get you out of this horrible country and safe somewhere as soon as we can go."

"Wal, thet's jest what we *ain't* goin' to do," said Miranda decidedly, "I ain't no wax doll whose nose'll melt off in the sun, an' thur ain't no tomyhawk goin' to tech me. We're goin' to git to work right here'n now an' teach them pesky Injuns some manners. You don't mean to tell me, Allan Whitney, thet you would sneak off an' take yer wife away to hide her in pink cotton while them dear misshuneries is settin' thar sorrerin' fer him"—she choked but went bravely on—"an' in danger, mebbe, needin' pertection. Allan Whitney, thet ain't you! I know you better'n thet! An' ef hevin' a wife hes made you sech a fool, baby'n, coward she'd better git hers'f tomyhawked right here an' now an' git out o' yer way. I wouldn't be worth my salt ef I couldn't stand by yeh an' he'p yeh do yer duty like the brave man yeh air. How long sence it happened?"

"Randa, dear, you don't understand. It's been going on several days. There's been a massacre. You know there are over seventy people in and around the mission and they've killed fourteen of them already. Dr. Whitman and his wife first, and some of the sick people; and over fifty of them have been taken prisoners. One man got away up to the fort and they wouldn't take him in. What do you think of that? I tell you this is a horrible country and I want to get you out of it."

"Name o' sense! Why didn't you tell me afore? Ain't you done nothin' 'bout it yet? You ain't goin' to give up an' let this go on? *Prisoners*! Them poor women an' children! You gotta git up a regiment 'mongst the settlers an' git out after 'em. How 'bout them es is killed? Hev they ben buried yet? Somebody oughtta go right down to the mission an' tend to thin's. Where's Nathan? Ain't he comin' back purty soon? He'n I c'n go down to the mission. Mebbe ther ain't nobody thar, an' 'tain't safe, so many wild animals as thur is round. You go git the settlers t'gether an' fight them Injuns! It's time they was taught a good sound lesson."

Allan stood staring at his wife in amazement and admiration.

"Randa, I can't. I can't have you go down to that horrible place, and I can't leave you here alone. I don't know where Nathan is. You're a woman, and you're my wife. I must protect you."

"Stuff an' nonsense!" said Miranda, hurrying around the cabin picking up things to take with her. "This is a time o' war an' you can't sit aroun' an' act soft then. Ain't I as good a right to act like a man in a time like this as you hev, I'd like to know? Ef I get tomyhawked I will, an' thet's the whole on it. It's got to come sometime I guess, an' my time ain't comin' till it's ready, an' you can't stop it ef it's really here. Sides, thet don't matter a hull lot. Thet ain't the way that misshunery man talked ennyhow, an' now he's gone I reckon we've got to do our best to take his place. Ef I git prisonered I bet I give 'em a lively time of it afore they git done with me ennyhow. Come on, Allan, don't you try to stop me doin' my duty, fer yeh can't ennyhow, an' it ain't reasonable at a time like this. Them pris'ners gotta be set free. We gotta be c'rageous an' not think o' oursel'es. Ef ennythin' happens to us this ain't the hull o' livin',—down here ain't. You go git the horses ready, an' I'll put up a couple o' bundles, an' I'll ride 'long o' you till I find somebody to go to Waiilatpu with me. Hurry up now, it ain't no use argyin'! I'm willin' 'nouf to go back East when I've done what thur is to do, but—not till then!"

Allan stooped and kissed his wife, a look almost of awe upon his face.

"Randa, you are wonderful!" he said softly. "I have no right to stop you!" and without another word he went out and saddled the horses.

CHAPTER 30

IN the Autumn after young Nathan Whitney went to Oregon his sister Helena was married to a farmer living near Fonda, and Prudence went to teach school up above Schenectady. Three months later their father died, quietly, unobtrusively as he had lived, the mask he had always worn not changed or softened by death. What secret emotions he had had died with him, and men read nothing from his silent face.

His wife Maria, not relishing the care of the younger children who were just grown to the annoying age, packed them off to their Aunt Jane in Albany and betook herself on an indefinite trip to New York. By the ordering of the will she had received enough money to make her comfortable during her lifetime, and the house did not belong to her, so she was free to go. She had few friends in the village where she had lived so many years, and preferred to leave it behind her forever.

The old house was closed. The grass grew tall in the yard, the hedges rough and scraggly, and cobwebs wrought their riotous lacery across doors and window casements, a lonely deserted sight for those who looked across from the windows of the Spafford house. Rose had often cast a wistful glance toward the vine-covered gateway as she threw open her windows in the morning, wishing she might see the familiar figure of Nathan and hear his cheery whistle as he came down the walk. He had been gone a long while and only one letter had come from him, in St. Louis on his way out.

But one morning in late glowing Summer the cobwebby shutters were thrown wide, and Miranda rested her plump, bare arms on the window sill and leaned out, drawing in deep breaths of her native air and smiling in broad satisfaction.

The years had passed, long in their waiting, changes had been fulfilled, and at last Miranda had come into her own. She was mistress of the great white house and she was happy.

Miranda, Allan and Nathan had been home for nearly a week, and they had been welcomed with open arms and glad smiles. They had told their tales of terror, bloodshed, peril and deliverance. They had visited their friends, heard the news, social, religious, political, and now they had come home. The house had been cleaned and polished to the last degree. The cobwebs were no more. Nathan was even now out in the yard with a big scythe mowing down the tall grass. The Whitney children, Samuel and the twins, were coming on the afternoon stage. Allan was going into the newspaper office with David. Miranda was content.

"Golly!" she said as she sniffed the cinnamon roses under the window, "Golly! I'm glad thur ain't no pesky Injuns 'round here. They may be all well 'nouf fer them 'at likes 'em, but not fer me. The misshunery business ain't what it's cracked up to be. I've hed my try at it an' I don't want no more. I don't grudge 'em all the things they stole out o' the cabin when we was off chasin' 'em, seein' they left me my rose quilt thet my little Rose made with her baby fingers fer me, an' I've only one regret an' thet's the risin' sun quilt they got, fer I don't 'xpect ever t' git anuther misshunery quilt agin; but then 'twas meant fer 'em in the beginnin' an' mebbe it'll do some good to 'em, an' convert 'em from the error of thur ways. They suttenly need it. Anyhow I ain't goin' to fret. I've got all I want, an' I'm real glad I've seen a mounting. It's som'pin' to go 'ith the stars."

Her eyes grew wide and serious, and a sweet look came around her mouth.

Across the street Rose stepped out on the front stoop with a broom wafting the cobwebs dreamily from the railing, and waving a graceful hand to Miranda. Nathan dropped his scythe and went over to her. Miranda watched them, a gentle look glorifying her face, and remembered how she used to come out on that stoop over there and look across thinking she might have been the mistress of this house but wasn't. How queer it all was! She was here with Allan, having the life of all the others she would have chosen if she had had the choice. Would it be that way when you got to heaven? Would you look back and see where you used to be, and look at your old self and wonder? How little the trials and crosses looked, now that they all were passed! You did get things on this earth, too,—stars, and mountains, and heroes—and happiness!

Miranda, in the gladness of her heart lifted her sweet, brown eyes, the merry twinkles all sparkling with earnestness, to the blue of the deep Summer sky above the waving tree tops, and murmured softly under her breath:

"Thanks be! Thanks be!" Then she took her broom and went to work.